"All women are different, Jackson,"

Kaly said, "and it's time you realized it."

She was lecturing him on how to deal with women? That was rich. "Let me tell you something, lady. I don't need a glory-hungry bookworm to teach me about relationships with the opposite sex."

"Your ignorance is exceeded only by your imagination," Kaly said in disgust. "Where do you get your ridiculous assumptions about people?"

"Based on experience," Jackson retorted flatly. "Mine. And the next time you need a thrill, read a romance novel. Then you won't need to get your kicks gossiping about my relationships with women."

"For your information, Jackson," she threw over her shoulder, "I have less interest in your personal life than I have in the mating habits of the reptile kingdom, although I'm sure the similarities are endless." She turned to walk away.

"Wait," he commanded.

Kaly turned around, knowing it was a bad idea.

"Truce?" Without thinking, he lowered his head. His lips were just a fraction from hers....

MARRY ME,
Cowboy

RANCHER'S CHOICE

Kylie Brant

RAWHIDE
& Lace

Silhouette Books

Published by Silhouette Books

America's Publisher of Contemporary Romance

To John,
who cooks, cleans and irons
while I'm at the computer.
Now, that's romantic!

SILHOUETTE BOOKS

ISBN 0-373-65338-7

RANCHER'S CHOICE

KYLIE BRANT

lives in Iowa with her husband and children. Besides being a writer, this mother of five works full-time teaching learning-disabled students. Much of her free time is spent in her role as professional spectator at her kids' sporting events.

An avid reader, Kylie enjoys stories of love, mystery and suspense—and she insists on happy endings! She claims she was inspired to write by all the wonderful authors she's read over the years. Now most weekends and all summer she can be found at the computer, spinning her own tales of romance and happily-ever-afters.

She invites readers to check out her online read in the reading room at eHarlequin.com. Readers can write to Kylie at P.O. Box 231, Charles City, IA 50616, or e-mail her at kyliebrant@hotmail.com. Her Web site address is www.kyliebrant.com.

Chapter 1

"No way in hell! Absolutely not!" Jackson Lowell Roberts III paced agitatedly around the Circle R ranch office. The contents of his whiskey glass splashed precariously as he pointed it at his brother. "This is the worst possible time to bring another person to the ranch, Jeff, especially a woman." He spat the last word as he would a curse. "I've got enough trouble around here trying to figure out who's stealing our cattle, without having to fend off unwanted advances or watch over the family silver."

The object of Jackson's wrath sat calmly behind his polished mahogany desk. Being the younger sibling of such a volatile man had given Jeff years of practice at dealing with his temper. "I told you, Jackson, I'm at a place in my book where I need Kalinda Scott's expertise," Jeff explained patiently. "She's going to be kept plenty busy as my research assistant. She won't upset things—you'll barely know she's here." Jeff raised his eyebrows at his brother's inelegant snort, but continued firmly, "Kalinda's credentials are top-notch. You don't have to get yourself in an uproar about having her stay at the ranch. This woman is different."

Jackson ran his hand through his thick dark hair, trying to control his anger. His brother's naïveté about women was more than just irritating—it was down-right dangerous at times. "Just like the last two women you hired to help at the ranch were different?" he asked caustically.

Jeff had the grace to look somewhat abashed, but quickly defended himself. "How was I supposed to know that Sara Richards had a rap sheet and a string of aliases?" he protested. "You have to admit, she really kept the place organized while she was here."

Jackson raised the glass to his lips and downed the contents before crossing to the decanter to pour him-self more. "She was only here long enough to case the house and learn the combination of the office safe," he reminded Jeff tersely. "We were damn lucky she was caught trying to fence Great-Grandmother's silver, or she'd be halfway across the country by now." He turned to eye his brother derisively. "You always were a sucker for dimples."

Jeff seized the opportunity to embarrass Jackson in return. "And my last secretary was a sucker for big macho cowboys," Jeff cooed mockingly. "She was just swept away by your strong shoulders and—" He broke off as he ducked the book on cattle breeding his brother hurled across the room at him.

"Your so-called secretary was more concerned with latching onto a healthy bankroll than with typing for you." Jackson remembered the erstwhile secretary,

Amber Holiday, with irritation. "She had ice in her veins and dollar signs tattooed on her butt."

Jeff grinned with huge enjoyment. "You'd know more about that than the rest of us, buddy. I seem to recall coming in here about the time Amber was offering to show you that very portion of her anatomy—among others."

Jackson glared narrowly at his brother, remembering that particular scene with distaste. The woman had believed absolutely in her own charms and had been vile-mouthed when Jackson had declined to sample them. He reminded Jeff silkily, "And that's just how you lost yourself a secretary, when I had to throw Amber and her dollar signs off the ranch. If you think I'm going to go through that again with this new bimbo you want to hire, you need your head examined."

Jeff recognized that tone. It usually preceded Jackson's verbally or physically dismantling the offender, and Jeff was not anxious to tangle with his brother. He quickly changed tactics. "This *woman* is a professional, Jackson," he stressed. "Kalinda Scott is a doctoral candidate in cultural anthropology at the University of Arizona. Her knowledge of Native American cultures will give my book the authenticity it needs."

"Then find a man to help you." Jackson's tone brooked no opposition. "All hell's breaking loose around here with this rustling going on and we sure don't have time to hold the hand of some dusty old-maid scholar."

"You know how much time I've spent trying to find someone right for this position," Jeff maintained stubbornly. "I've talked to department heads at several universities. And—" Jeff paused before bringing out his strongest argument ''—Dr. Morehead is Kalinda's adviser. He recommends her highly.''

Jackson's head swiveled as he gazed sharply at Jeff. Professor Allen Morehead had been one of the biggest influences in Jeff's distinguished postgraduate career at the University of Arizona. It was he who had encouraged Jeff to expand his master's thesis on the history of New Mexico into a book. The professor had also interested a publisher in the work. Jeff's first book had been so well received by the academic community that it was already being assigned as required reading in some college courses. Jeff felt he owed a lot to Dr. Morehead, and the two men shared a mutual respect.

Jackson rubbed his free hand tiredly over his face. He could feel himself losing ground rapidly after this last piece of information, but he gave it one more shot. ''I just can't believe that the only so-called expert you could find had to be a female. Couldn't Dr. Morehead recommend a man with similar qualifications...''

Jeff was already shaking his head. ''No one who would be free to spend the amount of time in New Mexico that I need someone for. Besides,'' he continued doggedly, ''I want Kalinda Scott. She lived on a Navaho reservation last summer while she was researching her dissertation. It's her knowledge and experience I need to help me with my book. Also, I think having another woman around will be good for Carrie. She's feeling a little confined with the pregnancy and will probably welcome having a woman to talk to.''

Jackson's look sharpened as concern for his sister-in-law momentarily took precedence over his argument with Jeff. ''She isn't having more trouble, is she?''

Jeff hastened to reassure him. ''So far, so good, but

the doctor wants her to take it very easy with this one. She has to have plenty of rest during the day and no stress.'' Carrie had already had two miscarriages, and both her husband and her brother-in-law were willing to do anything to help her avoid that nightmare again.

Jackson dropped his six-foot-three frame wearily into his oversize chair and leaned back, propping his boots on the large oak library table that served as his desk. ''I suppose that having another woman in the house would be good for Carrie,'' he grudgingly admitted. A sudden premonition occurred to him. ''You aren't both going to work in *here,* are you?''

Jeff shrugged matter-of-factly. ''My library is here, as well as my computer and all my notes.''

Jackson bit off a curse. ''It isn't bad enough that I have to put up with a pushy, greedy female living in our house, you actually expect me to share my office with her?''

''Our office,'' Jeff corrected him mildly. ''But don't worry. We'll be so busy you won't bother us.''

Jackson looked grim at this attempt at levity. He might have found himself outmaneuvered. He might even reluctantly admit, privately of course, that this Scott person seemed necessary. But he didn't have to like it, and damned if he would pretend to. ''I'm warning you, Jeff,'' he threatened darkly, ''if this woman causes any problems at all, with me or with the hired hands, she'll be out of here so fast your head'll spin.''

Jeff, sensing victory, grinned. ''Don't worry, Jackson,'' he quipped, ''I won't let my big bad research assistant harass you. If you want me to, I'll even chain her to her desk, so she can't chase you around yours.''

Jackson's visage grew darker. Jeff, ignoring the warning signs in his brother's cloudy countenance, rose from his desk and strode across the room toward him. "Think of it this way," he teased, slapping Jackson on the shoulder. "We've already experienced the worst with the last two women I hired. The third time is supposed to be the charm." Jeff dodged the elbow his brother jabbed at him and walked jubilantly from the room.

Jackson sank farther down in the leather chair and took a healthy swig from his glass. "Yeah," he muttered morosely, "a real charm."

Kalinda Scott moved lithely around the small bedroom in her Tucson apartment, emptying dresser drawers and returning to her bed with the clothes. She stepped nimbly around the fat white Angora cat sprawled lazily in the middle of the floor, but her progress was hampered as she was forced to work around the lump in the middle of her bed—her roommate, Susan.

"I still don't understand, Kaly," Susan complained querulously, "why in heaven's name you have to bury yourself on a ranch hours away from civilization."

Kaly smiled. Susan considered anywhere she was as civilization. And since she was never anywhere that lacked culture, nightlife and an unending supply of men, perhaps by her own definition she was correct.

"Summer is supposed to be a time to have fun, take a break. Last year you insisted on staying on that isolated reservation, and now this. If you really feel the need to work, surely there's something on campus that you can do." Susan shuddered delicately. She had an obvious disdain for gainful employment, which was one reason she was a perpetual student.

Kaly reminded her, "I do have to work this summer

if I want to be able to eat during my last semester of classes. This job will give me the money I need to pay you room and board next semester, and allow me to live in the manner to which I've become accustomed.''

Even Susan had to smile at that. Kaly was frugal out of necessity. Her progress through graduate school had been interrupted periodically as she took time away from her studies to earn enough money to continue paying for classes. These necessary breaks had lengthened the amount of time it took her to complete her doctorate, but while it was frustrating, at least she'd had the satisfaction of knowing she was making her own way.

Kaly stopped packing as a sudden thought occurred to her. ''My leaving this summer isn't going to put you in a financial bind, is it?''

Susan waved away her friend's worry. ''If I can't pay the rent on this dump, I can always call my folks. Which is another thing, Kaly. If you just need money, why don't you call your mom and dad?''

Kaly winced inwardly at this reference to her parents, but responded evenly, ''I'd never ask them.'' As usual, the thought of her family brought mixed emotions to her. Being the only daughter in a family with three older brothers meant that she had never had a lack of people in her life who thought they knew what was best for her. The conflicts had begun when Kaly insisted on playing Little League with her brothers. They had continued ever since.

Mr. Scott was a police sergeant and expected his family to respond as readily to his orders as the rookies at the precinct did. However, Kaly had rarely been amenable to his directives. She had entered the anthropology program at the University of Arizona in the face of her father's vehement protests. But if he'd thought that withholding the financial support he had given to her brothers would deter his daughter, he had been doomed to disappointment. Kaly's grades had earned her scholarships as an undergraduate, and she had become accustomed to working her way through graduate school. She loved her family, but living half a state away from them had its benefits. Her independent nature invariably clashed with her father's when they were together for long.

She turned to fix Susan with a look. "If my parents call before they get my new address," she ordered sternly, "you're not to discuss my summer plans with them."

Susan looked startled. "What's the big secret? Aren't they going to know where you are all summer?"

Kaly calmly continued packing. "Of course. I explained my plans in my letter. In the meantime, I don't want to have to deal with a phone call from my dad if he gets the urge to reach out and nag someone."

"I wouldn't blame him for trying to talk you out of this idea. Honestly, a ranch, Kaly!" Susan made it sound as though Kaly was going to travel to the Amazonian jungles.

Kaly made her way to the closet and returned to dump an armload of clothes on the bed. "I really do need the money, but it's the experience I'm after," she informed her friend. "Jeff Roberts is becoming a well-respected historian. I can learn a lot from him. His book is documenting the impact the white man's arrival had upon the Native American tribes living in the Southwest." Her voice rose in excitement even as she thought about it.

She tried to convince her friend, who still looked uncomprehending. "Don't you see? This job is perfect for me. The research I did last summer on the reservation is just what he needs. Give me a hand with this, will you?" She motioned to the mound of clothes.

Susan sat up on the bed and began a desultory attempt to sort and fold tops and jeans. She wished mightily she could someday see her roommate get as excited about a man as she did about her work. "I'll miss you, Kaly," she said, pouting. "You know what a scatterbrain I am. I'll probably even forget mealtimes. Who's going to see that I eat properly while you're gone?"

Kaly's eyes twinkled. "I guess I'll have to leave that to Charles." Charles was an accountant and Susan's new love interest, although Susan's relationships lasted no longer than her attention span.

"I'm hopeless in the kitchen. I'll probably waste away without you to do the cooking," Susan warned.

Kaly suppressed a smile. "Charles is used to playing with figures. I'm sure he'll be glad to watch over yours."

Susan sighed at her friend's lack of concern and flopped back on the bed. "One of us has to keep the men happy around here. And you—" she fixed Kaly with a gimlet stare "—definitely have not been doing your part."

Kaly responded as she always did when Susan started harping on her lack of social life—she ignored it. "Have you seen my turquoise blouse?" she inquired as she rummaged through her closet.

Susan shook her head. "No, and don't change the subject. It's not healthy the way you never date. I think you can get some illness from that or something."

"A heart disease, no doubt," murmured Kaly drolly.

"No, really, Kaly," Susan said seriously as she sat up and once again started folding clothes. "You can't count having coffee once in a while with one of the professors as a social life."

Kaly rolled her eyes at her friend's exaggeration. "I do go out occasionally," she corrected. "I can't help it if you never approve of my escorts."

"Hmph! Those dweebs!" Susan grimaced. "I think you accept dates only on the merit of how likely they are to provide a cure for insomnia."

Kaly laughed in spite of herself. "No. I pick them for their intelligence, or because we have a lot in common. I can't help it if your idea of a hot date is a cross between Evel Knievel and Tom Selleck. I like a little substance in my men."

Susan sighed. "The guys you date are full of a substance, all right, but I won't put a name to it. Honestly, Kaly, sometimes I swear you're a geek magnet." She looked at her friend soberly. "Don't you think it's time you forgot about that rat Philip and started really living again? It's been years."

At the mention of her ex-fiancé, Kaly's stomach sank. Susan was really on a roll this time. "I certainly am not still hung up on Philip, if that's what you mean. But he did teach me a valuable lesson about the basic untrustworthiness of the average male. All I want right now is to concentrate on my studies, finish my dissertation and find a job."

"You chose Philip mainly because he seemed so different from your father and brothers," Susan said wisely. "Just because you made one mistake doesn't mean you should swear off a real relationship with any other man. It's time you stopped being so darn careful, quit planning every aspect of your life and just let go!''

Kaly was irritated with Susan's amateur analysis, but was forced to admit to herself that there was some truth to it. She had thought Philip's ideas and personality were as far removed from her father's as possible. She and Philip had been recipients of academic scholarships in the same program in college and had shared similar interests. They had also, as they grew closer, shared similar goals. At least they had until Philip's hopes for his future had dimmed. Then Kaly had found out just how little she had really known the man she had planned to marry.

Others might be able to chalk up such an episode to experience, but Kaly could not forget how close she had come to making a colossal error or how dismal her judgment of men had turned out to be. ''I know you view caution as a major character flaw,'' she answered her friend dryly, ''but it works for me. One disastrous mistake a lifetime is enough. I'll leave the frantic social scene to you, thanks, anyway.''

Susan's face brightened. ''Why didn't I think of it sooner?'' she asked excitedly. ''This summer might be just the answer to your dull social life. You're going to be on a ranch with hordes of eligible men!''

Kaly cast her a quelling look. ''Jeff Roberts is married, and quite happily from all accounts,'' she said. ''Even you have been rumored to have some scruples where married men are concerned. Besides, I'm going to be heavily involved with his manuscript. There won't be much time for socializing.''

Susan's face became mulish. ''You can make time for some fun in the next three months, I would think.''

She looked thoughtfully at the casual clothes being packed neatly in the suitcase and made a mental note to add to the selection. She said tartly, "Your usual supply of academic dorks won't be around, so maybe you can expand your horizons a little. There's sure to be a whole bunch of men on a ranch. Don't they need cowboys to go on cattle drives or something?"

Kaly laughed. "I think you've been watching too many old Westerns on TV. But I promise," she said, forestalling Susan's argument, "if I meet somebody interesting, I'll go out with him. Will that satisfy you?"

But Susan was staring into space. "I wonder if you'll get to meet any rodeo riders," she mused. "I always thought there was something exciting about the way they risk their lives with those wild horses and bulls...."

Kaly rolled her eyes heavenward. "Susan! Give it a rest! Make yourself useful and help me close this suitcase." Susan obediently sat on top of the bag as Kaly locked it. "There," Kaly announced with satisfaction. "All done." She looked up and caught Susan's woebegone expression. "C'mon," she cajoled. "It's my last night in Tucson for months. Let's go out and splurge on dinner tonight."

Susan perked up. "Pizza?" she asked coaxingly.

Kaly agreed. The two grabbed their purses and headed for the door. "I swear," Kaly teased, "your appetite for pizza is exceeded only by your appetite for the opposite sex."

"I wouldn't go that far," Susan disagreed. "Although the thought of Charles smothered in anchovies and mushrooms does have a certain kinky appeal." The two women looked at each other and broke into gales of laughter.

Chapter 2

Jeff Roberts followed his brother into the ranch office and closed the door. He turned around to face Jackson, who was pacing the oak paneled room. Jeff spoke first. "We've been hit again."

The rage on Jackson's countenance was formidable. "Sometime in the last few days," he affirmed with barely controlled fury.

"Well, I'll be damned," Jeff said. "We've never had problems with rustling around here before, but now we've been hit twice. Have you called the sheriff yet?"

"Yeah, I called him as soon as I found out, and he said he'd be here later this evening. I don't expect much help from him, though. He sure hasn't come up with anything so far." Jackson strode to the window to stare unseeingly out at the landscape, his boots leaving dusty marks on the highly polished wood floor.

"How many head did they get?" Jeff asked.

"I'm not certain yet. About a dozen, I think." Jackson shook his head in frustration. "Nothing about this makes sense." He turned away from the window and crossed to a large map of the ranch pinned to the wall. "Sheriff Dumont said that normally these guys hit and run. But this is the second time they've struck at our ranch. And instead of stealing cattle from the most remote pastures, where it would take longer for us to notice—" Jackson indicated a couple of areas on the map "—they're hitting our closest pastures where we have the smallest number of head grazing."

Jeff frowned. "What does Dumont make of it?"

"He hasn't come up with much. He said that without a vehicle description, he doesn't have a lot to go on."

"What are we going to do?" Jeff asked somberly.

"We don't have a choice. We're going to have to keep some of the stock closer to the buildings," Jackson replied. "We can't afford to lose our prized breeding bull, or the cows we've bred with it. We'll have to keep them in one of the barns for the time being." Jeff nodded in agreement. The ranch was primarily a beef operation, but they'd expanded into breeding in the past few years. The cost of the purebred bull had been astronomical, but the investment was imperative for the future of the ranch. "I'm also going to have the men double up on night shifts, patrolling the pastures that are reached most easily by truck."

"There's no way we can patrol all the land," Jeff protested.

"Yeah, I know," Jackson conceded. "So we're going to have to bring the cattle in closer, narrow down the number of places we have to watch."

The brothers looked at each other with unspoken

concern. The danger in Jackson's plan was overgrazing on the land that the enlarged herd was kept on. Unable to forecast the summer rainfall, ranchers went to great pains to take care of their pasture land. Running too many head on any pasture ruined it in a hurry for a season, sometimes longer.

Jackson continued, "Dumont is checking with the neighbors to see if they've been hit this time. We'll have to wait and see if we're being singled out or if the rustlers are hitting several places in this area." He dropped tiredly into his chair. "All in all—" Jackson's voice was muffled as he rubbed both hands over his face "—it's been one hell of a day."

Jeff hesitated, sure that it was about to get worse. "You haven't forgotten what day this is, have you?" he said reluctantly.

Jackson raised his eyebrows inquiringly.

"My research assistant, Kalinda Scott, arrives today."

"Damn!" The epithetics that followed were usually reserved for the barn or some particularly recalcitrant cows. Jackson glared at his brother, as if blaming him for the timing.

"I told you last week when she was coming," Jeff defended himself. "With all the trouble lately, you must have forgotten."

Jackson groused irascibly, "How am I supposed to concentrate on our problems in here with some nosy broad hovering in the corner?"

Jeff took exception to his brother's tone. "Getting this book published is important, too. I told you before that there wouldn't be a problem with all of us working in here. You and I manage it all right."

"Yeah, but that's because you're not always sashaying your fanny around trying to get my attention," Jackson retorted darkly.

The visual image that his brother's words brought to mind tickled Jeff's well-developed sense of humor, but one look at Jackson's glowering expression made him swallow his laughter.

"Kalinda will be here to work, not to attract you," Jeff said diplomatically. "She won't be any bother at all. Professor Morehead said she has a very pleasant personality."

Jackson choked. "Pleasant! That's a word usually used by aunts who want to set you up with their ugly nieces. I can just imagine what this spinster anthropologist looks like."

Jeff blinked in confusion. "What makes you think she's ugly?"

Jackson looked at him impatiently. "You know what I mean. What kind of a woman would tie herself up in school for that many years, anyway? She must be a real bowser."

Jeff was drawn into the inane conversation in spite of himself. "What do you care? First you were concerned that she was some kind of female piranha who was going to come on to you. Now you think she's only in school because she can't attract a man?"

"There are only two kinds of women, Jeff," Jackson lectured his brother grimly. "Those who use their physical appeal to trap a man into providing for them, and those who have no physical appeal at all." He should know. He'd been damn close to the altar with a woman who had a beautiful face and a cash register for a heart. Her undying love for him had lasted only until she found someone with a fatter wallet and more time to dance attendance on her.

Jeff shook his head wryly. "You're too young to be so cynical," he said, only half joking. He knew Jackson had been badly burned in the past, but sometimes he was shocked anew at the effect his brother's experience had had on him. His jaded attitude of the opposite sex wasn't widely known outside the family. His personal life was the envy of every single man in the county, and a few of the married ones. Jackson never lacked a steady stream of women willing to take him up on the masculine promise in his intense blue gaze. But although he treated the many women he'd dated with unfailing politeness, none lasted more than a month or two. Jeff doubted any of them had the slightest idea how deep the scars in his brother ran. Or how determined he was to remain unattached.

"I can just picture her," Jackson continued, interrupting his brother's thoughts. He was enjoying baiting Jeff. "Hair cut as short as a man's, wearing jeans the size of Big Zeke, the livery man, and laced-up boots."

"Jackson!" At Carrie's mortified gasp, both men's heads swiveled around. Carrie was coming through the doorway accompanied by someone who could only be the research assistant. It was clear the women had heard part of the conversation.

Carrie appeared momentarily speechless, but Kaly was openly amused. "I have to plead guilty to a couple of your accusations," she said as she strolled gracefully into the room. "I do often wear jeans, but as to Big Zeke's size—" at this she looked questioningly at Carrie, who rolled her eyes "—I can't attest. I've even been known to wear hiking boots. But I haven't worn my hair short since my mother cut it in the second grade."

Jeff was the first to recover. Although visibly discomfited, he stepped forward to introduce himself. "Kalinda, welcome to the Circle R. I'm Jeff Roberts, and I'm sure Carrie introduced herself, didn't you, honey?"

Carrie's look encompassed both men and promised retribution later, although her voice was sweet. "Of course, dear. I greeted Kalinda and assured her of her welcome here," she said pointedly.

"And this is my brother, Jackson Roberts," Jeff said hurriedly as Jackson unfolded his long length from his chair and approached them. "Jackson, this is the research assistant Dr. Morehead recommended, Kalinda Scott."

Jackson's eyes narrowed as he quickly sized up the woman before him. She was a beauty, but the realization brought him no pleasure. She looked like trouble, he thought sourly, the kind of trouble he had spent the past few years steering clear of. The kind he had just warned his brother about. "Miss Scott," he said flatly, taking her proffered hand briefly.

Kaly was shocked as a current of electric pleasure flared at the simple pressing of their palms, although the contact was so brief she was left wondering if she had imagined the flicker of sensation. Jackson was already turning and addressing the others. "I've got things to do. See you at dinner." Nodding at Kaly, he placed his hat back on his head and left the room.

She blinked at his retreating back, then Jeff reclaimed her attention. "I'm looking forward to your input, Kalinda," he said earnestly. "I was very intrigued by what Dr. Morehead told me of your project last summer. I'm hoping you can clear up my confusion about—"

Carrie interrupted laughingly. "Jeff! She's spent hours on the road driving. You can certainly let her settle in before badgering her about work."

She took Kaly's arm and led her from the room. "Let me show you to your room, Kalinda. I'm sure you're anxious to freshen up and get unpacked."

"Call me Kaly, please. And yes, I can't wait to wash the dust away."

The two women strolled through the airy hallway and up the open oak staircase. Kaly marveled over the intricate woodwork and high ceilings.

"Yes, this old house is a real oddity in these parts," Carrie agreed. "Family history has it that Great-Grandfather Roberts built this home for his young bride. It's supposed to be an exact duplicate of Great-Grandmother Roberts's family home in Boston."

Kaly was led down a huge hallway and ushered through the first of many doorways. "I hope you're comfortable here," Carrie said as they surveyed the bedroom. "I moved in some chairs, a table and a TV, in case you want to work or relax in private."

Kaly stepped in and absorbed the aura of the room. The bed was an old four-poster with a lace-draped canopy. A large oak wardrobe stood in one corner with a highboy next to it. A matching lowboy with a huge mirror was against the wall opposite the bed. The room was done in white and yellow, with airy curtains to match.

"It's absolutely charming," Kaly exclaimed sincerely, turning her gaze to Carrie.

Carried looked pleased. "I'd hoped you'd like it. It's always been one of my favorites." She strode across the room and opened a door to show Kaly a large walk-in closet. "There should be plenty of room here for all your things. Peg, our housekeeper, will bring your suitcases up shortly. Let me show you to the bathroom. It's just down the hall.''

As the women walked through the hall, Carrie opened each of the remaining doors, showing Kaly the rest of the upstairs. Each room was furnished in a manner similar to the first, though none were as large. Carrie explained, ''Jeff and I have moved into a room downstairs at the back of the house.'' She grimaced. ''He seems to think that walking up and down stairs is too difficult for his fat pregnant wife.''

Kaly shot her a glance laced with sympathy. ''How far along are you?'' she inquired shyly.

''Just over five months.'' A shadow passed across her face. ''I lost the last two babies I was carrying, but the doctor says this time everything looks normal. We're taking extra precautions, though.'' She shot a droll look at Kaly. ''I have the world's two largest watchdogs in Jeff and Jackson. They make sure I follow all instructions to the letter. They pamper me shamelessly.''

Carrie indicated the closed door at the opposite side of the hall. ''That's Jackson's room. He had some construction done a few years ago and combined three rooms into one suite so he could relax upstairs if he wanted.'' She opened the door and showed Kaly, who remained motionless in the doorway.

The room was huge, easily twice the size of Kaly's, decorated in forest green and beige. It, too, was furnished with antiques. One part of the room was sectioned off from the rest with an overstuffed couch, a chair and an enormous rolltop desk. An entertainment center sat opposite the couch. Kaly's eyes, however, were riveted to the bed with its large oak headboard.

Carrie noticed the direction of her gaze and laughed. "That was built for Great-Grandfather Roberts. He was even taller than Jackson. Isn't it a monster?"

Kaly flushed as she involuntarily pictured the dark, brooding man she had met so briefly downstairs lying in that bed. She hurriedly pulled her eyes away and surveyed the rest of the interior. The frank masculinity of the owner was stamped indelibly on his private domain, and she felt uneasy, like a trespasser.

Carrie chattered on, unaware of her guest's discomfort. "Jack has a master bath off this room, so you won't have to share yours. When he remodeled he spared no expense on the bathroom. It has a huge sunken tub, Jacuzzi and separate shower." She looked mischievous. "I tell him that Jacuzzi is positively hedonistic. But truthfully, he needs something to loosen up those kinks after working with the cattle all day." She moved toward the door.

Kaly stepped thankfully out of the room and followed Carrie across the hall. "Here's the bathroom. Sorry there isn't one off your room," Carrie said, "but in these old houses, bathrooms weren't a high priority."

"Believe me, after growing up in a home where I shared the only bathroom with three brothers—all of them slobs—having any bathroom to myself is paradise," Kaly said wryly.

The bathroom was as quaint as the rest of the house. A large claw-footed tub dominated the small area. One look at the bathtub and Kaly began to long for a refreshing soak.

Carrie noticed the wistfulness in her gaze and laughed. "I know, I know, you'd love nothing more than for me to stop blabbing so you can cool off in

that tub. The towels are in here.'' She indicated a
small closet. ''Supper is usually at six, so if you'd like
to lie down after you unpack, you have plenty of
time.'' She eyed Kaly's pink suit and added, ''You
look terrific, but if you'd like to dress a little more
comfortably, we're pretty casual here. Besides—'' she
had a large smile on her pixieish face as she patted
the small bulge of her stomach ''—I'd hate to have
you look like a dream every day while I appear in my
maternity wear from Tent-and-Awning.''

The two women giggled companionably as they
walked back to Kaly's room. Her suitcases had been
brought up and set in the middle of the floor.

''I'll leave you to unpack and rest,'' Carrie announced. ''If you'd like to give me your keys, I'll have
one of the men take your car around and park it in a
garage. I'll just tell him to leave the keys in it, if that's
okay.'' She accepted the keys from Kaly and waggled
goodbye with them as she moved toward the door.
''See you at six.''

Kaly turned into the room. She thought longingly
of the big tub down the hall, then thrust the thought
resolutely away. First the unpacking, she planned, then
a long relaxing bath as a reward. She swiftly moved
a bag to the bed, where she popped open the top. She
stopped, nonplussed, before drawing one unfamiliar
garment after another from her suitcase.

None of these were items she had packed, but comprehension came swiftly. Susan! Her roommate had
obviously added a few garments she deemed necessary
to Kaly's wardrobe. She smiled in chagrin as she hung
them up in the closet. Only Susan would imagine a
silk shorts-and-top outfit was suitable ranch attire. She
might just have to splurge on a phone call to her de-

vious friend. Clothing wasn't the only surprise she'd sent along. Susan had also put some small foil packages in Kaly's purse. To her mortification she'd discovered them when she'd pulled out her billfold to pay a service station attendant for gas.

Kaly felt the heat of embarrassment rise to scorch her cheeks anew. If those telltale packages had fallen from her purse as she searched for her money... She shuddered. Susan had carried her motto of Be Prepared too far this time. Kaly vowed to give some serious thought to a fitting revenge for her interfering friend.

At last the suitcases were emptied. Kaly pushed them into the closet with a sigh of anticipation. She grabbed her robe and bath articles and headed for the long-awaited soak. Minutes later she was immersed to her chin in cool water and bubbles. She closed her eyes in pleasure and let her thoughts drift.

She smiled as she thought of Carrie's open friendliness. She already liked the little red-haired woman with the gamin charm. Jeff seemed nice, too, Kaly mused drowsily, from the little she had seen of him. He seemed to have an easygoing personality and a sense of fun. Jackson was much harder to read. It obviously hadn't bothered him at all that she had heard his unflattering verbal portrayal of her. Although he'd been polite, his dark blue eyes had remained distant.

A lassitude began to creep into Kaly's limbs, and she slipped more deeply into the water, allowing her mind to continue its meandering. The two brothers were physically similar enough to make their relationship unmistakable. Both were tall, dark and blue-eyed. But there the similarities ended. Jeff's eyes were a clear sky-blue, which reflected his sunny temperament. His brother's navy eyes were shrewd and assessing.

Though Jeff was almost as tall as his brother, he lacked Jackson's massive build.

Kaly shivered unconsciously, reliving that burst of awareness she'd felt earlier. She was used to dealing with men, through school and her jobs, but none had ever affected her as strongly as Jackson Roberts, and the knowledge made her uneasy. He was a dangerous-looking man. There was something threatening about him, something more than his size and his demeanor. She had felt almost dwarfed when he was near, and it had been all she could do not to take a self-protective step back at their introduction.

His dark features were too hard, too irregular, to be considered handsome in the conventional sense. Yet his was an arresting presence, more compelling than mere handsomeness. A forceful sensuality radiated from him, and Kaly knew he would overshadow more pleasant-looking men, making them pale by comparison. Those huge shoulders had strained his denim shirt, mute testament to the manual labor involved in running a ranch. Dark hair had peeked from his shirt's open throat, and she wondered if the rest of his chest was covered in a mat the same color as the hair on his head....

She sat bolt upright in the tub, aghast, her eyes flying open. Where had that thought come from? That was more worthy of Susan, to mentally undress every attractive male around. She, Kaly Scott, never harbored such musings!

Blaming her unaccustomed thoughts on weariness, she stepped out of the tub. She grabbed the thick towel she had laid out and began to dry herself vigorously. Jackson Roberts appeared much too arrogantly sure of himself; he was everything she detested in a man, and she mentally vowed to stay a safe distance from him.

She recalled his description of her, which her arrival had interrupted. She secured the towel around herself and looked closely at her reflection in the mirror. She examined her face, finding nothing remarkable about her wide green eyes, oval face and short straight nose. She had never focused much on her looks, usually finding them only a deterrent to being taken seriously. Her hair was her only vanity. Her dad always said the long thick tresses reminded him of honey.

Kaly made a face in the mirror and exchanged the towel for her robe. What difference did it make what Jackson Roberts thought? She thrust her arms through the sleeves and tied it at the waist. Unfortunately he probably wouldn't be the last man she met who indulged in gross generalizations about women. Although more women were studying anthropology than ever before, it was still a male-dominated field. She just hadn't been prepared to have to deal with such a man the entire summer. She hung her damp towel on the rack and headed back to her room.

As she crossed the threshold, she experienced the same lethargy that had almost overtaken her in the bathtub. She still had two hours before dinner. Pulling back the coverlet of the bed, she stretched out on the mattress, after first setting her wristwatch alarm. It wouldn't do to be late the first night she was here.

At a quarter to six, Kaly descended the front stairway and followed the hallway into the dining room. Upon awakening she had remembered Carrie's advice and put on a casual denim dress. She walked in just as Jeff was seating Carrie.

The two greeted her. ''You look refreshed,'' Carrie said brightly.

Kaly smiled. ''A cool bubble bath and a short nap were just what I needed.'' She looked at Jeff and said politely, ''I'm ready to work tonight if you'd like to get started.''

Jeff looked eager for a moment, but a warning glance from his wife made him subside. ''Carrie has promised to skin me if I so much as talk shop with you before tomorrow.'' He added teasingly, ''We're all scared to death of her around here, so we'd better do as she says.''

Carrie punched him lightly on the arm. ''Jeff! You'll make her think I'm a shrew!''

''But such a lovable little shrew, honey,'' Jeff joked, kissing his wife on the cheek. ''Kaly, would you like a drink? Or will you join my wife in a tall glass of milk? I was going to pour myself some wine.''

''A glass of white wine would be lovely, thank you.''

Jeff poured a glass and handed it to her, before turning away to fill his own. He returned with his glass and raised it high. ''A toast to our partnership,'' he proclaimed. He touched his glass to Kaly's, and Carrie raised her milk glass high.

Jackson's arrival at the table interrupted the levity. It was obvious he had just showered. His glossy brown hair glistened damply, his smooth jaw suggested a recent shave, and he had changed his shirt and jeans. ''What are we drinking to?'' he asked.

''To the successful completion of my book,'' Jeff announced. He winked at the women. ''How can I go wrong with these two beauties on my side?''

Jackson cocked an eyebrow but said nothing as he

joined them at the table. Carrie began telling the men about the phone messages she had taken for them during the day. Minutes later the swinging door opened and a tall rawboned woman in jeans and T-shirt came through and started setting food on the table.

"Kaly, this is Peg, our cook and housekeeper. We couldn't last a day without her," Carrie said.

Kaly greeted her and Peg smiled back. "Welcome, Miss Scott. I'm the one who keeps these three on the straight and narrow. This one here—" she nodded at a silent Jackson "—needs a powerful lot of guiding. Takes a strong hand to keep him in line." She didn't quail at all before the hard gaze he aimed at her.

"Do we have to listen to you jaw all night or did you actually plan to feed us sometime?" Jackson asked with deceptive mildness.

"You'll get your food," Peg scolded as she bustled about, bringing more and more dishes to the table. "I ain't never let you starve yet, have I? You don't look like you've missed too many of my meals." The others at the table laughed at her ribbing.

The mealtime passed pleasantly. Kaly politely answered the questions Carrie and Jeff put to her about her school career, dissertation and project experience. Good-natured laughter was heard as both brothers joked with Carrie about various mishaps she'd suffered when she'd first come to live on the ranch.

Soon after they'd finished, Peg brought out a cherry pie and a pot of coffee. The two younger women groaned in unison.

Kaly pleaded, "No more, please. I won't be able to walk away from the table as it is."

Carrie chimed in, "Same for me, Peg. I have a doctor's appointment soon, and if I put on any more

pounds, he'll have to weigh me on a livestock scale."
The two women sipped coffee while Jeff and Jackson
consumed alarmingly large slices of dessert.

Carrie rolled her eyes at Kaly. "Isn't that disgust-
ing?" she indicated the men's plates.

Jeff protested, "Not at all. It just proves that men's
metabolism is superior to women's." The two began
bantering amicably about the virtues of the two sexes.

Kaly watched in frank amazement as a second
wedge of pie disappeared from Jackson's plate. She
was embarrassed when he looked up and caught her
eyes on him, but she refused to look away. She was
not going to let this man intimidate her.

Jackson returned her look unwaveringly as he took
a sip from the strong black coffee in front of him. The
way the woman was staring at him, you'd think she'd
never seen a man eat after spending a hard day at
work. Most likely she hadn't, he decided. She was
probably used to absentminded professor types who
ate tofu and sprouts after a strenuous day cracking the
books. Well, he wasn't going to apologize for his appetite. The labor he did on the ranch burned off
thousands of calories daily. He ate to replenish those
needed calories, and he knew there was no spare flesh
on his frame. But her steady regard annoyed him, nevertheless. Still perusing her, he leaned deliberately
back in his chair.

"Kalinda." He drew the name out in a drawl.
"What kind of name is that?"

"It's a combination of both my parents' names. My
father's is Kasey and my mother's is Linda. My
friends call me Kaly."

"And what do your friends think of your spending
the summer on a cattle ranch?"

She smiled in amusement as she thought of Susan's exaggeratedly romantic view of life on a ranch. "I must admit that my roommate had visions of strong silent cowboys on endless cattle drives."

"Let's hope you don't share her ideas," Jackson muttered, already envisioning the possible problems with his hired hands if the beautiful woman before him decided to collect admirers.

Kaly was taken aback. Although his words were innocent enough, they were at odds with the flinty look in his eyes.

Jeff's amiable voice cut in. "Jackson, you're not harassing my assistant already, are you?"

"Not at all," Jackson denied deftly. "We were just getting acquainted." He rose from the table. "I'm going back out to the cattle barn." He shot a meaningful glance to Jeff. "Send any visitors out to see me there."

Jeff nodded, understanding that Jackson didn't want to mention the forthcoming visit from the sheriff in front of the women. Jackson strode from the room, and Jeff got to his feet. "I really have some work I need to get to," he said apologetically.

Carrie waved him away. "Go on. I'll just watch TV and do a little reading."

"And I'm going to go to my room and work on my paper," Kaly said. "I'll probably make an early night of it tonight."

"Get your rest," Carrie teased, knowing Jeff was still within earshot. "My husband is a real slave driver!"

"I heard that!" floated back through the doorway, and the women laughed.

Kaly returned to her room and set up the laptop

computer she had brought with her. A Christmas gift from her parents a couple of years ago, it had astounded her at the time, but had since proven invaluable to her in her studies. She placed a disk in the drive and brought the latest chapter of her dissertation to the monitor. Soon she was immersed in revising her work.

When Jeff Roberts looked out the window and saw the sheriff's car coming up the drive, he hurried out the front door to intercept him. "Evening, Sheriff."

"Jeff. How's that pretty little wife of yours?" Sheriff Roy Dumont was a portly man with a florid complexion. His was a labored, country charm that quickly had Carrie gnashing her teeth whenever they had a conversation. But despite his bumpkin appearance, he possessed a shrewd intelligence and insight that Jeff hoped would aid in this investigation.

"Doctor says she's doing just fine. Jackson's down at the south cattle barn and said to bring you there as soon as you arrived."

Jackson saw the two men as they entered the barn, and he approached them in long strides. "Sheriff," he said tersely.

"Jackson." The older man returned the greeting pleasantly. "I've been looking into your complaint and have some news for you. Seems a couple of your neighbors were hit this time, too. Blane and Schmidt reported some missing head shortly after I talked to you. Already been out to their ranches."

"Find anything?" Jackson asked impatiently.

The sheriff scratched his head. He plainly didn't like to be hurried. "Well, I found some tire tracks at Blane's, but haven't found out yet if they belong to one of his trucks or not. Didn't find nothing at Schmidt's. Same kind of operation that hit you, though. Not many head missing, and they took them from the pastures closest to the houses.''

Jackson exchanged a look with Jeff and cursed. ''How do you figure it, Roy?''

'''Pears to me that someone was bound and determined to fill up a truck with prime beef. How many head were you running in that pasture?''

''Close to eighty. The rustlers could have easily filled their truck here, without risking going to other ranches. It doesn't add up.''

''Well, mebbe it doesn't, mebbe it does,'' Roy mused. ''Let's say the rustlers only struck here, like last time. But they want a big haul this go-round— they're not gonna be satisfied with a measly dozen or so. What are the odds they can fill up a truck and have that big a loss go unnoticed for long?''

''Not a chance,'' Jackson stated surely. ''Any more than a dozen, and one of my men would have noticed, even from a distance.''

''Well, there you go then,'' the sheriff answered. ''The thieves wanted to buy some time. They were gonna get their truckload one way or another, but they figgered they'd risk hitting more than one place in a night for the extra getaway time it'd buy them. Instead of a few hours head start, they could count on at least a day, mebbe more.''

''Makes sense, I guess,'' Jeff said slowly, as Jackson mulled this over in silence. ''But it still seems like they're taking unnecessary risks. They could have hit the more remote pastures and still had a pretty good chance of being undetected for a while.''

''But getting to those pastures in the dark with a

truck that size would be a hell of a risk, too,'' Jackson said finally. "They'd have to travel farther, over rougher ground, to get to the herds. It would be easy to break an axle at night in some of those pastures.''

Roy nodded. "That's how I figger it, too.''

"But what are we going to do about it?" Jeff asked in frustration. "We can't patrol the whole ranch indefinitely. If we've been hit twice, what's to stop them from striking here again?''

"Well, I'll put another area watch on your place, of course,'' the sheriff assured him.

Jackson snorted. "Somehow I don't think that's going to help me sleep better at night, Roy. It sure didn't do much good the last time. We got hit again almost the minute the watch was over.''

"So you did. What do you make of that?''

"Make of what?" Jeff asked, looking between his brother and the older man.

"Jackson knows what I mean.''

Jeff's eyes swung to his brother's. "Jack?''

"He means maybe the rustlers knew there was an area watch on the place and knew when it was due to end.'' Jackson let out a sigh. "Because maybe the people who stole our cattle also work on this ranch.''

"What?" Jeff's mouth hung open in disbelief, but Roy was nodding and Jackson's jaw was like granite.

"You gotta look at all the angles, Jeff,'' the sheriff told him. "Now, I ain't saying it's so, but it's a possibility. We gotta look at all the possibilities.''

Jeff shook his head. "I don't believe it. Who do you suspect?''

Jackson shrugged impatiently. He didn't want to consider the idea any more than his brother did. He had hired most of these men himself, and the others had been here since he was a kid. He worked alongside them daily. He knew them, and he knew most of their families. He hated the ugly suspicion that kept cropping up in his thoughts ever since the ranch had been targeted, but as Roy had said, they had to consider every possibility, no matter how distasteful. "I don't suspect anyone, yet," he finally answered his brother. "I'm just keeping my eyes open."

"Still," Jeff muttered, "it's too unbelievable that one of our own men would be involved."

"Whoever it is," Jackson said flatly, "they won't get clean away. Nobody steals from me—I protect what's mine." His eyes were glacial when he looked at Roy and then at Jeff. "They better hope Roy catches them first."

The sheriff clapped him on the shoulder. "Don't worry, Jackson, these guys usually leave a trail. We'll find them. It'll just take a little time. In the meantime, I'll alert the markets to be on the lookout for brands from the three ranches."

Jackson heaved a sigh of frustration as Jeff escorted Roy back to his car. He leaned wearily against the side of the barn. Alerting the markets wasn't going to be much help if the rustlers changed the brands on the stolen cattle, which they undoubtedly would do. Nor did he have much faith in the protection a renewed watch would give the ranch. It looked as if he was going to have to rely on his own methods for guarding his cattle.

But instead of focusing on his strategy for protecting the ranch, his tired mind formed a picture of Jeff's new research assistant. Kaly's delicate features swam in front of him.

She was a pretty little thing, no denying it. And tiny.

She stood almost a full foot shorter than he was. In that pink suit she'd worn earlier she'd looked as dainty and fragile as a desert flower. Something about the way she wore her hair all pulled up in back made him want to see the golden tresses released to cascade around her shoulders, or better yet across his own bare chest.

His eyes snapped open. Hellfire and damnation! All he needed right now was to be thinking of Jeff's hired bookworm. He had a finely honed radar when it came to women, and it screamed a warning about this one. Women with her looks were practiced at using their physical appeal to seduce a man into providing for them, and that wasn't Jackson's style at all. His relationships tended to be hot, short and shallow, and that was the way he liked them.

It didn't take someone with his track record to be able to tell what this woman was. It was apparent in her looks, the way she had of strolling into a room, looking for all the world as if she owned the place. He didn't know her, but he recognized her all the same. As he had told Jeff, he knew enough about women to know what drove them, and any woman who looked like this one was used to having men fall all over her. But she was going to find things different here, Jackson vowed grimly. This was a working ranch, not a setting for an educated little hothouse flower.

His ex-fiancée had been a woman just as attractive as Kaly Scott, he mused with a sardonic twist to his mouth. Pretty, pampered and spoiled, she had spent all her time pouting for him to come and play with her and whining that it wasn't enough. And then she had found someone else just as spoiled and useless to play with full-time. The pain of her betrayal had faded in the years since, but the lesson she taught him had not. Women weren't to be trusted, and beautiful women were treacherous.

He shoved impatiently away from the wall and strode toward the house. Thinking about past mistakes was a waste of time, except as a reminder to avoid repeating them. Morning came early at a ranch. He still had a pile of paperwork to do before he could turn in.

Late that evening Kaly leaned back in her chair. She saved her work on her computer and shut it off. Stretching her tired shoulders, she readied for bed. As she ambled wearily back from the bathroom with her eyes at half-mast, she ran into a solid wall. Her eyes flew open. Jackson Roberts, looking as weary as she and very bad-tempered, held her away from his chest with two hard hands on her shoulders.

"Sleepwalking, Miss Scott?" he asked caustically.

She strove to respond evenly. "Just getting ready to call it a night. You seem to have been working late too."

Jackson closed his eyes briefly, remembering the events of the day. "You could say that," he murmured. His hands seemed to have a life of their own, sliding down her arms and back up again in an unconscious caress.

Pinpoints of pleasure radiated through Kaly from his careless gesture, and she jerked away as if she'd been scalded.

His eyes opened and she thwarted his biting question by mumbling, "Good night," and scurrying back to her room, leaving him staring after her reflectively.

Kaly slipped into bed thankfully. She'd been shaken anew by the sensations his touch so easily wrought, and it was a bad sign indeed. Despite Susan's preaching, Kaly knew exactly what type of man was best for her, and when she was again ready to let one into her life, he wouldn't be an oversize man of steel used to wielding power and giving orders. Next time she would choose a man who would cherish her independence, not trample it.

She rolled over and punched her pillow, trying to forget the feel of those hard hands on her.

Chapter 3

Immediately after breakfast the next morning Jeff and Kaly went into the office and worked out a schedule. They agreed that they would work together all morning, with afternoons saved for transcribing notes and Jeff's actual writing.

Jeff showed her to the small desk that would be hers. She was relieved to note that the computer on it was a model she was familiar with. Then he motioned Kaly to sit on the overstuffed couch, but remained standing. "As you know, my book details the settling of the Southwest," he began.

She nodded her understanding, a small smile tilting her mouth as Jeff started to pace in front of her. The good-natured man she was coming to know was lost as the earnest historian took his place.

"You need background information on the tribes living in the Southwest at the time," she filled in.

"Exactly," Jeff affirmed. "I want to provide more

detail than most historians do about the disruption this caused to the Indian way of life.''

''Where do you want me to start?'' Kaly asked, a little at a loss. Jeff sat down in his desk chair and whirled to face her. ''Start anywhere at all.'' He picked up a pad and pen and waited expectantly.

She gathered her thoughts for a moment and then took a deep breath. ''Several Native American tribes lived in the Southwest long before the first white man came,'' she began. ''There were the Hopi, Navaho, Apache, Pueblo and the Zuni. The Spaniards were the first whites to come into contact with them...''

The two worked all morning, with Kaly speaking and Jeff asking questions and making notes. They made lists of questions she would research later.

They broke for lunch and then worked until after four, when Carrie interrupted them.

''Jeff, your editor is on the phone. Do you want to take it now?''

Jeff stretched and looked at Kaly. ''What do you think? Did we get far enough for one day?''

Kaly picked up her glass of water, which had been refilled frequently, and took a swallow. She jested, ''If you keep me talking that much every day, I'll need new vocal cords after the first week.''

Jeff grinned. ''Okay, I can take a hint.'' He looked at his wife. ''See, Carrie, she's only here for a day, and already she runs the show.'' The three laughed. He continued more seriously, ''I'll take the call now. Why don't we call it a day, Kaly? This will probably take some time.''

Kaly rose to leave the office.

''Would you like me to show you a little of the ranch?'' Carrie offered.

"Not on horseback," Jeff warned his wife as he picked up the receiver.

Carrie made a face. "We'll take the walking tour," she promised him. The two women went outdoors and headed toward the first barn. There were several of the large red structures, all some distance from the house. "Jackson has added these to the ranch since he's been in charge," Carrie said.

"How long *has* he been in charge?"

"He's always been much more involved with the actual ranching than Jeff," Carrie explained. "Jackson followed his dad and the men around from the time he could walk. Jeff always had his nose in a book." She shot Kaly a mischievous glance. "Some things never change."

"This ranch must have been in your husband's family for some time," Kaly surmised.

"Four generations," Carrie affirmed matter-of-factly. "Jeff and Jackson's father added quite a bit of land to the original acres. It's about ten thousand now."

Kaly stopped and gaped at Carrie, sure she'd misunderstood her. "Acres?"

Carrie nodded. "Great-Grandfather Roberts claimed five thousand acres when he settled here in 1870, and each generation has added more."

Kaly pondered this information. It was amazing to think of that much land staying in the same family for more than one hundred years. "Is Jeff's father retired?"

Carrie shook her head sadly. "He died of cancer four years ago. Jeff was still in graduate school. Jackson had already returned from college and had been working with his dad. As their father got sicker, Jackson took over more and more of the management. By the time his father died, Jackson had been making most of the decisions for quite a while. Their mother died shortly after Jeff was born, so it's just the two of them.''

That explained Jackson's aura of command, Kaly thought. It was easy to see he was used to giving orders and having them obeyed.

The women approached the barn that Carrie said held the horses. ''We keep about twenty horses for the hands, as well as several for pleasure-riding. That used to be one of my favorite pastimes.'' She sighed wistfully, then looked thoughtfully at Kaly. ''There's no reason you shouldn't ride whenever you wish, though. Have you ridden before?''

''I used to ride quite a bit as a child,'' Kaly admitted. ''I haven't been on a horse in years, though.''

''I'll introduce you to Nate. He's been here forever and takes care of the horses. Whenever you feel like riding, just come out and he'll help you get a mount ready.''

A grizzled older man approached them from the opposite opening in the barn. He walked with the bandy-legged stride that bespoke many years on the back of a horse. As he drew closer to the women, he swept off his hat and greeted them. ''Afternoon, Mrs. Carrie. Hope you ain't here trying to sweet-talk me into saddling Misty for you.''

Carrie flushed and responded tartly, ''Rest assured, Nate, if I'd known what a tattletale you are, I never would have asked in the first place.''

The old man cackled. ''I just thought your husband might be a bit interested, seeing's how he was the one who told me you wouldn't be riding till after the little one's born.''

Cheeks still red, Carrie turned to Kaly and introduced her to the cowboy. "Nate's a real blabbermouth," she added, "so don't tell him anything other than the name of the horse you want to ride."

Nate cackled again. "Nice to meet you, Miss. Mr. Jeff already told me to help you out with a mount if'n you feel like riding."

Kaly looked longingly at the stable full of horses. "Tell you what, Nate," she said decisively. "I'll be out after supper. Just for a short ride, though," she warned as the man nodded approvingly. "You'll have to pair me up with a gentle one. I haven't ridden for years."

Carrie piped up with, "She can ride Misty, Nate." To Kaly she explained, "Misty's my mare, and she hasn't been getting much exercise lately. You'd be doing me a favor if you would ride her while you're here."

Kaly was touched. She knew most owners were fussy about who rode their horses. "Thank you, Carrie. I promise I'll take good care of her."

The women continued through the barn, stopping periodically to stroke the velvety muzzle of an inquisitive horse. On the other side of the barn was a corral area, where several men were gathered. Carrie walked up to the group and began introductions.

Kaly's head spun as she tried to keep the names straight. By the time Carrie finished, there were only four faces she could match names with. Tom was the one who looked like a kid, though he was probably in his twenties. He seemed shy, never looking either woman in the face as he nodded a greeting and ducked his head. Rod was an older, dark-haired man. Nick, the one Carrie introduced as the ranch foreman, intrigued Kaly the most. There was something almost familiar about him, although she was sure she'd never seen him before.

It jolted her to realize he reminded her of Jackson. The two men didn't resemble each other physically, but Nick had the same brooding air, and eyes that seemed to assess, then look right through a person. He nodded politely to Kaly, but not a flicker of emotion crossed his hard face.

The last man introduced was a different story. Larry Scott was a blond man about her own age with an open, engaging manner. Right away he played on the fact that they shared the same last name.

"I'm sure we're related. I'll bet we're kissing cousins, on my daddy's side," he joked, a teasing light in his eyes.

Kaly pretended to ponder. "I don't think so," she said. "I don't have any other relatives that resemble you."

Larry grinned easily and replied, "Just as well. Now there won't be any reason for us not to get married. We should, you know, just for the convenience. You wouldn't have to change your last name."

Before she could frame a laughing rejoinder, a sardonic voice spoke behind her. "I doubt the lady would find it convenient to marry someone of your limited means, Larry."

Kaly whirled around and came face-to-face with Jackson. He scowled down at her surprised features. He had seen the group of men as he rounded the corner of the barn and had hastened over, believing there must be a problem. He'd frozen when he saw the women, and watched in simmering anger as his usually levelheaded hands fell all over themselves to greet the lovely newcomer. After a long day filled with more than the average number of headaches, the scene caused his temper to ignite even more quickly than usual. When he spoke to Kaly, his voice was deadly. "Your job here is to help my brother, not to entertain my men. Stay the hell away from them, or you'll have me to deal with."

He ignored her openmouthed dismay and looked beyond her, addressing the men in a louder tone. "Seems to me that most of you guys have better things to do than stand around talking, but if you don't, stick around and I'll find something for you." Taking furtive looks at the boss's implacable expression, the men quickly dispersed, except for Nick, who walked over and began to discuss something with Jackson.

Kaly was speechless. There had been no misinterpreting his remarks this time. They had been blatantly insulting. She walked stiffly back to Carrie's side and waited until she finished her conversation with Rod.

Jackson glared after Kaly as the two women departed. When he'd noticed her here among his men, he'd seen red. It was the past repeating itself, when his ex-fiancée had interfered with every aspect of ranch work in search of a male audience. He recognized women like Kaly Scott, knew they needed to have men eating out of their hands, needed it like air to breathe. But he wouldn't let her turn his men into a bunch of hungry saps, making fools of themselves over her.

He turned back to his foreman, who was eyeing him knowingly. "Well, what?" Jackson snapped.

Nick shook his head. He knew better than to tangle

with his boss when he was in such a foul temper. "I'll go give Rod a hand with that truck," he responded, and left Jackson looking as if he'd like to take a bite out of someone.

Carrie steered Kaly back to the house. "The rest of the barns are for the cattle," she explained, unaware of Kaly's agitation. She had missed the exchange between Jackson and Kaly. "We can walk over there another time, if you'd like."

"I'm not sure we should," Kaly answered carefully. "Jackson didn't seem pleased to find us near the corral."

Carrie looked puzzled. "I don't know what's the matter with Jack lately. He hasn't been himself for weeks. It isn't like him to bite the men's heads off like he did back there. Something must be bothering him."

Kaly was beginning to get an idea of exactly what was bothering the rancher. At first she had thought they had angered him by invading his domain at the corral. But after more thought, she decided it was deeper than that. Her very presence at the ranch seemed to infuriate him, although she was mystified as to why he felt that way.

"He hasn't even been going out much in the evenings, and that's especially odd. Jackson's a real ladies' man," Carrie informed her. She took a quick look at Kaly's set expression and hastened to explain, "It's not that he's a Don Juan or anything. But he was hurt badly a few years ago by a woman he was engaged to. He's never talked about it—he guards his privacy—but I think the experience really hardened him. He plays the field these days."

It was no wonder, Kaly thought snidely, still smarting from his earlier remarks. Women obviously didn't want anything to do with Jackson Roberts once they got to know him!

After dinner that evening Kaly eagerly changed clothes and went to the barn. There she found Nate, who already had Misty saddled.

"Mrs. Carrie phoned from the house and told me you were coming," he informed her. "Misty's a beauty and gentle as a lamb. You shouldn't have no trouble with her. You ever lose your way riding her, just give her the reins. She'll head back here eventually."

Kaly thanked him and took off from the yard at a gentle trot. The horse's movements rocked her soothingly, bringing a measure of peace. The stark beauty of the land around her was dazzling in its contrasts, not unlike the man who ranched it. Jackson, too, was compelling to look at, but dangerous to the unheeding.

She could feel her earlier tension returning as she considered the man. She was still stinging from his remarks at the stable. She certainly didn't want to be at odds with Jeff's brother all summer; the next few months would be terribly uncomfortable if she was. But the more she thought about it, the safer that seemed. Somehow, she knew even without experiencing it that Jackson Roberts was capable of a formidable, wholly masculine charm, and she was eager to keep that fierce intent turned away from her. She already had proof she was susceptible to his intense sexuality. His most casual touch had shown her that.

She shivered. As unpleasant as it would be, she would prefer to be on the outs with him all summer. Their hostility would serve as a buffer between them. Kaly felt like a coward admitting, even to herself, that she needed such a protective barrier. But something deeply feminine inside her was aware she was emotionally vulnerable to the man, and she was determined he not learn of it. As long as she kept these unfamiliar feelings hidden, they couldn't be used against her.

The sight of a large black horse tethered to a fence post brought Kaly out of her musings. Her gaze searched for its rider, and she went rigid when she recognized the man leaning over the fence nearby. Jackson looked up and called out a greeting. After his show of temper earlier this afternoon, she was shocked and not a little wary of his cordiality.

"Surveying your kingdom?" she asked flippantly as she pulled up next to him.

The side of his mouth lifted. "Just taking a breather." He nodded to a nearby tree. "Tie up your horse and join me for a minute."

She sat frozen at his words. Her determination to maintain a distance from this man in any way possible was being put to the test much sooner than she'd imagined. She wasn't ready for another confrontation, she thought a little wildly. She needed time to marshal her defenses, to recover the inner calm she'd always been able to rely on. None of that calm remained right now. It had vanished at the first sight of his big tough body propped indolently against the wooden boards, every hard muscle outlined in the faded denim jeans. In spite of her earlier brave determination to stoke the flames of hostility between them, right now she felt an overwhelming urge to dig her heels into Misty's sides and gallop in the opposite direction.

When Kaly did not immediately obey but remained

seated on the horse, Jackson's face showed impatience. "Did you need help dismounting?"

His words jolted her out of her momentary indecision. At his offer, Kaly hurriedly slid down from the saddle and slowly walked the mare over to the tree, tying her to a branch. The last thing she wanted was for Jackson Roberts to put his hands on her again! Or worse yet, to think she was coyly inviting such an action. She could handle him right now. She didn't need time or planning to take what he dished out, nor to return more of the same. She threw her thick blond braid over her shoulder and asked with feigned nonchalance, "Think we can have a conversation without one of us drawing blood?"

He quirked an eyebrow at her. "I'm willing to try if you are." He raked her with his gaze, slowly taking in the long lithe legs sheathed in worn denim. Jackson felt an unfamiliar pang of remorse for his behavior at the corral. She wasn't responsible for his bad temper then, any more than she could help being exactly the kind of woman he'd sworn off forever. Beautiful women were spoiled by men. After receiving all that attention their whole lives, it was understandable that they demanded it as their due.

He ruthlessly squashed the sentiment. Listen to yourself, he thought derisively. Now you're making excuses for her! That should have told him just how dangerous Kaly Scott was. He had no intention of getting involved with her, but the last thing he needed was for her to complain to Jeff about his behavior. For his brother's sake, he had to get on a casually polite footing with the woman and stay on it.

It was this decision that had made him invite her to join him, but she was approaching him with all the enthusiasm of a calf to branding. He was annoyed, even though he knew her distrust was deserved. It also irritated the hell out of him to be so sharply aware of how the soft fabric of her jeans molded to her shapely thighs.

Kaly walked toward him, searching for a neutral topic. "I've been enjoying the scenery on my ride," she finally offered tentatively.

"It's a little bleak out here for some people," he said quietly. "Not everybody can see the beauty of this land."

Kaly cocked her head, her innate curiosity taking over her earlier resolve. "But you do." She spoke with certainty.

Jackson nodded, his gaze roving over the horizon. The unending roll of pasture, the mountains in the distance, the rock formations that jutted up from nowhere—the sheer majesty of earth and sky was breathtaking to him.

"Carrie was telling me a little about the ranch this afternoon," Kaly offered, tactfully leaving out the episode when Jackson had appeared at the corral. "She told me how huge it was. Is that why I haven't seen any cattle yet?"

He pointed in the direction she had been riding. "If you ride five more minutes that way, the fence line becomes barbed wire. That's the east pasture. We have about 150 head there. The others are scattered in different pastures all over the ranch. That way we don't have too many head grazing in the same spot. Some of the other cattle are kept isolated."

"Why is that?"

"Bulls are separated to keep them from fighting each other and getting injured." Jackson didn't go into the reasons the bulls fought, which had to do with breeding. No use shocking the city girl with the facts of life on a cattle ranch. "Females with new calves are by themselves for the first few weeks." He couldn't resist a wicked jab. "Like most females, mama cows can be a little touchy."

Kaly ignored the ribbing. "My grandparents have a farm in Arizona, near my home. They keep some horses and raise Herefords."

"Good beef cattle." Jackson nodded. "We have mostly Brahmans here."

At Kaly's blank look, he elucidated, "Brahmans are a strange-looking breed if you haven't seen any before. They have a big hump at the back of the neck. Make a grunting sound, instead of a moo."

"You're lucky you're able to do what you love." At Jackson's quizzical look, Kaly clarified, "The ranch, I mean. It's obvious you wouldn't enjoy anything else."

Jackson nodded. "I wouldn't be happy in a nine-to-five, necktie job, that's for sure. Cities are great for evenings out, but after a couple of days they begin to close in on me. I nearly went crazy sometimes at college."

"I'm surprised you went to college," Kaly remarked.

"Why? Can't believe that an ignorant cowboy could hack the big university?"

"No," she murmured. Whatever other qualities Jackson Roberts appeared to possess, ignorance wasn't one of them. "I just have a hard time picturing you off the ranch."

He cast her a quick glance. "I hated being away," he affirmed. "Sometimes I'd come home and spend the whole weekend camped outside, trying to get enough of it to last me when I got back to school.'' He stopped abruptly then, but Kaly was nodding her understanding.

''I know what you mean. I used to love to stay in the country with my grandparents. I felt so free there. Nobody ever expected me to behave a certain way or placed restrictions on what I could or couldn't do.''

Jackson eyed her keenly. ''You don't like restraints?''

''They're very uncomfortable,'' Kaly answered lightly, and he nodded.

Kaly scanned the vast meadow before them. She mentally congratulated herself for agreeing to stop and talk to him. Maybe she'd been too hasty when she'd vowed to stay at odds with him. Here they were, having a normal conversation, and lightning hadn't struck, the earth hadn't cracked, nor had there been any other major catastrophe. It might just be possible to maintain a civil relationship with Jackson Roberts, without having to resort to erecting a stone wall between them.

''You never did tell me what made you decide to come here.'' At her confused expression he expanded, ''To the ranch. Why would you be interested in coming way out here for your summer vacation?''

''Jeff is building a reputation as a fine historian. It's an honor to be able to work with him on this book.''

''We're all proud of Jeff,'' Jackson allowed. ''He was always the brainy one in the family. But what do you usually do in the summer?''

''I've gone to summer school when I could afford it, worked when I couldn't. I spent most of last summer on a Navaho reservation, researching my dissertation. Working with Jeff this summer will be a valuable experience, and it'll pay for my classes next fall,'' Kaly explained.

He was silent as he digested this. When he spoke again, his tone was guarded. "You're putting yourself through school?''

She nodded. ''I've received scholarships, so that's helped, but the doctoral program is expensive. I work to pay for classes. That's why it's taken me a bit longer to complete the program. I only have another semester before I finish up, though. Assuming, of course, that the final draft of my dissertation is accepted.''

So the lady wasn't as pampered and useless as he'd first figured, Jackson thought. He'd assumed that some indulgent parents were bankrolling the school career, giving in to their precious daughter's every whim. But obviously he'd been wrong. He had no use for people who expected handouts, who weren't willing to do honest work for what they wanted. He had to respect, at least, the way she had managed to do just that.

Unaware of the direction of his thoughts, Kaly added idly, ''Dr. Morehead is a big fan of your brother's. He's convinced my work on Jeff's book will benefit me as much as it will Jeff.''

Of course. Jackson's face twisted at her words. If he hadn't been so disgusted with himself, he would have laughed out loud. What a fool he'd been to consider even for a moment that Kaly Scott was different from any other woman he'd known. So it wasn't money she was after; it was prestige. He supposed this job did look good to her; it was a way to earn a buck and get some glory from working with his brother at the same time. But to his mind, using a man to pad her résumé was just as bad as trapping one for his bank account.

"Well, that sure figures," he muttered sardonically.

Kaly was bewildered at his sudden change in attitude. The man's moods were as difficult to follow as a maze. "What?"

"That's what it always comes down to, doesn't it, with women like you. Using a man for whatever you think you need." Jackson was annoyed with himself for forgetting for even a minute what kind of woman she was. Oh, she might be smarter than most, but that just made her more shrewd, better able to get what she wanted from a man before the guy even knew he was a target.

His last remark was the spark that lit her own usually even temper. "And what is that supposed to mean?" she demanded. "A woman like me?"

He smiled cynically. "Women who are motivated to get what they want, no matter who they hurt. Some women want money—" he shrugged "—with you it's fame. Hell, at least you're honest about it."

Kaly clenched her hands tightly into fists to squelch the urge to sound her palm smartly on his hard cheek. Never had anyone infuriated her so quickly. "Only cretins make such ridiculous generalizations about people. Just because you had a bad experience with your ex-fiancée doesn't mean you have to be suspicious of every other woman you meet."

Jackson froze. He didn't welcome comments on his personal life from anyone, not even family, which this woman damned sure wasn't. He slowly straightened and turned toward her. "What the hell do you mean by that?" he asked menacingly.

Kaly realized she had crossed a dangerous line, but

she was past caring. She wasn't going to back down, not before his insults or his temper. "I meant that all women are different, and it's time you realized it," she continued recklessly. "You're not the only person in the world to have gotten hurt, you know."

Jackson glared down at her narrowly. She was lecturing him on how to deal with women? That was rich. Especially after he'd just found out what had really motivated her to come to the ranch. "You and Carrie had quite a little chat this afternoon, didn't you? Well, let me tell you something, lady, I don't need a glory-hungry bookworm to teach me about relationships with the opposite sex."

"Your ignorance is exceeded only by your imagination," Kaly said disgustedly. "Where do you get your preposterous assumptions about people?"

"Experience," Jackson retorted flatly. "Mine. And the next time you need a thrill, read a romance novel. Then you won't need to get your kicks gossiping about my relationships with women."

Kaly pushed herself away from the fence. "I should have known that this friendly act of yours was phony," she said icily. She headed back to where Misty was tied. "For your information, Jackson," she threw over her shoulder, "I have less interest in your personal life than I have in the mating habits of the reptile kingdom, though I'm sure the similarities are endless."

Jackson watched her walk away with narrowed eyes. Maybe he'd been rough on her just then, but he was really touchy about certain subjects, and without even trying, Kaly brought all of them out. He felt his anger abate a little. A man would have to be made of stone not to appreciate the gentle sway of her tush as she stalked toward her horse. And that was one thing no one had ever accused him of being.

''By the way—'' Kaly half turned back to him for a moment ''—the benefit I mentioned from working with Jeff? I was referring to the research I'd be doing all summer for him. Dr. Morehead and I agreed that it would also help me prepare for the written and oral exams I have to take at the end of my doctoral program.''

She took some satisfaction from the flicker of surprise that crossed his face and turned back to the mare. Reins in hand, she prepared to mount.

''Wait,'' he commanded.

For a heartbeat he didn't think she would obey, but then with exaggerated patience she turned and drawled, ''What now?''

He was silent for a long moment. Then he finally allowed, ''Maybe I was out of line a minute ago.''

When he said nothing else, her eyebrows rose. ''Is that supposed to pass for an apology?'' she asked snootily.

He propped an elbow against the fence and waited, but saw no softening in her countenance. ''Well, hell,'' he said mildly, ''that's not the way you're supposed to act when a man says he's sorry. You're supposed to be full of compassion, pat him on the head.''

Kaly pursed her lips to prevent a smile. ''I'd like to pat you on the head with a pickax.''

A corner of his mouth kicked up. ''God, you're such a snot.'' He chuckled. ''I'm surprised you weren't beaten regularly as a child.''

Kaly looked smug. ''I was a fast runner.''

He grew more serious. ''So I'm forgiven?''

She pretended to consider, then said with mock reluctance, "Oh, I suppose. It's so tedious to watch grown men grovel." She turned to Misty again, planning to mount. Jackson moved to her side.

"Here, let me give you a hand," he started, and Kaly turned back.

"That's not necessary...." She swallowed. He was very close. And very big. She took an involuntary step closer to the mare.

The hands that Jackson had extended to help her into the saddle seemed suspended in midair for a moment, before he slowly lowered them to settle on her arms. She seemed to be holding her breath, or maybe he was the one not breathing. Oxygen seemed nonexistent.

Without thinking, he lowered his head an inch. Kaly's lips were pink, slightly parted and very inviting. A fraction away from her lips he whispered, "Truce?"

Kaly's lips quivered. She knew this was a bad idea. A terrible idea. Ill thought-out and impulsive and... "Truce," she whispered back. And watched that well-formed mouth approach hers before she let her eyelids flutter shut.

His lips were enticing, the gentleness of his kiss at odds with his rock-hard demeanor. He brushed his mouth over the bow of hers, once, twice, then again. With his tongue he traced the seam of her lips, probing intimately. Kaly dropped the reins, bringing her hands up to press against his chest.

Jackson opened his eyes and released her lips. A millisecond passed before her hands smoothed up to his shoulders and his mouth came down again, without gentleness this time, to take her on a journey of swirling arousal.

Kaly felt her knees weaken. His tongue swept her mouth in sensual possession and filled her with his taste. It dueled with hers, enticing her to return the pleasure. His tongue skated along her teeth and flicked the sensitive roof of her mouth.

Her world tilted. This was unlike any kiss she'd ever had. Jackson kissed her with complete assurance in his own masculinity, and her body recognized that assurance and reveled in it. Without conscious thought, she allowed her body to soften against his harder one.

His mouth lifted a fraction from hers. He demanded gutturally, "Kiss me back, Kaly. Kiss me the way I'm kissing you." Almost fiercely he sealed their mouths again.

Kaly was not sure she had the experience to obey his erotic demand, but she was helpless to deny him. Her pointed tongue made timid forays into his mouth, playing hide-and-seek with his own. A jolt shook his big body at her flirtatiousness and he ground his mouth over hers. One hand dropped to caress her hip and pull her hard against him, letting her feel the very physical effect she had on him.

Kaly's heart hammered crazily. Her arms slid up his huge biceps to twine around his neck, one hand sliding into the thick hair at his nape. Never had a kiss aroused her to such hunger. Sweet, hot fire rolled through her, and she pressed even closer to the muscled planes of his body. Her nipples tightened shamefully, straining petulantly from behind the lacy confines of her bra. Frissons of passion raced up her spine and desire began to flame in her belly.

The kiss seemed endless as their mouths twisted together, their tongues locked in tender torment. Jackson raised his head slightly, his breath still touching her face. Kaly opened her eyes and looked up into his navy ones. Desire had tautened the already hard lines of his face and smoked his eyes. He stared down for a second into the cloudy green eyes below him, and the passion he read there made desire claw in his gut. He had too much experience to mistake the arousal in the woman before him. Reason gone, he again lowered his head, intent on sampling more of her sweet passion.

At that moment, one of the horses stamped its foot and whinnied gently. Jackson froze. Memory poured back through him, of where they were, who she was. Mentally he cursed as he attempted to quiet his raging hormones. He pulled Kaly's arms from around his neck and put her away from him. Turning slightly, he ran one shaking hand through his hair.

"God almighty, Kaly, that almost went too far."

She was dazed at his sudden departure. "It did? I mean...it did, yes." Why had he stopped? She had wanted it to go on and on. She didn't want to think. Then his words penetrated her consciousness, and she backed up, eyes widening in shock. "What was I doing? I don't even like you," she blurted unthinkingly.

Jackson, his pride stung, glared at her. "Well, I was having a real hard time remembering that a minute ago. It sure didn't feel like a solo act to me."

She glared back at him. "I'm sure your memory is controlled by your libido. The two never work simultaneously."

He barely controlled his frustrated desire as he snapped back, "Look, however it happened, we have to make sure it doesn't happen again."

"It can't." Kaly wrapped her arms around herself, suddenly cold.

"It won't."

They looked at each other for a long moment. She was awash in shame. "I'm going back to the house," she muttered. Without waiting for a reply she quickly mounted Misty and turned the mare in what she hoped was the way she had come. Kicking the horse gently, she urged it to a trot, anxious to put as much distance as possible between Jackson and herself.

Kaly bit her lip to prevent the tears she could feel pooling in her eyes. The last few minutes had been so unlike her! She had never been a flirt, never known how to tease. Relationships had always seemed so simple. Two people met, they had things in common, and they became friends. Sometimes that friendship progressed to something deeper, more meaningful. That was the way it had been with Philip and her. She wasn't a prude, but she had always felt that physical intimacy was wrong if the two people didn't share a genuine caring and respect for each other.

Her cheeks flushed, she made a clicking sound to hurry Misty along. Somehow she was uncertain whether her convictions could withstand the assault of Jackson Roberts's expertise. She'd known he was dangerous, had known it the first time the man had touched her. Now she knew he was lethal. The barn came into sight and Kaly headed for it.

He's way out of my league, she thought, and shivered. She must never get that close to him again.

Jackson stayed by the fence for a long time after Kaly had ridden off. His body still ached with the determination it had taken to push her away. The suddenness of his desire for her had astounded him. He had touched her on impulse, and after that there had been no thought involved.

As much as he hated to take any time away from the ranch right now, Jackson grimly conceded he was going to have to resume dating. He was a man with rigid control, but also one with a healthy sexual appetite. If he remained celibate much longer, he was very much afraid he was going to make a mistake with Kaly Scott. That would be a very costly mistake indeed.

Even as he made that decision, his thoughts crept back to the woman he had so recently held. Jackson had had a lot of women, not as many as had been attributed to him, but enough. They had always been attracted to him, drawn by that go-to-hell attitude that was so much a part of him. Yet it had always been second nature to keep a part of himself remote from the woman and what they shared. His passion had never ruled him; he had always maintained tight control over it.

But when Kaly had responded as she did, inching that sweet tongue of hers into his mouth, he'd felt as though his body was going to explode. Every thought had been wiped from his mind, and he had only felt. Felt what her mouth tasted like. What her small lithe body felt like pressed up against his. How the womanly curve of her hips... Damn!

He thrust himself away from the fence impatiently. This wasn't doing him any good—he was getting hot again just remembering. He strode quickly to his horse, untied it and mounted awkwardly. He promised himself he wouldn't lay another finger on Kaly Scott. She reminded him too clearly of the mistake he had made in the past, and it wasn't one he was eager to repeat.

As he headed back toward the ranch he clenched his teeth against the ache in his groin, which showed no signs of subsiding.

Chapter 4

For the next few weeks, Kaly and Jackson avoided one another as much as possible. Each time she thought of the enigmatic rancher, she flinched inside, remembering with uncomfortable embarrassment how she'd responded in his arms. Never before had she reacted to a man with such total abandon. The only way she was able to forgive herself for that lapse was by promising herself repeatedly that she would not allow it to happen again.

But Kaly couldn't help the involuntary leap of her pulse each time she saw Jackson. Her newfound sensual awareness of him was as unexpected as it was unwelcome. That made her doubly grateful for the rarity of their meetings.

She was certain that one reason for his infrequent appearances was his renewed dating. Even Carrie had commented on it, noting it was unlike Jackson to order all his personal calls forwarded to the barn, instead of

having messages taken for him. She had laughingly
surmised that maybe he was getting serious about
someone again. That remark had brought an inexplicable tightness to Kaly's chest. It had been bad enough
dealing with the guilt she felt at how easily he'd
brought her to passion. To now find herself one of a
crowd made her feel stupid, as well.

One afternoon she was working in the office, transcribing notes while Jeff took Carrie to her doctor's
appointment in Albuquerque. When the door pushed
open and Jackson strode in, Kaly stared at him in
shock. He seemed just as nonplussed. After a moment,
she cleared her throat nervously. "Jeff and Carrie are
in Albuquerque," she informed him.

He nodded bemusedly. "Yeah." Then, collecting
himself, he explained, "I mean, I know. I just have
some work to do in here." He gestured in the direction
of his desk, but made no move toward it. His eyes
stayed on her. What with running the ranch and evenings out, he hadn't seen much of her since the incident in the pasture. His frenzied social life was an
attempt to remove him from temptation, but instead,
it was threatening to rob him of his sanity. He finally
moved in the direction of his desk, keeping Kaly in
his view. She had turned back to her computer screen
and her fingers fairly danced over the keyboard, mute
testament to the fact that his presence disturbed her
not at all.

His mouth twisted. Here he was knocking himself
out to stay away from her, burning the candle at both
ends, and she sat over there as poised as could be.

Peg's voice came over the intercom. "Jackson,
phone for you."

"Okay," he answered, and Kaly's fingers faltered

as he picked up the receiver. She wished fervently he had used another extension. She doubted her ability to sit by with equanimity and listen to him make yet another date.

Soon it became apparent that the caller was Jeff. Jackson's tone got terser, his comments shorter and more infrequent. Kaly finally gave up pretending she wasn't listening and turned to face him, worry stamped on her face. His was impassive, impossible to read, and she wanted to shake him. ''Is something the matter?'' she hissed, finally unable to stand the suspense any longer.

He shook his head at her, but she wasn't satisfied and waited impatiently for him to hang up the phone.

''Carrie's fine,'' he said, forestalling her anxious question. ''But on the way to the doctor she started having contractions. They stopped after an hour or so, but with her history, the doctor wants to play it safe. He's ordered stress tests to be taken every morning for the rest of the week.''

''Oh, poor Carrie and Jeff,'' Kaly answered softly. She could only imagine the heartache they must have suffered over the previous miscarriages. ''They must be so frightened.''

''Yeah,'' Jackson replied tersely, staring fiercely at the toes of his pointed boots. ''But Jeff said they're hopeful. It could be false labor. If nothing shows up on these tests, it's a good sign. They're going to stay in a motel, rather than drive back and forth every day. Jeff said not to worry about it.''

Kaly said sympathetically. ''But you can't help worrying, can you?''

He was silent a moment before replying, ''Carrie's been through hell the last couple of pregnancies. Jeff, too. I sure don't want either of them to have to live through that again.'' He sighed. "But there's nothing we can do except wait for news. He said he'd call with the results every day.'' Jackson scowled at the phone as if blaming it for the situation. "I hate waiting.''

"I'm surprised,'' Kaly responded tongue in cheek. "You're usually such a patient man.''

"One of my many good qualities,'' he agreed solemnly, and she made a face. Then her eyes widened in amazement when he approached his desk and sat down, swiveling his chair to turn on the computer on the table next to his desk.

"What are you doing?'' she asked unthinkingly.

"I told you, I have to work. I hope I won't bother you,'' he said with mock politeness.

"But you never work in here during the day,'' she objected, not caring that he was gazing at her interestedly, obviously noting that she kept track of his habits.

"I need to be outside running my ranch during the day,'' he agreed, "but there's a load of paperwork that goes along with this job, and I've been neglecting it lately. Now I have to get caught up before I get buried in it.''

Kaly turned back to her own computer. Not for the world would she have reminded him that his busy social life in the past few weeks might have caused this overload. Her fingers hit the keys with more force than necessary. She didn't know how much work he had to do, but she hoped it wouldn't take long. Because she was dismally aware that her powers of concentration were nil in his presence.

As the hours passed, Kaly learned that she *was* able to work side by side with Jackson. At first the silence in the room seemed heavy with tension, and she was as inefficient as she'd feared, retyping the same paragraph three times before she caught her error. But gradually, as Jackson made no attempts at conversation and seemed engrossed in what he was doing, she relaxed. She made her way through most of the work Jeff had left and began to wonder how she was going to keep busy the rest of the week.

Her gaze snuck to the man across the room, who was cursing under his breath. He had been muttering for the past several minutes, and now he was glowering fiercely at the screen and uttering dire threats at it.

Kaly's mouth twitched. If it was one thing she understood, it was the sheer frustration of feeling that a machine was outsmarting you. "Is something wrong?" she asked.

"There's something wrong with this damn computer," he snarled. He caught the amusement on her face and warned her, "And don't give me that stuff about a computer being only as smart as the person running it, or I won't be responsible for my actions."

Kaly laughed. "I wouldn't dare," she promised. "I've been there too many times myself." She watched him for a moment longer as he continued to push keys in vain. "Maybe I can help," she offered hesitantly. He looked up and she added quickly, "It's the same kind as the one I'm using, isn't it? I may have had a similar problem before."

He shrugged. "It's all yours."

She rounded his desk and Jackson pulled up another chair for her in front of the computer. "What are you having difficulty with?"

"It won't bring up the file I requested." He sent another threatening glare at the screen. "I've used every command I can think of."

"It could be in the retrieval or just a problem with the way it was saved," murmured Kaly as she typed in a command. "What did you name the file?" She turned to look at him at the same time he brought his face closer to see what she was doing.

Tendrils of hair had escaped from her braid, and one brushed his cheek as she turned her head. It felt silky against his skin, and he wondered, for what seemed like the hundredth time, how it would feel to free the satiny skeins and bury his face in them.

He shifted uncomfortably to relieve the ache that the image brought. Already he could feel his skin heat from that single tantalizing touch. Staying away from Kaly was proving more difficult than he had imagined. It was hard to remember that she represented everything he normally steered clear of, especially since his memory was exquisitely accurate when it came to recalling how she had felt in his arms.

Kaly looked at him in concern when he didn't answer her question. "Jackson?"

His eyes met hers, startled, and belatedly he became aware that he had neglected to reply. "Ah...the name?"

"The name."

"Yeah." He cleared his throat, wishing he could clear his head as easily. She was looking at him as though she suspected he'd come down with some dreadful malady, which was not far from the truth. She'd be stunned to know she was the cause of it. "I've got it under 'Markets.'"

Kaly typed in the word and chewed her lip when

the computer failed to find the file. "Are you sure that's what you named the file?" she asked. "I don't see it listed on the menu."

"Of course, I'm sure." Jackson spoke with certainty. He paused for a few seconds before correcting himself. "I'm pretty sure."

Kaly raised her eyebrows, waiting.

"Okay, I thought I did, but I'm not positive, all right?" he amended grouchily.

Kaly buried her face in her hands.

"I can't help it if I'm computer-hostile," Jackson continued, aggrieved. "If God meant us to use computers, he'd have put microchips in our brains."

"I won't even touch that one," Kaly said wryly, raising her head.

"Jeff's always hounding me about the way I save files. He's the computer expert here—messed around with them quite a bit since college. It was his idea for me to use one for ranch business."

"They can be real time-savers," Kaly remarked, "especially with as much paperwork as the ranch must generate."

"That's how he convinced me," Jackson agreed, "but he forgot to add that they only save time when the person running them knows what the hell he's doing."

He sounded so irritated Kaly had to laugh. "Well, it's not that bad," she said diplomatically. "The market information is probably buried somewhere. All we have to do is bring up each file and look inside it."

Jackson eyed her speculatively. "I'll bet you know a lot more about it than I do. Maybe you could—"

Kaly guessed what his suggestion was before he finished making it. "Oh, no," she said firmly. "I'm sure that's what Jeff does every time this happens. He straightens it out and you never learn a thing.''

He attempted to look innocent at this accusation, but Kaly could have told him he was wasting his time. Innocent was one look that face could never achieve. There was a hint of wicked light dancing in his eyes and entirely too much experience stamped on his tanned, masculine features for him to pull it off.

She sniffed silently. No doubt that beseeching tone and guileless look had been practiced to a fine art and were wildly successful with the women who paraded through his social life. But it wouldn't work on her. She hadn't survived three brothers without learning something about the way men could manipulate others to do their bidding.

But she had never felt this clutch in her stomach when faced with their requests, either.

''I'll help you,'' she said, stressing the second word, ''but you have to pay attention. And it wouldn't hurt to take notes this time, either, so you can clean up your own messes from now on.''

Jackson looked smug at her acquiescence, but quickly found that she had been completely serious about demanding his attention. Not only did she insist he take notes, but after showing him what to do, she sat back and made him bring up each of the files. She coached him on the techniques for opening and renaming the files so he'd be able to find them later. When he finally found the file containing the missing information he had been looking for, he couldn't prevent a delighted grin.

''Well, I'll be damned!'' he crowed. ''We did it.''

Kaly returned his triumphant smile. But when he reached out an arm and gave her a hug, her smile froze on her face. Electrodes of pleasure ran a current up her side and radiated throughout as if on a circuit. Her breathing grew short, and panic welled up inside her. If a casual gesture like that had the power to evoke such electric pleasure, what chance did she have to withstand his considerable sensuality?

She stood up suddenly, almost upsetting her chair in her haste. "Congratulations." Her voice was strained. "I'll let you get on with what you were doing while I finish the work Jeff left me." She walked quickly back to her desk and ignored the puzzled look he sent her.

Kaly stared resolutely at her screen. It was painful to keep her distance from Jackson while he cavorted with a different woman every night. But it would be impossible to stay remote if he touched her again. She had to keep her self-preservation instincts firmly in place around him—it would be all too easy to fall prey to his charm.

She began typing a list of his most unattractive traits to keep in mind when she felt herself weakening. *A* was for...arrogant, she nodded as she typed. Certainly that. He had too much power and women came too easily for him to be otherwise. *B* was for bossy, Kaly typed automatically. That had been obvious from the start. *C* was for controlling, and that was the most frightening of all. She had spent most of her life fighting for the right to make her own decisions, and her independence had been too hard won for her to relinquish it to any man. *D* was for domineering. This was getting too easy.

"What?"

Kaly started at the sound of Jackson's voice. She

looked up to see him gazing quizzically at her. "What?" she repeated faintly.

"It sounded like you said *E*." He had a curious look on his face.

"No," Kaly denied swiftly. "I mean, I was just talking to myself." She squared her shoulders resolutely and began to finish up the notes she was transcribing for Jeff. She would do well to remember the words she had hurriedly erased from the screen. Every womanly instinct she owned warned her that this man could be devastating.

The next few days passed with surprising ease. Jeff called with good news each day, as the tests showed that Carrie was having no more contractions. Jackson came in after lunch each afternoon to work, and after a while Kaly offered to help him.

"Really?" His response was too quick to hide his eagerness.

"Sure. I'm at loose ends until Jeff gets back. Is there anything I can do?"

Jackson showed her a ledger filled with figures. "If you can just read each line off for me to enter on the computer, I think it will go a lot faster."

And it did go well. They switched places after lunch, with Jackson reading the figures, and worked companionably for the rest of the week. Simply by their proximity, Kaly learned more about Jackson in those days than she had in all the time she had spent at the ranch.

Despite his insistence that Jeff was the brains in the family, Kaly knew differently. Behind his desk hung his degree from the University of New Mexico. "What did you major in?" she asked him curiously.

He didn't look up from the computer. "Double majored in agricultural economics and animal sciences, minored in marketing."

Kaly's eyebrows rose. "What did you do in your free time?" she quipped, more than a little awed at his impressive studies.

This time he did look at her. "Mostly hung around the computer labs, designing software." They both laughed at his jest.

When the last figure was entered, Jackson made an exaggerated display of saving the work as she had taught him. Kaly clapped appreciatively. He leaned back in his chair, stretching his arms over his head. "We are done, partner. Dinner tonight should be a real celebration."

"Don't tell Peg that," Kaly warned. "I'd hate to see how much more food she could come up with if she thought it was a special occasion."

He smiled faintly, not responding while he studied her face. She was a constant surprise. The past few days he'd seen her quick intelligence, as well as her ready wit. She seemed to have a perfectly even temper, though he knew from experience that when riled she could give as good as she got. Teasing memories of what else he knew about her from experience tantalized him, and he dropped his gaze to her lips, intent on their pink fullness.

"What's the matter?" Kaly asked, surprised at the almost breathless quality of her voice.

"Hmm?" His eyes didn't move from her mouth.

"You're staring," she felt obliged to point out, and then finally his dark eyes met her own.

"Am I?" At her bemused nod, he said, "Well, maybe that's because I—"

"Jackson?"

They were both startled by the simultaneous rap at the door and the greeting. Nick walked into the room, but stopped short at the sight of the two of them staring at him. He looked from one to the other carefully, then focused on Jackson. "Got time?"

Kaly rose from her seat with haste and walked swiftly back to her own desk. There she busied herself tidying up stacks of papers already arranged in neat piles. The prolonged silence in the room finally penetrated her embarrassment, and she glanced at the two men. They were both watching her patiently, saying nothing.

It occurred to her, finally, that they didn't want to speak in front of her. She decided she could die of mortification just as easily out on the porch.

"I think I'll get some air," she said with feigned indifference, and made a quick exit.

When the door closed behind her, Jackson indicated for Nick to pull up a chair. He knew why his foreman was here. He had taken Nick into his confidence regarding Roy's suspicions about the rustlers working for the Circle R. Even if the sheriff's hunch was right, Jackson knew without a doubt Nick wasn't involved. He'd given the man a job when no one else in the world would, and he trusted him in a way he trusted few others.

"What do you have?"

"Not much," Nick admitted. "Some of the men owe money, that's nothing new. Rod's always strapped raising those kids of his. Trevitt's been gambling again. Larry bought himself a fancy new motorcycle—to impress the fillies, I suspect."

Jackson snorted. "Didn't he just buy a pickup last year?"

"Yep. He's still got that, too."

That drew his boss's attention. "Either he's come into some money we don't know about, or he's in hock up to his eyebrows. Which is it?"

Nick shrugged. "Probably in hock. You know how Larry is."

Jackson's mouth hardened. "God, I hate this," he muttered. He didn't like the feeling he got from snooping around in his men's lives. He sure wouldn't take kindly to someone doing the same to him. Not for the first time, he damned Roy for planting in his mind the ugly suspicion that one of his own hands was involved in this mess. "Anything else?"

The foreman shook his head.

"Hell, we're probably chasing our tails," Jackson said in disgust. "Well, let me know if you hear any more."

Nick nodded and left the room.

It could just as easily be someone from another ranch, Jackson thought grimly. Word traveled fast in these parts; his men might not have been the only ones aware of how long the sheriff's area watch would last. And now that Blane and Schmidt had lost cattle to the thieves, wasn't it just as likely that a hand from either of their ranches was in on it? It was probably even more likely that Roy had come up with this cock-and-bull idea so he wouldn't have to go out and find the real rustlers, Jackson thought sourly. He reached for the phone, meaning to call the sheriff, but then he dropped the receiver back into the cradle.

It wouldn't hurt to wait until after supper to call. His temper would be a little more under control by then, and he was undecided whether he even needed to repeat to Roy what Nick had told him. He rose from his chair and headed to the dining room.

Kaly was already seated, and she watched as Jackson mixed himself a drink. Without comment he poured her a glass of white wine and handed it to her.

Kaly raised her eyebrows as she accepted it. "It's customary to ask what a person would like to drink before deciding for her."

"What's the point?" He shrugged. "I already know you like white wine."

"The point," answered Kaly dryly, aware of the futility of explaining, "is to give the other person the chance to make a decision for herself."

He stared at her impatiently. "Are you trying to tell me you don't want that wine?"

She gave up. "The wine is fine."

Jackson studied her for a moment over the rim of his glass. "It may surprise you, Kaly," he said finally, "but some women find it flattering when a man remembers what they drink. Others don't even mind if a man orders for them in a restaurant."

Kaly's pained look told him what she thought of that practice.

"And there are still others—" here his voice lowered to a husky drawl "—who enjoy very much using their fingers to feed a man his whole meal, morsel by morsel."

Kaly met the devilment in his navy gaze squarely. "Those women should be seen to," she said clearly, "and chemically altered."

Jackson chuckled. It was obvious that his attempt to get a rise out of her had succeeded. "You're an independent little thing, aren't you?"

"I've had to be," she informed him. "If I'd waited for a man to dictate my life, I'd be living a very different one."

His eyebrows rose. "Oh? Such as?"

"I would have been safely enrolled in my hometown college, majored in home economics and graduated with my MRS degree."

Jackson's eyes crinkled up in amusement. "Whose plan was that?"

"My father's."

"But you went your own way because you don't like being dictated to."

"Do you?" Kaly countered.

"Touché." Jackson raised his glass in a salute.

They sat down at the polished walnut table as Peg came through the swinging doors with steaming dishes of food. Soon the table was filled with platters and bowls, and Kaly shook her head in amazement. "Peg, you keep forgetting that there are only two of us eating," she said, only half joking.

"You don't need to be eating like a bird," the older woman scolded, "and Jackson takes a lot to fill up. Has a hollow leg, that one does." She bent her head closer to Kaly's as she went by and said in a loud whisper, "Making sure he's full will keep him from taking a bite out of you." She continued to bustle around the table, chuckling.

Jackson eyed the color flooding Kaly's cheeks with interest. "I don't know," he murmured suggestively. "I'm betting that a bite of Kaly would taste quite... sweet."

Kaly mentally damned the blush she could feel heating her face. "Save it," she managed to order lightly. "I'm not one of your women, Jackson, remember?"

He remembered. God, did he remember! He was reminded by his instant reaction every time her hand grazed his, every time she walked by with that pert little wiggle she had. Or when he engaged in a fantasy of untwining her hair from that braid and finding out for himself if it was as thick and smooth as it looked. His body recalled in erotic detail how soft and supple she had felt in his arms.

And his brain remembered all the reasons she should never be there again.

Kaly interrupted his thoughts. "Tell me about the ranch," she said. "Carrie says you've been running it for some time."

Jackson nodded. "Ever since my dad died. He was one hell of a fighter. He kept this place going through droughts and low prices, and managed to build it into a well-respected beef operation. He kept trying till the end, but cancer was the one thing he couldn't beat."

"You must have learned a lot from him," Kaly observed quietly.

Jackson considered her statement. How could he explain the bond that had existed between his father and himself? It went deeper than that of parent and son. He put his fork down and reached for his glass. "He taught me...everything," he finally said. "How to ride, shoot and rope. I learned every aspect of ranching from him. He taught me to respect the land that gave us a living, to see its beauty and to put back as much as we took from it." He wiped his mouth on a napkin. "He was concerned about the environment and ecology long before it was fashionable, and he drilled into both Jeff and me the dangers of taking our natural resources for granted. Education was important to him, too—ranching isn't an occupation for the uninformed.'' He finished quietly, ''But most of the things I learned from him could never have been taught in a classroom, or read in a book. You have to live them.''

Peg's entrance interrupted the look of understanding that passed between the two of them. As she began to clear the table, Jackson stood up. ''Would you like to take a walk in the gardens?'' he offered. ''Peg's got a whole mess of roses out there she's always bragging about.'' This was offered in a tone guaranteed to be overheard by the housekeeper.

''Best rosebushes in the county,'' Peg said proudly. ''Been taking home so many ribbons from the fair the last few years I've purt near covered a whole wall with them. And you just remember, mister,'' she said as Jackson and Kaly walked toward the French doors, ''keep your hands off them, or you'll answer to me.''

Kaly had to bite her lip to keep from laughing at the look of mock fright that crossed Jackson's face, but she noticed as they walked that he was careful to do as Peg had ordered.

The brick paths between the flower beds were narrow, and she was uncomfortably aware of each time her arm brushed Jackson's. She edged away, trying for her own peace of mind to keep a little distance between them.

Jackson noticed her movement and commented on it as he stopped momentarily to light a cigarette. ''You're not afraid of me, are you, Kaly?''

She turned to eye him askance. ''Afraid?'' She shook her head firmly. ''I'm not afraid of you, or any other man.''

He didn't answer, just kept watching her steadily as he drew on his cigarette.

''Well, okay, I have to admit that Charles Manson gives me the creeps,'' she added cheekily.

His mouth quirked, but he didn't interrupt his perusal of her. ''Maybe 'afraid' was the wrong word. How about 'wary'?''

That observation was too close to the mark, and she was honest enough to admit it to both of them. ''Yes.''

He narrowed his eyes against the smoke curling up between them. ''Why?''

The question hung in the air as their eyes continued to meet. Why, indeed? Kaly searched for a truthful answer that wasn't overly blunt. ''You're too...'' Here she floundered. Too everything. Too big, too gorgeous, too successful and way too sure of himself. Too used to power and control and too easy about wielding them.

Jackson waited for her to finish, but when she didn't, he continued helpfully, ''Too sweet?''

She choked. Not hardly.

''Too smart?''

Most assuredly. Her mind still reeled from the management skills displayed in the thick ledgers and records he kept.

''Too darned handsome for my own good?'' His eyes were dancing, but her heart agreed. God, yes. For his good or anyone else's.

''Probably,'' she affirmed primly.

His hand went to his heart in shock. ''A compliment from Miss Scott? Will wonders never cease?'' His grin was a white slash in his darkly tanned face.

Kaly was visibly uncomfortable. ''I'm sure a man like you is very aware of your appeal to women.''

His eyebrows rose at this. ''A man like me?'' When

she didn't go on, he prompted her. "And what kind of man am I?"

She met his eyes squarely, despite her discomfort with the turn this conversation was taking. "Experienced."

Jackson tilted his head slightly to blow a stream of smoke away. "You don't get to be my age without some experience, Kaly. Or your age, either," he added. "Why does that bother you?"

She shook her head. "Let's drop it. I don't want to make the mistake again of offering unsolicited observations on your personal life," she said, referring to their discussion in the pasture.

"I was out of line," Jackson answered. "I thought we'd agreed on that. And I'm curious. Go ahead and tell me how you see me. I'm a big boy. I can take it."

After a long pause, Kaly did as he requested. "You're used to having your own way," she said slowly. "You've had a lot of responsibility with the ranch, and you're accustomed to giving orders."

"What's so bad about that?"

"Nothing," said Kaly, "when it's related to work. Only when you respond to people that way."

"You're saying I'm bossy," Jackson interpreted.

She almost laughed when he used one of the same words she had used to describe him to herself. "If the boot fits," she said sweetly.

He took another long drag on his cigarette, considering what she had said. He couldn't deny her words, not completely, anyway. Running the ranch required constant decision-making, and he didn't bother to tiptoe around his men—he told them what to do and they did it. He thought he was a bit more diplomatic with others, but apparently the lady saw things differently. "Go on," he invited.

Kaly plucked a waxy green leaf from one of the flowering plants nearby and began to shred it. She still doubted the wisdom of continuing in this vein, but he had, after all, invited it. "You use your experience with your ex-fiancée as a shield to keep women at a distance," she said finally.

"I don't know if you've noticed," he drawled, "but I like women to be pretty close."

"Physically, but not emotionally," she said firmly. "You don't let anyone get close enough to hurt you."

He was silent for so long that Kaly thought she had ignited his temper again. But when he spoke, his voice was quiet. "Spoken like someone who's been there. How about it, Kaly?" He met her eyes soberly. "Who caused you to be so cautious?"

He saw entirely too much, she thought uncomfortably. "I was engaged once, too," she admitted.

"And?"

"And I was wrong about him," she said slowly. "It frightened me to realize how poor my judgment was."

Jackson dropped his cigarette to the walk and ground it beneath his heel. "It puts a damnable dent in your pride," he agreed. "But you didn't let it destroy you. You got on with your life. So it sounds to me like we're not so different, after all."

Kaly mulled this over. They had in common the experience of being hurt by a person they'd chosen to marry, and that couldn't help but affect the way they responded to members of the opposite sex. She was uncomfortable with the feeling of kinship this knowledge brought. It had been difficult to ignore his pull when she had known little about him, but now she felt an emotional closeness, as well, and that terrified her.

She felt suffocated suddenly, by his nearness and their disclosures. "Do you know what time Carrie and Jeff will be back tomorrow?"

"Jeff said they'd head back after the test tomorrow morning," Jackson replied, "so expect them around noon or so."

Kaly turned back to the house. "I think I'll go for a ride."

"It's getting pretty late," Jackson observed. He raised his hands to stem her response. "I'm not trying to tell you what to do. I just want you to be careful. Lots of critters come out at dusk, and some of them might spook Misty. Just head back in plenty of time, that's all."

She nodded, and Jackson watched her make her way back to the house as he shook another cigarette from the package and lighted it. He was frankly grateful to be alone. He was still uncomfortable with how easily she had read him. She had called him mostly right, he acknowledged. How the hell she'd managed that with his well-practiced defenses, he didn't know.

Or maybe he did. He drew on his cigarette deeply, then blew perfect rings in the air. If she had been right about him, he knew with absolute certainty that he had read her equally well. Her failed relationship had caused her caution around men, and she had figured him out so easily because his feelings were probably similar to her own.

He remained where he was, in uncustomary idleness, and reflected on the unlikely understanding they had just reached. He didn't have time for this; he needed to get down to the barn. There was still some

light left, and he should talk to Nick, plan the men's
duties for the next day. He also needed to make that
call to Sheriff Dumont to check on the investigation.

But he was immobile for the next several minutes
as he continued to draw on his cigarette. His mind
wasn't on mending fence or finding missing cattle. Instead, he was wondering about the man who had gotten close enough to hurt Kaly Scott.

Chapter 5

Carrie and Jeff arrived home before noon the next day, and Peg fixed a celebratory lunch. The test results had convinced the doctor that Carrie's pregnancy was progressing normally, and they couldn't conceal their relief at the news.

"I hope now you're persuaded—" Carrie's droll look encompassed both her husband and brother-in-law "—that it's safe to stop treating me like a porcelain doll. The doctor was as certain as he could be that the baby is healthy." Her tone was smug. "He said I could resume my normal activities."

"He said within reason, Carrie," Jeff stressed.

Jackson put in, "No use taking any chances, Carrie. It won't hurt to continue being extra careful."

Kaly smiled in commiseration at the beseeching look Carrie threw her. "She isn't talking about training for the Boston marathon, you know," she told Jeff teasingly. "She just means that now you can ease up a little."

"For instance," Carrie said, shooting her husband a side glance, "you can stop carrying me up and down the porch steps! It's bad enough at the ranch, but when you insisted on carrying me up the four steps to the doctor's office, people thought we were demented."

Even Jackson had to smile at that. But Jeff's jaw squared. "Fine," he agreed. "You can use the porch steps. But we're still not moving our room back upstairs until after the baby comes. You don't need to be climbing stairs unnecessarily." His tone said the subject was closed, and Kaly blinked at him in amazement.

She had never heard that note in his voice, nor seen his face as serious as it was now. For the first time since she'd met him, Kaly saw an obvious resemblance to Jackson's implacable manner, and it surprised her. It was so at odds with Jeff's usual cheerful personality. Obviously his concern for his wife brought out his most protective instincts, and she secretly thought it was rather sweet. Still, she couldn't help sympathizing with Carrie. She knew too well what it was like to chafe at restrictions.

Kaly's musings were interrupted as Jackson's chair scraped back and he got to his feet. "Well, some of us have work to do. We can't afford to laze around in the city for days." He grinned when Carrie wrinkled her nose at him. "We're glad to have you back, Carrie, especially with the good news. Kaly almost drove me nuts worrying about you."

Kaly's eyes widened. "Look who's talking." She confided in an aside to Jeff and Carrie, "As you know, Jackson never learned that patience is a virtue." Her audience grinned appreciatively at the truth of her statement. "He practically ordered the phone to ring, then pounced on it when it did."

"Just to ease Kaly's mind." He winked at them before strolling to the door. "I never had the slightest doubt what the outcome would be." Kaly rolled her eyes and the others laughed at his feigned nonchalance.

"I'm ready to get back to work, Kaly," Jeff said after the dishes had been cleared away. At her nod, he looked at his wife. "What are you going to do this afternoon, honey?"

"Oh, don't worry about me," Carrie said airily. "I always manage to keep myself busy."

"That's fine as long as it doesn't include lifting, bending, climbing, riding..."

"How about breathing?" Carrie muttered under her breath, but Jeff heard and pretended to consider.

"Well...okay," he said finally, giving her a hug. "But take it easy, huh?"

Kaly made her way to the office, leaving Jeff lingering over his wife's lips. By the time she had the computer booted up he'd joined her, and they worked steadily all afternoon. After a brief supper they put in a few more hours, unaware of the passage of time until Carrie's voice floated in from the hallway.

"If I don't get some company out here pretty soon I'm going to do something desperate. I'm thinking about going out to break that ornery horse Jackson bought."

That brought Jeff immediately to his feet and halfway to the door before he recognized the jest. "I guess that's my wife's not-so-subtle way of telling me we've worked long enough," he said in amusement, turning to Kaly. "We'll pick up where we left off tomorrow morning."

"Jeffrey Roberts!" This time Carrie appeared in the doorway. "You know tomorrow is the Blanes' barbecue. You haven't forgotten that, surely."

"Of course not," Jeff proclaimed, with an exaggerated patience that clearly attested he had. "But working a couple of hours in the morning won't hurt, will it? The barbecue doesn't start until after lunch."

Carrie eyed him suspiciously. "Excuse my disbelief, but I know how difficult it is for you to quit working once you've started."

"We could work until noon and then while you're gone I could type up the notes," Kaly volunteered.

Carrie eyed her askance. "Absolutely not, Kaly! We wouldn't think of leaving you here by yourself. Besides, you need some time to relax, too. We'll leave about one tomorrow, and be sure to bring a swimsuit. The Blanes have a pool."

Kaly opened her mouth to protest, but Jeff shook his head at her. "Carrie's right. You're coming with us tomorrow. It'll be good for you to get away for a bit."

After promising to take part in the outing the next day, Kaly headed to the barn for a quick ride. But she was careful to head back toward the ranch well before dusk fell, heeding Jackson's warning of the day before. Though not particularly timid, she was not eager to encounter any of the night creatures he had alluded to.

Engrossed in unsaddling Misty, Kaly jumped when a hand fell on her shoulder.

"Hey, settle down." Larry Scott laughed. "I didn't

mean to scare you. Just wanted to ask if you needed some help with that mare.''

Kaly smiled, her hand over her heart. ''You did startle me,'' she confessed. ''I didn't hear you come up.''

Larry lifted the saddle off the horse and Kaly removed her bridle, then began the careful rubdown and grooming she always did after riding the mare. Larry leaned against the stall, surveying her.

''I haven't seen you around much lately. Jeff keeping you glued to that office of his?'' he inquired.

''We do stay busy,'' Kaly said with a nod. ''And now that he and Carrie are back from the city, we'll be back on our schedule again.''

Larry spoke lightly. ''I'd like to help take your mind off your work for a while if you'd go out with me some night.'' He smiled and waggled his eyebrows with mock lechery. ''How about it? You can forget about everything except having a good time.''

Kaly laughed in spite of herself. ''I'd like that,'' she answered.

His smile broadened. ''Great! How about next Saturday night?''

''Sounds good,'' she responded as she hung up the currycomb. Together they latched the stall and walked out of the barn.

''See you next week,'' Larry said. Kaly nodded and walked back to the house. It seemed empty, though Kaly knew Jeff and Carrie were probably watching TV in their room. She headed upstairs and took a bath before going back to her own room and working on her paper for a little while.

As she slipped into bed later that night she mentally

congratulated herself. She had managed to keep so busy all day that she hadn't thought of Jackson Roberts.

Much.

Jeff was true to his word the next morning. They quit working before noon to get ready for the barbecue. But when Kaly descended the stairway at one o'clock it was Jackson, not Jeff and Carrie, she saw. He had one hand in his pocket jingling his keys impatiently.

She stopped midway for a moment and stared, transfixed. The cutoffs he wore were obviously a favorite, worn white in places, and they fit snugly. They were fringed with blue and white threads, which intermingled alluringly with the hair on his thighs. A red cotton-knit shirt was tucked in, and he wore sneakers without socks. Her eyes traveled slowly downward and then wandered back up his legs, lingering on the strong calf muscles that bulged from his lower legs up to the solid thighs, flat stomach and wide chest. Red was definitely his color, she mused as she studied the contrast it made at the vee where his shirt was open at the neck. His dark hair and skin stood out against the brilliant color, and she shivered involuntarily at his compelling attractiveness.

She had failed to consider that Jackson would accompany them, and she was suddenly filled with misgivings. She had somehow felt drawn closer to him in Jeff and Carrie's absence, and she had not yet been able to put those feelings into perspective. He was the same man she had believed him to be, had warned herself about. Yet now she was aware that he was so much more, and the newfound knowledge threatened her normally cautious nature.

Jackson looked up when he heard footsteps on the stairs, his impatience dissipating as he watched her approach. Her hair was pulled back into a jaunty ponytail. She wore a fuchsia collegiate T-shirt, denim shorts and flat white sandals. He swallowed as he watched her slim legs descending the steps toward him. She had, he decided, the best-looking pair of legs he'd ever seen on such a petite woman. He tore his eyes away from her trim ankles and asked, "Bring your swimsuit?"

"I'm wearing it under my clothes," Kaly responded. "I wasn't sure how long these things usually last, but I put a sweater and a pair of long pants in the bag in case it cools off tonight."

Jackson nodded absently. "It'll probably be dark when we get home." The thought of Kaly in a bikini danced across his mind and he mentally groaned. He wished he'd had the foresight to plan to drive alone to the party, but that would have been difficult to explain to Jeff and Carrie. Not that it would have made much difference. He was still going to have to face an entire day in her presence—in her skimpily clad presence, probably—and the thought made him want to grind his teeth. There were usually plenty of people at these things, and he'd have to do his best to mingle, staying well away from the temptation she provided. He snuck one last peek at her legs and wished mightily for a pair of blinders.

"All set?"

At Carrie's voice, both Kaly and Jackson turned. "Jeff's brought the car around. Do you want to slip your things into my bag, Jack?" He did so, and then slung the striped beach bag over his shoulder. "How many times do you have to be told not to be carrying things?'' he lectured his sister-in-law. Kaly and Carrie smiled at the incongruous sight he made and followed him out the door.

When they arrived, the party appeared to be in full swing. Mrs. Blane met them as they walked toward the house, and Jeff introduced Kaly to her.

''I'm so glad you came, dear,'' the woman told her sincerely. ''The more the merrier, I always say. Oh, and Jackson,'' she gushed, ''I'd hoped you make it.'' She tapped him on the arm coyly. ''Lots of pretty young things have already asked about you.'' She lowered her voice to speak to Kaly. ''You watch out for this one. He's a heartbreaker.''

Kaly watched as Jackson struggled not to scowl at the woman. ''So I've heard,'' Kaly murmured dryly. Jeff and Carrie laughed at his discomfiture.

''Just go out back—you'll know everybody here. I must check on the food,'' she said, and hurried off.

''Half-wit,'' Jackson muttered darkly.

''Jackson, be nice,'' Carrie remonstrated, openly amused. ''She can't help but be enthralled with the thrilling secondhand accounts of your romantic accomplishments.''

''After all, you do your best to keep the countryside abounding in gossip,'' Jeff put in. He added in an aside to Kaly, ''The three hottest topics of conversation around here are the markets, the weather and the name of Jackson's latest conquest.''

Kaly was silent. Despite their joking tone, she recognized the truth in their words, and hearing it bolstered her determination to fight the attraction the man held for her. She couldn't imagine anything more distasteful than being the subject of gossip among the neighbors. Jackson Roberts was hell on women, those foolish enough to become involved with him, but she wasn't going to be one of them. That she promised herself.

"There are usually snacks all afternoon and we'll eat about six," Carrie informed Kaly. "You can swim or sun, and sometimes there's a game of volleyball. Do you play?"

"Oh, some," Kaly answered blandly. She had played on a volleyball team for three years in high school and enjoyed playing for pleasure.

They rounded the corner of the house and saw that it was already crowded. People of all ages sat at picnic tables and on lawn chairs, while others stood near the keg of beer or lounged by the pool. Jackson stopped to talk to a group of ranchers, and Carrie and Jeff escorted Kaly around, introducing her to their friends.

After a while people began to gather around the volleyball net, and Jeff cocked an eyebrow at Kaly. "Looks like a game is going to start up. Want to play?"

Kaly looked at Carrie, who waved them away. "You two go ahead. I'll find a seat where I can watch." She lifted her face for Jeff's quick kiss, and then Kaly and Jeff headed off. They were hailed as they showed up in the midst of the crowd and were quickly claimed by a team.

Jackson was already in place on the opposite side of the net, and Jeff whispered a warning to Kaly. "Watch out for Jack. He's got a wicked spike." And his words proved true in the next few minutes. Jackson spent more time in the net than out of it, and helped score several points for his side.

When it was Kaly's turn to serve, Jackson set it easily from the middle row, but a teammate bobbled it, and Kaly's team got the point. Her smile broadened when she saw Jackson's visage grow more determined. She aimed each of her serves at him, hard and fast, and he returned each of them himself.

"Hey, Roberts, is this a private game, or do you mind if the rest of us play?" gibed one of Jackson's teammates. He turned his head to grin at the man, but before he could answer, Kaly's next serve hit him in the chest, scoring another point for her side. Jackson sent her a look promising retribution.

He relentlessly returned each of her next serves, but several more points were scored by Kaly's team before one of her teammates tripped and missed the ball. As the game continued, the two teams ran neck in neck. Near the end of the game they were tied.

It was Jackson's turn to serve, and the glare he gave Kaly looked menacing. He served the ball high and hard, intending it to drop at her feet, earning his team the final game point. Kaly dived for it, setting it for Jeff, who spiked it. Two men on Jackson's side collided and failed in their effort to return it, and then Kaly's team had the serve. Jackson returned the ball straight at Kaly. This time when she hit it, she looked at Jackson while sending the ball to a woman on the other side of the court. His whole team had expected the ball to go to Jackson, and it landed harmlessly at the woman's feet, winning the game for Kaly's team. There were catcalls and cheers before Jeff held up Kaly's arm and called, "Our secret weapon!"

"Not so secret," someone joked, slapping Jackson on the back. "If your brother could've kept his eyes off Kaly and on the ball, we'd have killed you." Jackson reacted to the bantering good-naturedly, arguing that he'd had to play single-handedly.

Carrie strolled up then and congratulated Jeff and Kaly. "C'mon," she said. "Let's go get something to eat. You, too, Jackson," she called to him, beckoning him to join them. "You must be starved after your ignominious defeat."

"Sure, rub it in," he groused amiably. "And where were you when we needed an unbiased line judge?"

Jeff hooted at that. "Unbiased? Looked to me like you were getting all the breaks! If you'd been in the net any more you'd have had to wear it home."

They filled their plates with snacks and found an empty table to sit at. Carrie cast a disgusted look at their heaped plates. "You don't know how lucky you are not to have to watch your figures."

Kaly smiled in sympathy, but Jeff quipped, "Oh, I don't know, Jack spent quite a bit of time watching Kaly's. Isn't that how you lost the game, Jack?"

Jackson picked up a chip and threw it at him. "I demand a rematch," he responded. "We were just being easy on you, because your team had an obvious lack of talent." They all laughed at his words.

They spent a pleasant afternoon, lolling around the sparkling water and talking to friends and neighbors. Kaly couldn't remember the last time she'd enjoyed herself so much. When Carrie finally asked, "Who's ready for a swim?" the group around the table groaned in unison.

She scolded them for their laziness and bullied them into rising. The women found some vacant loungers and shucked their clothes to reveal the swimsuits beneath. When Kaly turned to the pool the first thing she noticed was Jackson's bare chest. Her mouth went dry. His massive torso made an inverted triangle, narrow-

ing at his waist. Her fingers itched to comb through
the curly mat covering it.

She raised her eyes to find him staring fixedly at
her, and she frowned. "What's wrong with you?"

He swallowed hard at the enticing picture she made
in her swimsuit. A black one-piece, it was more sedate
than most, but still showed off her curves enticingly.
The sight of her in it made sweat break out on his
forehead.

"Nothing," he muttered. He was suddenly in desperate need of some cold water. Preferably ice cold.
But first he grinned wickedly. "Remember the volleyball game?" He stalked her slowly. "It's payback
time." And before she could react, he scooped her up
and swung her high out over the water.

Kaly hit the surface with a splash and swam back
to the side underwater. As Jackson scanned the pool
she grasped his ankle and pulled with all her might.
Thrown off balance, he struck the water. She laughed
delightedly when he surfaced again, treading water
and shaking wet hair out of his face. "I guess it is
true what they say," she taunted. "The bigger they
are..."

She never finished. Reading the intent on his face,
she dived away from him, just managing to escape his
lunge toward her.

She darted this way and that in the pool, always
remaining just out of his reach. Jackson pursued her
with lazy determination, and she was aware that she
escaped him only as long as he allowed it. He abruptly
ended the game when she began swimming rapidly in
the opposite direction toward the ladder. In a few
strong strokes he reached her, then crowded her
against the side of the pool.

He looked down at her. "You sure seem in an awful hurry," he mocked.

"Just tired of swimming," she lied indifferently, but she could tell from the amusement on his hard features that he was not misled.

"Already?" he queried. "But you seemed to be having such a good time a few minutes ago."

He loomed over her, and Kaly felt the hard edge of the pool pressing into her. The breadth of his shoulders overshadowed her, and she felt small and incredibly vulnerable. The sun turned the water droplets on his skin into miniature rainbows. She watched, fascinated, tracing the progress of one drop as it meandered across his chest. She tore her eyes away from the fascinating display. He was blocking the ladder, so she started inching along the wall, away from him.

Jackson noticed her attempt and kept pace with her. "Careful," he warned when the water was at her chin. "You don't want to…get in too deep."

Kaly continued inching away, until the pool took an obvious descent and she was forced to cling to the side to stay above water.

Jackson moved to stand in front of her again. His superior height still left him head and shoulders above the sparkling pool and he stretched his long arms out to rest on either side of her face, effectively trapping her. His voice, when he spoke next, was husky. "I'd think a cautious gal like you would be nervous about getting in over her head."

She was helpless to look away from that compelling gaze. "I am," she replied softly. "Believe me, I am."

His eyes darkened at her response to his double entendre, and for just a moment, the rest of the party faded away. For once, Kaly gave in to her desire to drink her fill of him. He was so good to look at. His words, though, had been more than just provocative. In her mind, they sounded prophetic for the two of them, should they ever give in to the desire that was constant between them.

Over her head. Yes, she thought a little bitterly, that's exactly what she would be. If she gave in to this man's dangerous attraction for her, she'd be in *way* over her head. And while she was going down for the last time, he would be as he was before her now, virtually untouched by it all. She had no doubt he could drown her in sensation, but then what? There was no lifeguard for a broken heart.

Kaly abruptly sank beneath the water and under his arm, swam to the ladder and ascended it quickly. This time Jackson didn't follow her, and she was thankful. She found the lounger with her bag on it and searched for her comb. She spent the next several minutes working the wide teeth through her wet hair and repeating silent warnings to herself about the danger of uncharted waters.

And of sharks.

When the dinner gong sounded, Kaly and Carrie changed in the bathhouse before they again joined the throng filling their plates with food. Jeff came along and Kaly could feel herself growing tense, expecting Jackson at any moment. But when he didn't appear, she began to relax. Someone took out a guitar, and soon the soft strumming filled the air.

After a while, Carrie and Jeff excused themselves, making their way slowly around to various groups of people, stopping at each to visit. Kaly was content to remain seated on her own for a time, enjoying the peacefulness of the evening, before a voice sounded above her. ''The men in these parts must be even denser than I thought, leaving you to sit alone.''

Kaly looked up to meet the admiring eyes of the stranger before her. ''I'm Paul Whitfield,'' he said. ''Do you mind if I sit down?''

''No, of course not,'' Kaly responded politely, and introduced herself as he sank into a chair at her side. ''I'm Kaly Scott. I'm working with Jeff Roberts this summer.''

Paul widened his blue eyes appreciatively. ''You're Jeff's research assistant? I just got here, but I've already heard about your showing on the volleyball court. It seems I missed quite a game.''

''I don't know about that,'' Kaly said demurely. ''I'm sure the story has been greatly embellished with each telling.'' She studied the blond perfection of the man before her. His face was flawlessly handsome. He reminded her of a picture that had hung in her bedroom of the angel Gabriel. All he needed was the robe and sword, Kaly thought whimsically.

''My ranch is just down the road from the Circle R,'' Paul volunteered.

She knew enough by this time to realize that, in these parts, ''down the road'' meant at least several miles. She was still astounded by the size of the properties required to house the huge herds of cattle.

''Did you grow up with Jeff and Jackson?'' she asked curiously.

Paul grimaced. ''I'm not from here originally, no,'' he answered. ''My family is from the East Coast. For some unknown reason, my father decided several years ago to go into early retirement and start living like a cowboy. My sister and I had no choice but to follow him.''

''You don't like it here?''

''Oh, I've gotten used to it,'' he answered smoothly. ''After my father died and my sister moved away, someone needed to stay to look after things. God knows, there's not much around here for entertainment, so when I feel the need for more elegant surroundings I fly to Europe for a while. But I always come back. What about you? Where are you from?''

''I'm going to school in Tucson, but I grew up in a small town,'' Kaly replied. ''Tell me about your travels,'' she invited, and Paul obliged. He told her funny stories about mishaps in his journeys, and they compared notes on the archaeological marvels overseas.

''What have you been doing in your free time?'' he quizzed later, after he had fetched them soft drinks.

''Not much,'' Kaly replied. ''I'm working on my doctoral dissertation—that takes up most of my nights. But I do enjoy exploring the ranch on horseback. It relaxes me.''

''How about the Robertses? Are you getting along with them okay? You must be pretty brave coming out to spend an entire summer with people you don't even know.''

''They've been wonderful,'' Kaly answered warmly. ''Jeff is a perfect boss and Carrie is great. I'm enjoying myself so much it doesn't even seem like a job.''

Paul watched her, his eyes alight with interest. ''You haven't mentioned Jackson,'' he noted. ''How do you get along with him?''

Kaly could feel herself grow rigid just at the mention of the man's name. Paul sounded as if he was making more than idle conversation. "I don't see much of him," she responded carefully. "I'm sure running a ranch of that size keeps a person busy. You probably know that yourself."

"It does take work," Paul answered, "although my operation isn't near the size of the Circle R. And I know for a fact that it doesn't take all of Jackson's time, either." He shook his head. "That man has quite a reputation." When Kaly remained silent he shot a quick look at her. "I don't mean to be filling your ears with tales. It's just…" Here he hesitated. "Well, he was almost my brother-in-law, you know."

Kaly blinked in shock. "No," she murmured, "I didn't know." She'd never heard that Jackson's ex-fiancée had been a neighbor.

"It's old news." Paul shrugged. "And I think these things usually work out for the best. Maria, my sister," he added, "is married and happy enough, I guess. She was really hurt when Jackson jilted her, but she's put all that behind her now."

Kaly said nothing, but she couldn't help but wonder at his words. What had caused Jackson to call off the wedding? Had he finally realized he couldn't be happy tied down to one woman? Or hadn't Maria been malleable enough for him? Whatever the reason, the decision had definitely left a lasting impression on him. It colored the way he saw women, Kaly knew. But, though curious, she was uncomfortable listening to Paul speak of it. She knew Jackson well enough to know he'd be furious at the idea of others discussing his personal life, although from what she'd heard it was a primary topic among the locals.

Paul's voice broke into Kaly's continued silence.

"Listen to me," he said wryly. "I'm beginning to sound like some of these old busybodies who spend their afternoons gossiping on the phone." He gazed intently at her. "I'm sure you and I could find much more interesting subjects than Jackson Roberts to discuss." They talked desultorily for a while, Paul making her smile several times at his portrayals of the meetings he'd had to endure that day. Kaly enjoyed his company, but after a time she noticed Jeff and Carrie standing near the house.

She excused herself, saying, "I'd better check and see if the Roberts are ready to go. I don't want to hold them up if they are."

Paul rose when she did. "It was my pleasure to meet you, Kaly. I look forward to seeing you again."

Kaly headed in the direction she had last seen Jeff and Carrie, but they were no longer in sight. She moved slowly through the crowd still gathered, but in the growing darkness it was difficult to discern faces. Finally she decided to see if they had already gone to the car parked in front. She headed around the corner of the house and made her way carefully through the yard.

"Hey, lady, haven't you heard of the big bad wolf?" a voice said near her shoulder, and Kaly shrieked softly in surprise. She jerked around and barely made out Jackson's form leaning against the house.

"You creep," she fumed, her heart still racing. "You did that on purpose."

"Did what?" He chuckled. "I was just noting that it was awful dark for you to be wandering around. How was I supposed to know you jump a mile when you're startled?"

"Lucky that wolves don't frighten me," she informed him, still smarting from her earlier alarm. "Or I'd be terrorized at finding the biggest wolf in the countryside lurking in the shadows."

All amusement left his voice when he answered. "If you're referring to me, you're dead wrong. You just spent the last hour cozying up to the biggest predator in the country."

Kaly wasn't sure which surprised her more, his reference to Paul or the fact that he'd been keeping tabs on her. "Paul Whitfield seemed very cordial."

"I'm sure he did," he said. "Charm's his middle name."

She was quickly growing impatient with his sarcasm. "Are you sure it's Paul you object to, or is it the entire Whitfield family?" As soon as the words left her mouth, she wished she could call them back. It was a cheap shot and completely out of character for her. But Jackson didn't seem angry when he replied.

"No, I'm not holding any grudges against Paul because of Maria. Hell, I doubt he even knows the truth about what happened between his sister and me."

Kaly was filled with remorse. Though she hadn't responded to the little that Paul had said about Jackson, she still felt like a sneak for having listened to it and, even more, wondering further about it. "We weren't discussing you," she told him uncomfortably. "He just mentioned your relationship to his sister in passing."

"And you weren't curious in the least," he taunted.

"If I had any questions I'd do you the courtesy of addressing them to you," she answered steadily.

"And are you asking?" he countered.

At her silence, he sighed. And then he shocked himself by revealing what he had told no one other than Jeff. ''Maria needed a lot of things, and I doubt one man could supply them all. But I called the wedding off because I caught my bride-to-be in bed with another man.'' He instantly regretted his revelation. The last thing he wanted was her pity.

But she didn't give him any. ''Maria Whitfield—'' her tone bespoke amazement ''—must have been a fool.''

He shot her an amused glance and shrugged. ''I doubt it. He was old enough to be her father, but rich enough to give her anything she wanted. Since she liked money, she was mighty smart to grab it when it came her way.''

''But you're...'' Kaly bit her tongue to prevent herself from uttering the rest of that sentence. Jackson read her meaning easily.

''I'm not rich, Kaly, not in that league, anyway. The Circle R is a working ranch, and while we have good assets, our capital is mostly tied up in livestock and equipment. It takes a hell of a lot of money to buy purebred stock, and that's what's needed to branch out into a breeding operation.'' He stopped here, certain she wasn't interested in the financial operation of a ranch.

Kaly touched his arm tentatively. ''I'm sorry, Jackson.''

His arm tensed reflexively under her fingers. ''For what?''

''For dredging all this up. I'm sure it's not your favorite topic of conversation.''

He relaxed imperceptibly. ''Not hardly, but then it doesn't matter much anymore. It stopped mattering a long time ago.'' That was the truth, but it didn't explain his uncustomary loquaciousness with her. He certainly wasn't in the habit of swapping sad stories with any other woman of his acquaintance. What was it about her? he wondered, his eyes dropping to that small hand still on his arm. She broke through his guard the way no one else ever had.

The tension that seemed to surround them all at once made it difficult for Kaly to breathe. Belatedly she removed her hand from the furnacelike heat of his forearm. If she was so determined to skirt the magnetism he exuded, she was going to have to avoid touching him. And avoid being alone with him. She became suddenly aware of how secluded the area was. But her limbs seemed leaden, as if unwilling to move away.

''We should—'' Kaly barely recognized the breathless utterance as her own ''—find Jeff and Carrie.''

''Should we?'' Somehow he seemed closer, although she couldn't recall either of them moving.

''They're probably ready to go....'' Her voice trailed off. He had tipped his head down as if listening to her, but that movement put his lips alarmingly close to hers. In the darkness his mouth seemed to be the only thing she could see. The only thing she could concentrate on.

''They may be looking for us,'' she whispered, as his face came nearer.

''They haven't found us.'' His mouth stopped a fraction from hers.

''We weren't going to do this.'' Her voice trembled slightly.

''We weren't?'' The husky question was breathed across her lips.

"We decided it was a mistake." She swallowed as his lips barely brushed hers.

"A mistake."

"One we don't want to repeat," she said, searching desperately for words to stop him, to stop herself, for she wasn't sure she would have the strength to deny him once he kissed her again.

But her words finally penetrated what was left of his own instincts of self-preservation, and he pulled away. "No," he agreed shakily, mentally damning himself for needing her reminder, "we don't." He moved from her and wished an emotional distance was as easily achieved. "Let's go," he said brusquely, and they headed toward the front of the house silently, each wishing fervently they didn't face a twenty-minute ride home in the same vehicle.

Chapter 6

For the next several days Kaly didn't have to worry about avoiding Jackson and the spell he seemed to weave around her so easily. He made himself scarce around the house. Once again he was absent from the table at mealtimes, and though no one commented on it, Kaly knew what was motivating his absences.

She was certain that their conversations had made him as uncomfortable as they had her. She recognized that Jackson was normally reticent about himself, which made his openness with her quite out of character. He had to find that frightening. She did.

So he must have gone running back to his other women. The thought was like a vise around her heart. She knew that it was his way of protecting himself, and her, from giving into the almost palpable desire between them. She knew what he was doing, but she still hurt at the thought of it.

She didn't recognize herself like this. She had always been sure of what she wanted, and she knew that Jackson Roberts was a man to be avoided at all costs. Why, then, did she get a sick feeling in her stomach each night she heard that he was out again? She'd always been a firebrand with her family, giving as good as she got, but no one, not her family and not Philip, had ever caused the turbulent emotions she'd experienced since meeting Jackson Roberts.

She groaned. There, she'd admitted it. She had loved Philip, but the feelings he'd stirred in her, even in the most intimate of times, couldn't touch what she'd felt when just kissing Jackson. Instead of despairing at the rancher's renewed aloofness, she should be grateful he was making it easier on both of them to ignore this involuntary reaction they had to each other.

Kaly refused to acknowledge the bleakness that accompanied her thoughts. Jackson was doing what was best for both of them, and she would follow his lead. A cool, rational mind would always take precedence over heated mutual attraction. As long as she kept that firmly in her head, she would easily avoid the temptation.

Dinner that evening was a surprise to everyone, because Jackson joined them. Jeff teased him about not having a date, but his brother just fixed him with a look and the subject was dropped.

After dessert, Jackson announced, ''We got an invitation today. Some neighbors are having an impromptu get-together tomorrow night and invited all of us to come.'' His look around the table encompassed Kaly.

''Great!'' Jeff exclaimed. ''The barbecue last weekend was a good time. This will be the perfect way to relax from all that work Kaly's had me doing this week.'' He winked at her.

''Sounds like fun, Jackson,'' Carrie agreed. ''Who's having it?''

Jackson kept his eyes on his coffee cup, sipping the steaming brew cautiously. ''Paul Whitfield.''

There was silence at the table for a long moment. Jeff was the first to regain his voice. ''Paul? But he hasn't done much entertaining since…I mean…'' He faltered at Jackson's pointed look. ''He didn't say anything last weekend about it.''

Jackson's cup clattered against the saucer as he set it down. ''No, he didn't,'' he agreed impassively, ''but what difference does that make? Last-minute parties have never bothered you before.'' His chair scraped back as he stood up. ''It's at seven tomorrow night. I'll probably be late, so go on without me, and I'll see you there.''

Three silent faces looked at one another as Jackson left the room. Jeff exchanged a puzzled look with Carrie. She shrugged a little at him, before glancing at Kaly and flashing her a brilliant smile. ''Let's go upstairs and pick out our clothes for tomorrow. Parties at the Whitfields have always been far more formal than we're used to around here.'' Ignoring Kaly's protests, she came around the table, took her by the arm and fairly dragged her from the room.

By six-thirty the next evening, Kaly was ready to wring Carrie's neck. She had gone through Kaly's closet the night before with the determination of a fashion buyer, then found nothing in it suitable for the evening. Next she'd insisted that the two of them look through Carrie's own closet. When Carrie had pulled a dress from a hanger and proclaimed it perfect for her, Kaly hadn't had the heart to argue with her. But now, as she looked into the mirror, she was experiencing major misgivings.

An unfamiliar reflection stared back at her. The emerald material of the garment shimmered and made her eyes look greener. The dress was held up by tiny spaghetti straps and showed much more bosom than Kaly was comfortable with showing. It was not tight fitting, but did hint at every curve she had. She frowned into the mirror. At Carrie's suggestion, she had left her hair down. Kaly would have been much more confident wearing it in a chignon, but had compromised and pulled it back on either side with tortoiseshell combs. Black strappy sandals and small studs in her ears completed the outfit.

A horn sounded outside, signaling Jeff and Carrie's readiness. She sighed and picked up her purse, heading toward the door. The evening stretched interminably before her.

The party was in full swing when they arrived. The Robertses introduced Kaly to an alarming number of people, and she recognized many more from the barbecue the previous weekend. When the music began, she lost track of Carrie and Jeff as she was continuously escorted to the dance floor.

Jackson entered the large room well after the party had started. He swept the surroundings with a jaundiced eye. John Whitfield had added this room on to the original ranch house when he had brought his family to live here. They always referred to it as the ballroom, which was ridiculous, considering that most of the people here were more at home at a country-and-western dance than at a fancy dress ball. His hand loosened his tie slightly. Certainly he was more comfortable in jeans than dressed like a banker.

He reflected on his meeting with the sheriff, which had caused his tardiness this evening. For once Jackson had been unable to give his undivided attention to his plans for protecting his ranch. Instead, his mind had persisted in returning again and again to the woman so often in his thoughts these days.

Kaly was dancing with a neighbor of the Robertses, Justin King, when Jackson first caught sight of her. He froze in the act of accepting a drink from a servant as his eyes followed her. She was laughing up at the older man, despite the fact that King was well-known for having two left feet. Jackson felt a tightening in his gut. He'd never seen her with her hair unbound, although he'd certainly imagined it enough lately. She looked utterly desirable with her dark gold mane hanging loose. The combs holding the thick tresses away from her face framed its oval shape and drew attention to those knockout cheekbones and eyes. He surveyed her dress and frowned in disapproval. Dammit, it was cut way too low. Every man she danced with would get teasing glimpses of the creamy tops of those high breasts.

Jackson felt the burning sensation of desire curl through him. The dress alluringly draped the curves that had been branded on his brain since he'd seen her in a swimsuit. He never should have laid his hands on her at the pool, not even in fun. His temperature had risen so alarmingly that he'd had to do several laps before he could leave the water without embarrassing himself. And seeing her tonight wasn't much better. It was too easy to remember how her body had felt pressed tightly to his, so tightly her breasts had flattened against him and nearly sent him into orbit. Sweat popped out on his forehead at the mere memory.

He raised the drink to his lips and tossed down half of it, his eyes not leaving Kaly. He'd done his best these past few weeks to wipe her from his mind. But neither distance nor the scores of dates he'd gone on had succeeded in stamping out the fire that started in him every time he saw her. His renewed social life hadn't alleviated the hunger he felt. If anything, it had heightened it. The women he dated didn't put him on edge, nor did they surprise revelations from his normally tight lips. And they didn't interest him at all.

His lips twisted in self-derision. He'd convinced himself that his attraction to Kaly was due to his recent unaccustomed celibacy. He'd confidently believed that resuming his relationships with women would quench the passion she torched in him. What a fool he'd been. It was Kaly who had his thoughts straying from ranch matters; it was Kaly he dreamed about on too many nights. It was her name on his lips when he awoke from those dreams, sweating, shaking, the bedclothes in a tangled heap.

Working himself half to death the past few days hadn't made him forget her, either. It had only succeeded in shortening his temper. The men walked around him visibly nervous, and his foreman, Nick, was on the verge of snarling back at him.

"Glad you could make it, Jackson," a smooth voice said from behind his shoulder.

He turned slowly. "Paul." He nodded to the band. "Looks like you've gone all out tonight."

Paul's dark suit highlighted his blond good looks, and he was, as always, meticulously groomed. A slight smile crossed his lips. "Well, everyone seemed to be having such a good time last weekend, and it's been a while since I've returned my neighbors' hospitality.'' He studied Jackson for a moment. ''I know I've been traveling quite a bit the last couple of years, but now that I'm back, there's really no reason for me to be a hermit, is there?''

''No reason at all,'' Jackson replied.

Paul relaxed imperceptibly. ''Have you spoken to Dumont lately?'' he inquired, his light blue gaze sweeping the room before returning to Jackson.

''Just left him, in fact,'' Jackson said, nodding.

''So you heard I was the latest victim of the blasted rustlers.''

Jackson nodded silently.

''Thirty head probably doesn't sound like much, but I run a much smaller herd than you. I'll feel the loss.''

''Thirty head is a bigger hit than any of us have taken at one time,'' Jackson said. ''Sounds like the thieves are getting bolder.''

''What do you think Dumont's chances are of catching them?'' Paul asked.

Ed Blane and Doug Schmidt joined them at that moment. Jackson shrugged at Paul's question. As impatient as he was with the slow progress of the investigation, he also understood the sheriff's predicament.

''Dumont's sharp enough,'' he answered finally. ''The vehicle description you gave will sure help.''

''How in the Sam Hill did you manage a vehicle description, Paul?'' Ed asked. ''Did you catch them in the act?''

Paul gave a short laugh. ''I passed a couple of pickups and a truck full of cattle about a mile from my ranch on my way home last night. Can you believe it? I didn't think much of it until my men told me about the missing head this morning. Then I remembered those trucks and called Roy. I sure wish I'd paid better attention last night.''

''Too bad,'' Doug mumbled in disappointment. ''You might be the only one to get that close to the rustlers.''

''I got close enough to remember some details about one of the pickups,'' Paul said grimly. ''It was a two-tone Ford, white and navy or maybe black. Had a fancy grill, too.'' He chuckled self-deprecatingly. ''Heck, I noticed it because it caught my eye. I always have to look twice when I see a new-model pickup.''

Ed and Doug nodded in agreement. But Jackson had frozen at Paul's description of the truck he'd passed. He, too, had seen such a pickup and admired the sharp contrast of white and navy. He and some of the men had joked that with the fancy grill and wheels, the truck was good only for showing off.

The truck belonged to Larry Scott.

Jackson's mind raced furiously. Roy had told him that Paul had gotten a good look at the truck, but this was the first time Jackson had heard it described. He considered phoning the sheriff with this last bit of news, but then just as quickly decided against it. Larry Scott wasn't going anywhere; he'd keep until tomorrow. And in the meantime he would have Nick do some checking into the man's whereabouts the previous evening.

Jackson forced down the scalding taste of revenge filling him. He might be known as a hard man, but he prided himself on being a fair one. He hadn't voiced his earlier suspicions about the hired man when talking to Roy. He hadn't felt right about it; the evidence had been too damn flimsy. But this new information changed everything. And if Larry Scott turned out to be involved, he'd personally nail his low-down hide to the wall.

Jackson was disturbed from his vengeful thoughts by the continued conversation of the men around him. "Well, at least we have a little more to go on than before," proclaimed Ed. He shook his head ruefully. "They must have nerves of steel to keep hitting the same area and outwitting us all. Makes me feel like a downright fool."

Jackson gave a feral smile. "Thieves are lazy, and these rustlers don't appear to be all that bright. They've been lucky so far, but their luck won't last forever." Paul nodded in agreement.

Schmidt and Blane continued to discuss the rustling with Paul, and Jackson only half listened. He watched with narrowed eyes as Kaly passed from Justin King's arms to Jeff's. Seemed as if she had danced with every man here tonight except him. Maybe it was time to change that. He took a sip from his forgotten drink. Maybe it was time to change a lot of things.

He was willing to admit he may have been wrong about Kaly Scott. She was nothing like Maria—she didn't have a cash register where her heart should be. But in her sweetness lay another kind of danger. It would be too easy to be drawn close to her, to trust her. And once a man trusted a woman, all hell broke loose. But he wasn't going to be trussed up like a Thanksgiving turkey by his feelings for a woman. He'd never allow that. He was an old hand at keeping a part of himself untouched.

That didn't mean, however, they couldn't share something enjoyable. He frowned slightly. Convincing Kaly was a different matter. She was a wary little thing. But it wasn't ego that told him she'd been fighting their attraction as much as he had. He'd have to go slowly, calm her fears. His hard mouth curled in anticipation. He looked forward to persuading her.

"Jackson! I asked you if you were going to dance with me." Jackson slowly pulled his eyes away from Kaly and looked at the redhead by his side. From the petulance on her perfect features, it was obvious she'd made her request more than once. Jackson smiled charmingly and allowed himself to be led to the dance floor. He could wait.

Jeff was teasing Kaly unmercifully about her having to put up with Justin King stomping all over her toes. "I'd better tell Carrie to have a bucket of ice water ready for you once we get back home." At her uncomprehending look he added, "Your feet are probably so bruised by now that tomorrow you'll be hobbling around barefoot."

Kaly punched him lightly on the shoulder. "If that happens I'll make you carry me," she threatened. "It's your fault I had to dance so long with him."

"My fault?" Jeff looked wounded. "How do you figure that?"

"Because—" Kaly smiled sweetly "—dear Mr. King was busy explaining what an impact he'd had on your choice of careers." She laughed at Jeff's comical face. "He claims that he whetted your interest in history when you were but a lad, listening untiringly at his knee of his accounts of past glories of the King family and their contribution to the settling of the West."

Jeff groaned feelingly. "If that man's stories had anything to do with my decision to write, I'd be writing fiction, not history," he said. "He used to tell the biggest whoppers I ever heard, and it always took forever to get away from him.''

Kaly laughed, but then stopped short when she caught sight of Jackson dancing. He looked wonderful. She'd never seen him so dressed up. Jeff often wore slacks and dress shirts around the house, but she'd only seen Jackson in jeans and plain shirts, befitting the manual work he did. He made a devastating picture, and her eyes feasted on him hungrily. He wore a beige suit with a light blue shirt and striped tie. He looked incredibly handsome but not much more civilized than he did in his work clothes. There was something savage about his manner, something a little dangerous about his face that gave him an untamed look, despite what he wore.

At the moment, however, she thought waspishly, he was very close to wearing his partner. Kaly noted with unaccustomed jealousy the way the woman was running her fingers through the hair at his nape and tried not to recall when her own hand had done the same.

Jeff noticed Kaly's changed expression and danced her around so that he could unobtrusively follow the direction of her gaze. When he saw his brother, he said in surprise, ''Hey, Jackson made it. I never saw him come in.'' He glanced back down at Kaly and seemed about to say more, then hesitated. Finally he asked uncomfortably, ''He hasn't been, ah, bothering you, has he, Kaly?''

Kaly's heart jumped, and she could feel herself blush guiltily. Her eyes flew to his and then away. ''What are you talking about, Jeff?''

''I'm talking about Jackson and you. Jack's got a blind spot a mile wide about women. Sometimes he can be a bit hardheaded. I hope he hasn't offended you in some way.''

Kaly could feel herself go weak with relief. Her pulse was still beating madly in response to her mistaken interpretation of Jeff's words. Bother her? Yes, it would be safe to say that Jackson Roberts did, indeed, bother her. But not in the way Jeff meant.

"We understand each other better than you think," she responded. "And we get along fine, don't worry. Of course he's never there, so that helps," she added dryly.

"Yeah, he's been pretty busy lately." Jeff frowned, seemed about to say more, then shrugged and looked inquiringly at Kaly. "How about it—shall we give our feet a rest and get something to drink?"

"You'd better go rescue that wife of yours," Kaly ordered lightly. "She looks like her worst nightmare has come true. Mrs. Blane has her trapped again."

Sure enough, when the two looked at Carrie, she was nodding politely to the older woman's chatter. She caught her husband's eye at that moment and gave him a beseeching look. Jeff grinned down at Kaly and squeezed her hand. "Looks like you're right. Mrs. Blane is probably giving her a rundown of every minute of the labor and birth of her only child, for the fourteenth time. Carrie has threatened to throttle the woman if she had to sit through it again."

"Go, then." Kaly laughed. "We don't want Carrie to have to give birth in a jail cell."

"I'll keep Kaly company, Jeff," a smooth voice behind them offered.

Jeff greeted their host. "Hey, Paul. Nice of you to invite us all."

"Well, it gave me a good excuse to see Kaly

again,'' was his laughing rejoinder. Paul gazed down at her admiringly. ''I've been waiting all night for a chance to dance with you. But I'm not surprised you've had so many partners tonight. You look fantastic.'' Kaly was a little discomfited under his openly admiring gaze, but acquiesced when he asked her to dance. Paul took her in his arms and moved her onto the floor, while Jeff made his way across the room to his wife.

''Are you having a good time tonight?'' Paul inquired.

''Yes, I'm having a wonderful time,'' Kaly responded warmly. ''I love dancing, and your band is excellent.''

He looked satisfied. ''They're not bad for these parts, I guess. We don't often get the chance to shed jeans and cowboy hats around here. I enjoy the change.'' Here his voice dropped. ''And I wouldn't have missed the opportunity to see you in that dress for anything.''

Kaly smiled slightly. He was flattering her outrageously and made no effort to hide it. She knew he was charmingly glib, but decided there was no harm in him. As long as she remembered that he probably reacted similarly to any unattached woman, why not enjoy his company? Certainly it was a relief to engage in such lighthearted conversation with a man. There were no undercurrents in his words, nor did she have to choose her responses carefully. All in all he made a delightful companion, and she allowed herself to be amused by him. It was much better than spending the evening following Jackson with her eyes.

The music stopped, but Paul made no move to relinquish her. The next song was slow. He drew her gently to him and they began to sway to the melody.

"Excuse me," a deep voice interrupted them. "I believe this is the dance Kaly promised me." Jackson cut in smoothly and danced Kaly away, with no more apology to her partner. Paul stood staring after them, a frown of displeasure marring his handsome features.

"That was certainly rude," she observed icily when she recovered from her surprise.

Jackson eyed her lazily as he moved her capably around the floor. "The only way to get what you want is to reach out and take it," he responded. "Did I interrupt you in the middle of a conquest? He seems pretty smitten already, although I have to warn you, his tomcatting reputation is legendary."

"I'm sure your phone numbers are written on the same bathroom walls, then," Kaly replied sweetly, "because I've heard the identical thing about you."

Jackson shrugged his massive shoulders and continued gazing down at her. Up close she looked even more delectable, and the view his height afforded him made him warm, then frown. "Is that dress the fashion for anthropologists in Tucson? Seems a little drafty to me."

"Oh, then it must have been gallantry on your part that had you holding your last partner so closely. You were trying to keep her warm?"

Jackson looked satisfied. "That's me. Gallant to the end." He allowed a tiny smile to cross his hard features. "Is it my imagination or are you jealous?"

"Steven Spielberg should have your imagination," Kaly scoffed. "If reality were half as exciting as your fantasy life, you'd never survive it."

Jackson threw back his dark head and laughed boisterously. Kaly looked around surreptitiously, embarrassed to find others were looking at them. Jackson drew her closer, still chuckling. "You certainly have a smart mouth on you, Miss Scott." He lowered his head and whispered throatily, "I'd much rather have it on me." He nipped her ear.

Kaly pulled her head away. She ignored the tiny shivers that raced down her spine at his audacity. "Have you been drinking, Jackson?" she asked suspiciously. She could think of no other explanation for this sudden change in his behavior.

"Why would you think that?" he countered, his navy eyes alight with interest and amusement. His hand on her back slipped intimately to her derriere, and she stiffened in shock. But before she could protest it moved to the small of her back, leaving her wondering if she had imagined the caress.

She tried to find the necessary words to answer him, but her mind seemed to have been afflicted by the same lethargy stealing into her limbs. "You...I mean," she faltered, cursing inwardly at the breathless quality of her voice. "This sudden display of attention is a bit careless, isn't it? We decided weeks ago to avoid this."

"Hmm, my memories of that day are completely accurate," he murmured in her ear. "Remember? It was that day by the fence when I kissed you, and you—"

"I remember!" Kaly's whisper was strangled, and her hand tightened in his. "Which is why I don't understand why you're acting like this!"

He responded by bringing her hand to his lips, where he dropped a kiss into it and then cupped it tightly again in his own. Laughter laced his voice as he teased, "Don't you really mean—" here his voice changed to falsetto "—oh, my, Mr. Roberts, this is so sudden."

His clowning surprised a gust of laughter from her, which she swiftly tried to suppress. "You," she said with as much sternness as she could muster, "are incorrigible."

"You laughed," he pointed out reasonably.

"I'm not laughing." She bit her lip to still its quivering.

"Then why is your body trembling against mine?"

Her breath hissed in at his knowing remark. "Revulsion?"

"Kaly." Jackson placed a soft kiss on one bare shoulder and smiled in satisfaction as she shuddered wildly. "If you don't know the difference between passion and revulsion, I'll be glad to teach you."

Kaly was beginning to feel cornered. "Jackson, why are you doing this?" There was a pleading note in her voice. "Think about it. We've spent weeks avoiding this very thing."

"Weeks of getting to know each other better," he said in a low voice, serious now. "Weeks of being attracted, weeks of being tempted."

She began to have difficulty breathing. "This is not what we need."

Jackson looked pensive. "You're wrong. I think it's exactly what we need. It hasn't done us any good to pretend to ignore each other." He paid no attention to her sharp intake of breath. "As far as I can tell, staying away from each other hasn't put the fire out in me." He turned inquiring eyes down to her face. "How about you?"

"How many pounds a day of raw meat does it take

to feed that ego of yours?'' Kaly's tone held amazement. Taking a quick look at his skeptical features, she added, ''I can assure you I've been much too busy to think about you at all.''

''Little liar,'' he chided. ''Chemistry like that doesn't go away by itself. I should know.''

''Oh, here comes the line. What are you going to suggest now? That we have to give in to the chemistry, douse the fire?'' Kaly asked sarcastically.

Jackson smiled down at her in satisfaction and hugged her closer to his chest. He lowered his head and murmured, ''Why, Miss Scott, I'm shocked! However, I do think you may have hit upon an idea. I'm agreeable if you are.''

Kaly gnashed her teeth. The man shook her equilibrium, baiting her into making remarks that embarrassed her as soon as they left her mouth. She tore herself out of his arms as the song ended and muttered, ''I'm going to get some air.''

She found her way to a washroom, where she lingered as long as she could. Still loath to reenter the party, Kaly found the doors to the terrace and slipped outside, grateful for the opportunity to prolong her escape. Another couple was there, engrossed in each other, so she moved to the far end of the terrace, where she could stand near the railing in the shadows. She sighed in remembered embarrassment. What was it about that man that put her mouth into overdrive? Jackson could infuriate her with a few well-chosen words from his chauvinistic mouth.

''Hiding?'' a voice growled in her ear.

Kaly whirled around and groaned audibly. ''Don't you take a hint, Jackson?''

The ember at the end of his cigarette flickered in

the darkness. "May I point out that I was here first? And to answer your question, not very well, I'm afraid. When I want something I'm like a dog with a bone."

"I'm sure you share several other characteristics with the canine family," Kaly agreed sarcastically. "Our conversation is over. Finished. Let's go back to avoiding each other again. I know I was happier."

Jackson studied her. "I don't think that's what you really want," he said finally. "You're as aware as I am of the electricity between us. It won't do any good to run from it."

Kaly turned away, wrapping her arms about her middle. "Jackson, please," she whispered rawly. Why was he doing this? What could possibly have happened to change his distrust to outright pursuit? And what was she going to do about it? She longed for some distance between them, preferably miles. She needed time to regroup her defenses, time to remember all her very rational reasons for staying away from him.

He wasn't going to give her that time.

Jackson dropped his cigarette and nonchalantly ground it beneath the pointed toe of his boot. His body crowded hers, his hands cupping her bare shoulders and drawing her back against him. He dipped his head, nuzzling her hair, her neck, before answering. "Let's see what you really want," his husky voice dared her. "Kiss me the way you did in the pasture. Just once. Then tell me you don't feel anything for me."

"Oh, really." Kaly's voice dripped with disdain. She tried and failed to suppress the immediate leap of excitement she'd felt at his words. "Do you honestly think I'm going to respond to such an infantile attempt to manipulate me?''

He turned her around and pulled her into a loose embrace. His lips inched closer to her own, his breath brushing her face as he whispered, ''Do you know how many questions you ask? Well, all I'm asking is that you have the courage to find an answer.'' He touched his lips to hers softly. ''Just...one.''

Kaly stood stiffly in his arms, determined to withstand the onslaught of his kiss. She'd prove to him once and for all that sexual attraction did not take precedence over logical reasoning. It didn't require a scientific mind to figure out what he was doing. She could remain unmoved by his blandishments. She could!

Jackson lifted his head slightly. He smiled down at her with pitying amusement. ''Afraid, huh? I really thought I sensed more of a competitive spirit in you. But you're too frightened to take me up on my challenge.'' He gave a satisfied smirk. ''You must have it worse than I do.''

That did it! He was right, damn him. As childish as it seemed, as fatuous as his taunts were, she could never resist a dare. It was a flaw that her brothers had used against her time and again. When she was ten she had been ready to jump off the garage roof because Rick had said she couldn't. Only the arrival and anger of her oldest brother had saved her from herself that time. Now she was about to give in to a challenge again, just because the look on Jackson's arrogant face, so smug and superior, made her blood boil. She'd show him she was more than a match for a know-it-all cowboy! Kaly reached up determinedly, pulled his face close to hers and fastened her lips on his.

Jackson pulled back and mocked, ''That's not a kiss. At least not the kind that's going to determine anything. What's the matter? Scared of what will happen if you really let yourself go?''

She nearly gave in to the urge to kick him in the shins, but became determined to get her revenge another way. This time she drew his head down to hers and kissed him gently, licking his lips and scraping her teeth over them. Her tongue probed at his mouth and she nipped flirtatiously at his chiseled lower lip. The reason for the kiss faded from her consciousness as enjoyment of her explorations filled her.

A jolt shook Jackson's big body at her boldness, and he roughly pulled her closer to him and took over the momentum of the kiss. No longer was he a passive recipient. His mouth claimed hers avidly, greedily convincing hers to open, to grant him access to the moist chamber. Kaly conceded willingly, already lost under the relentless pressure of his mouth on hers, of his tongue sweeping the recesses of her mouth with practiced expertise. Their tongues twined together like lovers eager for the pleasure each could give the other.

At last Jackson tore his mouth away from Kaly's, breathing heavily. He leaned his forehead against hers, struggling to regain the control he'd lost so rapidly. ''I'd say the electricity is definitely there,'' he muttered hoarsely. ''Sparks fly every time we touch each other.''

Kaly looked up at him dazedly. ''Science was never my favorite subject in school,'' she murmured, fighting to keep her hands from smoothing back the dark hair that had tumbled down his forehead.

''Well, I'd certainly give you an A plus in chemistry, based on that display.'' Jackson slackened his grip on her and stepped back. The two looked at each other solemnly, uneasy with their reaction to the kiss.

"Here you are, Kaly." Paul's jovial voice sounded behind Jackson and both started guiltily. Neither had been aware of their host's arrival, so absorbed had they been in each other. "I'd hoped to convince you to finish that dance Jackson interrupted."

Kaly took one last look at Jackson's impassive features and said, "Thank you, Paul. I think I do feel like dancing some more." She took Paul's outstretched hand and accompanied him back into the house.

Jackson lit another cigarette as his narrowed gaze followed the couple's exit. It would be a little while before he was fit to return to the house, he acknowledged wryly. Every time he touched Kaly he was rocked by how easily she set him off. So much for his famous control. And she was still running from the feelings he awoke in her.

He leaned back against the railing. She could run a little longer. Then he and Miss Kaly Scott had some unfinished business to take care of.

Chapter 7

Paul monopolized Kaly for the rest of the evening. He had a sharp sense of humor, but Kaly was hard-pressed to recapture the earlier enjoyment she'd found in his company. That was Jackson's fault, of course. More than once her eyes strayed to him, but he never seemed to look her way. He appeared to be having a marvelous time, squiring one woman after another onto the dance floor. His seemingly easy dismissal of what had happened earlier between them was puzzling, but not entirely unwelcome. She had been shaken anew by the passion that had so quickly flickered to life between them. It had been a relief to be given time to recover.

And so it was with a great deal of dismay that she heard his voice behind her saying to Paul, "Sorry to deprive you of your dance partner, but I'm ready to leave, and Kaly's riding back to the ranch with me."

She whirled around to face Jackson's implacable

visage. "I came with Jeff and Carrie. I can ride back with them," she answered.

"Look around, Kaly. Jeff and Carrie left a while ago with a group to go have a midnight breakfast in Los Pueblos. I told them I'd drive you home."

She studied him closely. She almost believed he had engineered this situation. Almost, except that he'd been ignoring her for two hours. He was the last person she wanted to be alone with right now, but the man in front of her seemed a far cry from the amorous lover on the terrace. In fact, impatience was implicit in his face and stance.

Paul interceded. "I'd be glad to see Kaly back to the ranch, Jackson." He gazed meaningfully at her. "It would give me a chance to spend more time with her."

Kaly reluctantly turned him down. "No, thanks, Paul," she said. "It would be silly for you to make the trip when I could ride with Jackson."

Paul looked nonplussed, then recovered enough to squeeze her hand and murmur, "I'll be in touch, Kaly. Count on it."

Kaly felt acutely uncomfortable under Jackson's derisive stare. She extricated her hand and murmured a good-night to Paul. She looked around one last time as Jackson's relentless hand at the small of her back was directing her toward the door.

"I really should say good-night to the other guests."

"I already said your goodbyes for you."

That stopped her in her tracks. "You don't know how I appreciate your acting in my behalf," Kaly retorted, her tone implying just the opposite.

"You're welcome," he responded imperturbably.

The car ride was silent, disquietingly so. Kaly gazed out the side window into the darkness.

When Jackson finally spoke, she jumped. "I hope you didn't give Paul the wrong impression by spending so much time with him tonight. He's been known to move pretty fast when he wants something, and you were giving him plenty of encouragement."

Kaly was stunned by the accusation. She turned to gaze at him in astonishment, but he continued to face the road. The darkness hid his expression, but his profile was etched in granite.

"Paul," she said, stressing his name, "was a perfect gentleman. Unlike someone else I could name."

Jackson ignored the reference. "I'm just saying that it wasn't smart to use him like that. He's the kind of man to expect something in return."

"Pardon me?" Each syllable dripped icicles. "What do you mean 'use him'?"

This time Jackson took his eyes briefly off the road to answer her. "I mean that you were using Paul to make me jealous tonight, and it was a dangerous game. You shouldn't give out signals like that to men when you have no intention of following through with them."

Kaly was almost speechless. How like him to throw out so many illogical, outrageous statements that she wouldn't be able to decide which to respond to first. But she'd had enough of his sudden switches of attitude and his earthy remarks. "I don't know why you think I would need to use Paul for any reason. He's an intelligent, charming man. Why wouldn't I want to pay attention to him for his own sake?"

Jackson answered laconically, "Because you want me. I know it and you know it. You don't need to play games to get me jealous. He'll just get in the way, and I don't share what's mine."

"The only way I 'want' you is boiled in oil!" Kaly's tone was scathing. "And I would never sink so low as to use one man to gain the attention of another. You must be mistaking me for one of the dozen other women you danced with tonight."

She barely waited for the car to come to a halt in front of the house before she slipped out the door and hurried up the walk, ignoring Jackson's calling her name behind her. By the time she reached the front door, though, Jackson was there, opening it for her. Kaly sailed through without speaking and continued into the hallway, heading for the stairs.

"Wait a minute," Jackson said as he shut the door behind them and moved toward her. But it was the ringing of the phone, not his command, that made Kaly halt. Jeff and Carrie didn't appear to be home yet, and she hoped suddenly that this call wasn't bad news. She laid her purse on the walnut Queen Anne table in the hall and hurriedly followed him into the office. Jackson looked up, saw her and held the receiver out silently. Alarmed, her eyes asked wordless questions, but he was turning away to pour himself a nightcap.

She answered hesitantly. "Hello? Oh, Paul." She looked up to see Jackson's eyes on her as he approached her and handed her a glass of wine. She shook her head, so he placed it on the coffee table in front of the couch. He remained standing, listening to her end of the conversation unabashedly.

Acutely aware of Jackson's interest, Kaly kept her responses to Paul short. "Yes, I got home all right. You didn't have to..." She listened for a few more moments and responded weakly, ''That sounds fine. I'll talk to you later, then.'' She hung up the receiver and turned toward the door, loath to hear the sarcastic remarks she was sure were on Jackson's lips.

But the door to the office was closed, and six-feet-three inches of rugged male were propped against it, surveying her over the rim of his glass. ''Sweet of Paul to call and make sure you made it back okay. Staking his claim already?''

Kaly ground her teeth. ''Move away from the door, Jackson. I have nothing else to say to you tonight.''

He studied her lazily. ''I disagree.''

She glared at him. ''This is absolutely childish,'' she fumed.

''But effective,'' he pointed out. ''You may as well sit down. We have something to discuss, and you're not leaving until we're finished.''

Kaly looked around the room in frustration, but her only exit, short of climbing through the window, was blocked. Unless she chose to try to walk through two hundred pounds of solid muscle. She sat down on the couch. ''Where did you learn your charming manners,'' she snapped. ''Terrorist Tactics 101?''

Jackson shrugged. ''I'm not going to let you avoid this any longer, if that's what you mean.''

Kaly raised her eyes as if supplicating the heavens. ''I sense a serious lack of brain activity going on here.'' She looked back at him and said, enunciating distinctly, ''I'm not trying to avoid anything, Jackson, and most assuredly not you. I just want to go to bed. You know, that place where normal people spend the majority of their sleeping hours? And I'm going to bed because I'm tired. Not because I fear you, but because I fear what more of this banal conversation will do to my powers of concentration. Is any of this making sense to you?''

Jackson's eyes narrowed and he clenched his whiskey glass tightly in his big fist. ''Keep pushing, Kaly,'' he invited softly. ''You'll get a firsthand demonstration of what I can do to your powers of concentration.''

She looked away at his words. She remembered only too well how little control she'd had each time in his arms. She decided that baiting him was probably not the safest way to bring this evening to an end. She changed tactics abruptly.

''I'm tired, Jackson, and I just want—''

''You just want to escape upstairs and hide. Hide from what's happening between us, from the feelings you have every time I kiss you and from making a decision about what to do about them,'' Jackson announced. He wasn't going to let her hide anymore. He'd give her all the time she needed once she admitted what was happening between them and agreed to give it a chance.

Kaly shot him a fulminating look. ''Why do you keep telling me what it is that I want and feel? There is nothing for me to decide. I already know what I want in my future, and it doesn't include you.''

''You may have your schooling and hopes for a career mapped out, but you don't have the slightest idea what you want beyond that. You think you can just fill your life with those two things and that it'll be enough. Well, it just doesn't work that way. I know, because I've tried it. No matter how busy you are, you still need more in your life than work.''

If Kaly hadn't been so incensed she would have

been amused at how similar his dialogue was to her roommate's. "Are you quite finished, Dr. Freud?"

Jackson grinned wolfishly. "Not by a long shot." He left his post at the door and walked over to sink down on the couch next to her, picking up her wineglass and pressing it into her hand. "And neither are you. Because no matter how much you want to deny it, this attraction between us isn't going to go away. It's just getting hotter and hotter. At least, that's the way it's been for me. For you, too, if the way you kiss me is any indication."

"Will you quit it? There is absolutely nothing between us!" Kaly shot up from the couch, and this time Jackson didn't try to stop her. He watched as she paced agitatedly in front of him. "Okay, I'll admit there's a certain…" She searched vainly for a word to describe what was between them.

"Attraction," he supplied.

"…attraction between us. But I for one am sure I can handle this…this…"

"Chemistry." Jackson sat back. He was starting to enjoy himself.

"…without giving in to…"

"Sex," offered Jackson.

Kaly paused and stared daggers at him. "I was going to say lust, and I will thank you to stop putting words in my—"

"Mouth."

"Stop that!" demanded Kaly. "You make me so mad I could—"

"Spit?"

The contents of her glass were streaming down his face before she was even aware that she'd moved. She stared at the results of her loss of control in horror.

Even more terrifying was the calm, almost negligent ease with which Jackson mopped himself off with his handkerchief. Then he rose from the couch. Kaly took a few steps back. She was ready to run at the first signs of retribution.

Jackson slowly slipped his stained suit jacket from his muscled shoulders, all the while maintaining eye contact with Kaly. Next he untied his tie and pulled it from his shirt.

Kaly measured the distance to the door and dismally acknowledged that she'd never make it. Her eyes swung back to Jackson, who was unbuttoning his damp shirt.

"Um, Jackson?" Kaly wet her lips nervously while she inched her way toward the door. "You understand that was an accident, right?"

He remained silent, slowly moving the next button through its hole.

She moved a few more inches, speaking desperately. "I didn't plan to do it. I didn't even know I was going to do it until I did it. I mean, doing it wasn't something I meant to do. That's what I mean. And you pushed me, Jackson, you know you did. But still..." A few more inches to the door, another button. "But still, Jackson, I won't hold a grudge if you won't, so let's let bygones be bygones..."

Kaly's speech ended in a yelp as she swung open the door and made a rush for freedom just as Jackson lunged for her. She fled, using all her natural grace, as well as fear for her safety, to impel her. She was halfway up the hallway stairs before she realized she no longer heard the sound of his booted steps behind her.

Instead she heard, "Aha."

She turned warily to see Jackson leaning nonchalantly against the hall table, tapping her purse against one of his palms. "What do you suppose we have here?" he continued, as if to an unseen audience. "Why I do believe that it's Miss Scott's purse, containing, no doubt, all sorts of personal belongings." He grinned wickedly as he pointed it at her. "How badly do you want this back, honey?"

Kaly groaned inaudibly and mentally cataloged the items in her purse. While she certainly didn't want to have to watch Jackson pull out her personal belongings and snidely comment on each, she'd like nothing better than to call his bluff and let him have the darn thing. After all, it wasn't as if there was anything really important... Kaly closed her eyes and cursed inwardly. She had never gotten rid of those embarrassing foil packages Susan had tossed in her purse as a joke. Kaly hadn't wanted Peg to find them in her waste can, so she'd left them in her purse, and had forgotten about them until now. She eyed Jackson uncertainly. She wouldn't survive the humiliation if he found them. She just hoped she wouldn't have to abase herself too badly in order to get the purse back.

She seized on the off chance that he would see reason. "Why don't we act like adults here? Just toss it to me, Jackson, please?"

But Jackson was already shaking his head. "Don't see how I could do that, Kaly. I'd hate for something to fall out of it. You'll just have to come back down here and get it from me."

Still Kaly stood, her mind racing furiously. It wouldn't help to get her purse back if she also landed in his clutches. She doubted very much that Jackson was a forgiving person. She peered at him dubiously, chewing her lower lip. Despite his attempt at an angelic expression, pure wicked fire glittered in his dark blue eyes. He was obviously plotting something.

Jackson, apparently growing tired of her inactivity, drawled, "Maybe this purse isn't yours, after all. Could be I made a mistake about that. I'll just open it up and look through it for some ID—among other things." He fingered the clasp suggestively.

Kaly was galvanized into action. She descended the stairs with her hand extended and said in a conciliatory tone, "Jackson, please give me back my purse."

He held it out. "It's right here. Come and get it."

Kaly stepped a little closer to him, reaching but not able to grab the purse. She stopped, eyeing him nervously.

"You'll have to get closer than that," he coaxed. "C'mon, I don't bite. At least," he amended with a devilish grin, "not anywhere that would show."

Kaly approached and grabbed for the purse, but Jackson threw it aside and caught her by both wrists, easily restraining her.

He laughed down at her teasingly, his teeth gleaming whitely in his tanned face. "Well, well, what do we have here? Almost looks like you're throwing yourself at me."

She struggled madly, but was no match for Jackson. His grasp was not hurtful, but she was held firmly. She decided that a rational approach was in order.

"All right, Jackson. You've had your fun. Please give me my purse and let's forget about this."

Jackson cocked his head. "Aren't you forgetting something?"

Kaly gritted her teeth. "I apologize for throwing my wine on you, but you were asking for it." Any real remorse she had felt about her actions was fast dissipating with his tormenting behavior.

Jackson made a *tsk*ing noise. "Didn't your mama ever teach you that following an apology with the word 'but' kinda takes away from the thought? Let's try it again. I'll help you. Repeat after me, 'I apologize, Jackson…'"

Kaly briefly contemplated giving him a hard knee where it would do the most good, but one look at the light in his eyes made her think again. He was enjoying this, the big ape. If swallowing her pride was the only way she could extricate herself from this ridiculous situation, she wanted to do it before she choked. "I apologize, Jackson…" she mimicked.

"…for getting you wet…" he continued.

"…for getting you wet…"

"…when you looked so handsome…"

Kaly looked askance at him. "You've got to be kidding."

His lowered brows assured her he wasn't.

She gave in. "…when you looked so handsome…" she repeated flatly.

"…and I promise not to do it again, no matter how jealous I get." He waited in anticipation.

She could feel herself losing control once again. "I am not jealous of your harem!" she shouted in frustration. "You were probably dancing with me to make your other women jealous, though you could have spared me. If they were any more interested, they'd devour you."

"I'm not using you to spark anyone else's desire. I wouldn't put you in danger like that." He lowered his voice confidingly. "My ladies don't take kindly to competition."

Kaly answered pointedly. "They don't have any from me, I can assure you. Just stay away from me, and we'll all get along fine. Now, let go of me." She was surprised when he released her with exaggerated care. She turned once more for the stairs. His voice followed her.

"Am I the first man you've ever run from, Kaly?"

Her back stiffened at the truth in his words. "I'm not running from you."

"That's funny. It sure looks that way from here."

She forced herself to ignore the low, suggestive voice and to continue toward the stairs.

"Running is your last chance, isn't it? You only have two ways to deal with me. When words don't work, run like hell. That's your battle plan, right? Well, you can run from me all you want, but how are you going to run from yourself?"

She grasped the banister tightly, her steps faltering. She closed her eyes tightly. She hadn't realized she was so transparent. He was right, damn him, and she was very much afraid of the power that gave him over her.

She didn't realize he had moved until she felt a hard hand push her hair back and a kiss press to the pulse below her ear.

"Stop," she insisted, an uncontrollable shiver racing down her spine.

"I can't stop," his husky whisper sounded in her ear. "And neither can you. Quit trying to deny what you feel."

"I don't feel anything," she denied desperately, her words at odds with the break in her voice.

His hands were on her shoulders then, turning her

around while she trembled from just that touch. His head lowered and against her lips he whispered, "Liar." Then his warm mouth settled over hers.

Kaly used her elbows to try to gain leverage against his chest. She couldn't let him do this to her again, she thought despairingly. But it was getting harder to listen to her head when her body was screaming another message....

He increased the pressure on her mouth, entreating her to open for his tongue, to give him the response he knew she was capable of. He could feel some of the stiffness leave her body and pulled her even closer. He kissed her jaw line, her throat, and nibbled the sensitive cord of her neck. He could feel the rapid pulse there, and his excitement rose. He moved his lips back to hers, and this time they parted for him readily.

Kaly swayed into him. Her tongue entwined with his, savoring the taste and texture that was uniquely Jackson. A little sigh escaped her, and she gave in to the demands of his mouth. It was what she wanted, too, she acknowledged dizzily, the heat and excitement that she'd found only with this man. His mouth ate at hers, as a starving man consumed a meal, and her own hunger skyrocketed. Her blood was thrumming through her veins, flooding her body with heat, making her breasts tingle and her thighs ache. Her mouth twisted under his, desperate for more of him.

He sucked each of her lips in turn, the thin upper one, then the fuller, more sensuous lower one. His teeth gently worried the pad of her lower lip, teasing her until she captured his mouth again, demandingly. Jackson cupped her delicate face in his hands, then threaded his fingers through her long mane. He lifted his mouth from hers, freeing the combs that held back the heavy fall of hair. Dropping them to the floor, his hands roamed unfettered in the blond tresses as he once again lost himself in the taste of her mouth. He reached for her hand, guiding it to his half-naked chest. He pulled his mouth from hers reluctantly.

''Touch me,'' he rasped. ''I want to feel your hands on me.'' Again he took her mouth, confident his wishes would be carried out.

Kaly's hand trembled against those hard muscular planes. She moved it slightly, testingly. The mat of hair on his chest curled enticingly around her fingers and she gave in to the urge to rake them through it, pulling softly. She felt the hard shudder that passed through him at her actions and grew bolder. Her other hand joined the first, kneading, caressing. She soon grew impatient with the barrier his shirt presented and unbuttoned several more buttons. Now she was free to roam unhindered, to explore the haze of dark masculine hair shading the smooth skin. She found the pebbled hardness of his nipples, and her fingers fluttered away shyly. But his hiss of indrawn breath beckoned her, and her fingers crept back to the blunt nubs, scratching them lightly as she continued with her play.

Jackson's breath was coming in short bursts. He had wanted her hands on him, but hadn't reckoned on the combustible combination they would make. He lost the remnants of his rigid control and welded his mouth to hers. His kiss was rawly carnal, implicit in its demand. He moved her back several steps, never relinquishing her mouth, then pressed her back against the wall. With the easy masculine assurance that was so much a part of him, he slid one hand up to cup her breast.

Kaly jerked involuntarily as his big hand covered her. She could feel the heat of him through the thin silk and trembled at the flood of desire that coursed through her. The cut of the dress hadn't allowed for a bra, but she'd thought the lining would hide that fact. Now she could feel Jackson's warmth as though he was touching her bare skin, and she was shocked by the force of her craving. She rose up on her tiptoes and pressed closer to him, forcing a firmer contact, even as her hands continued their own mindless exploration of him. The tip of his thumb unerringly found her nipple and rubbed over it lightly. Kaly felt as though her body was on fire. She whimpered against his mouth and unknowingly clenched her fingers tightly against the corded muscles of his shoulders.

Jackson was beyond thinking, but his body was aware of what she wanted. He moved his hands upward and caught the thin straps of her dress in his fingers. He dragged them slowly off her satiny shoulders, causing the dress to gape, allowing him free access to her ivory breasts. He pulled away from her mouth and looked down to survey the treasure he'd uncovered.

Kaly felt seared by his intent regard. His face was drawn taut with passion, and he looked wilder, more primitive than ever before. His eyes were slitted sapphires as he silently perused her.

Jackson closed his eyes tightly for a moment, struggling for sanity. Her breasts were larger than they appeared when she was clothed, each firm round globe completely filling his large palms. Her coral-colored nipples were already puckered with arousal. He swallowed hard and said thickly, "You're beautiful, Kaly.

I want to taste you. I need the feel of you in my mouth.''

Kaly shivered in anticipation at his words. He bent her back over his arm and arched her breast up to him. His mouth closed over her nipple hotly, sucking strongly.

Kaly cried out brokenly as his avid tongue and lips worked their dark magic. His cheeks flexed as he drew more and more of her breast into his mouth. She felt him moving her, until the hall table was against her hips. Jackson lifted her slightly, so that she was barely seated on the edge, and moved in between her thighs. He removed his mouth from one breast and replaced it with his hand. He treated the other to the same favor, suckling, nibbling, as he stroked its twin.

Kaly was beyond rational thought. Whorls of color burst behind her closed eyelids. This spiraling excitement inside her left no room for anything else. Nothing she had experienced in the past had prepared her for this raw power, the savage passion she had unleashed. He was wildly aroused; she could feel the hard length of his masculinity pressed against her softness, and everything womanly inside her reveled in it.

Jackson's hand reached under her dress and smoothed up over the silk of her thighs, her hips, between her legs. She whimpered again then, whether in protest or supplication neither of them knew. One of his long fingers feathered along the lace band of her panties and then stroked inside. Kaly keened softly as he tenderly explored her womanly folds.

All the blood in Jackson's body pooled below his belt. His pulse hammered and his hormones screamed demandingly. This was too hot, too out of control for more teasing. Jackson's other hand left her breast and dropped to unfasten his pants. He moved closer between her legs, intent on making her his, when a sound made its way to his consciousness. He stood rigidly, shaking uncontrollably, as he listened.

He pulled slightly away from Kaly and made the mistake of looking down at her. The sight before him almost made him lose his resolve. Her heavy-lidded eyes were still slumberous with desire, and her lovely breasts rose and fell rapidly with her breathing. He steeled everything inside him and straightened her dress down over her hips, then slipped her straps up. "You'd better hightail it upstairs," he advised, his voice raw. "It sounds like Jeff and Carrie are home."

It seemed to take forever for Kaly's passion-fogged brain to understand the meaning of his words, even as she watched him adjust both their clothing. Then she heard the voices herself, coming alarmingly closer, and she swung panic-stricken eyes to Jackson's.

"Go on. I'll stall them," he said brusquely, and Kaly didn't wait any longer. She flew up the long stairway on shaky legs, leaving Jackson to turn abruptly back to the office. The toe of his shoe sent one of her combs skittering across the parquet floor, and he bent to scoop them both up and slip them into his pocket. He moved quickly to the office and grabbed his forgotten drink, walking behind his desk to sit down, needing its barrier to shield his still prominent desire.

He was mentally cursing his brother's timing when the front door burst open and Carrie's voice called out to him.

"In here," he growled. The office door banged open and Carrie approached him with fire in her eye; Jeff trailed sheepishly behind.

"Jackson Roberts, what do you and your brother

mean by keeping me in the dark about the rustling that's been going on?''

Jackson gazed pointedly at Jeff, who shrugged helplessly. ''Wanda Blane let it slip when we were having breakfast. Once Carrie heard a little, there was no stopping her until she had the whole story. You know how she is.''

Jackson glanced back at Carrie, who had both palms on the front of his desk, looking as if she could cheerfully kill him. The last thing he was in the mood for right now was placating a fire-breathing redhead. He shifted uncomfortably. On the other hand, it might distract his mind, which had joined the rest of his body in an agonizing, disappointed chorus.

''Now, Carrie,'' he soothed gruffly. ''We didn't want to upset you. This whole thing will be cleared up soon, and we didn't want to put any stress on you and the baby. Right, Jeff?''

Jeff agreed. ''That's what I've been trying to tell her, but she seems convinced there's some kind of conspiracy just to keep her in the dark.''

Carrie straightened and addressed the two brothers scathingly. ''Being pregnant does not drain away IQ points. I think you both owe me an explanation of all the details, and in the future I want to be told about anything that affects the ranch.''

Jeff hurried to his wife and spoke calmly. ''All right, Carrie, maybe you should have been told in the beginning.'' He ignored the scowl Jackson aimed at him and went on, ''We just didn't want anything to upset you during this pregnancy. Call us overprotective, but you know we'd do anything to help make this easier for you.''

Carrie was only partially mollified. Her look encompassed both men. "I'm going to bed now, but I expect to hear a complete account tomorrow, or I'll call the sheriff and find out for myself." She stalked out.

Jackson shot Jeff a commiserating look. His brother probably had had his ears blistered all the way home, and the night wasn't over yet. Carrie had a wicked temper when roused. He didn't envy his brother.

Carrie came back into the office, holding out a purse. "This is Kaly's, isn't it? What's it doing on the floor in the hallway?"

Jackson shrugged as nonchalantly as he could. "How should I know? She probably dropped it on her way in. I wouldn't take it to her now," he said quickly, as Carrie started to leave the room. "She went to bed quite a while ago. She's probably asleep."

Carrie looked at him strangely and replied, "I'll just leave it on the hall table, then, where she'll be sure to see it in the morning." She pointed it at him. "But don't think I'm going to let you off the hook. I still want to talk to you and Jeff tomorrow."

Jackson muttered, "Yeah, yeah," as she and Jeff left the room and made their way to their suite at the back of the house. When they were gone he picked up the phone and dialed Nick's number. Tersely he told him what he had learned tonight about Larry. "Find out where he was last night and let me know. I'll wait to hear from you before I call Roy."

He replaced the receiver and downed the remainder of his whiskey before rising to pour himself some more. He contemplated the contents of the glass and wished heartily that the liquor would wash the sweet taste of Kaly from his mouth.

He dropped heavily into his chair and raised the glass to his lips. It was going to be a long, torturous night.

Chapter 8

Kaly lay on the velvety grass beside Cherry Stream and surveyed the leafy canopy above her. She wished she could blame the fuzziness in her mind on having had too much to drink last night, followed by very little sleep. However, she knew that the feeling of dread and the utter confusion she felt were the result of what had happened last night with Jackson.

She folded her arms beneath her head. Nothing in her limited experience had prepared her for the tumult of emotions he wrought so easily in her. Never had she contemplated giving herself to a man in the hallway of his home! Heat blazed in her cheeks at the recollection.

Everything inside her had shrunk from facing anyone at the breakfast table. She'd slipped out at first light, hoping the surrealistic peace of the scenery would imprint itself on her tangled emotions. And after a time the quiet charm of the place proved lulling, and she slept.

Something disturbed her slumber, but it wasn't enough to wake her. She continued to doze peacefully until she felt a sweet, warm pressure on her lips. Her lips parted and her arms came up to languorously grasp the broad shoulders above her. She purred at the feelings awakening inside her, and her tongue darted out to taste the masculine lips. Her eyes flickered lazily, then widened. She came upright with panic and pushed strongly at Jackson's chest, nearly making him topple down the grassy slope.

Kaly jumped up and stormed at him, ''Just what do you think you're doing?''

Jackson got up and brushed the grass from his muscular, jean-clad thighs. ''Waking you up, and quite pleasurably, I thought.'' He cocked a well-formed eyebrow at her. ''Until you changed from a purring kitten to a spitting mountain cat.'' He leaned down to pick up the two combs he had dropped on her chest a moment ago, which were now lying in the grass at his feet.

Kaly scrubbed her mouth with the back of her hand. ''You have some nerve, sneaking up on me when I was asleep,'' she fumed, still shaken by how easily he'd crept into her dreams. ''You're lucky I didn't shove you into that stream.''

Jackson leaned against the tree. ''You're the lucky one. I wouldn't be as civil about a total dunking as I was about a little wine in my face.''

Kaly flushed at his reference to her loss of control the previous evening but pointed out, ''You would have deserved it. You don't have a gentlemanly bone in your body.'' She snatched the combs from his hand and tucked them into her pocket.

He crossed his booted feet and surveyed her. ''I thought we covered that ground last night.''

Kaly raised her hands to her face, sweeping aside the wispy curls that had floated away from her braid. She stopped, struck by a sudden thought. ''Did you follow me here?''

''No, I did not follow you here,'' he said. ''You happen to have selected the prettiest hiding place on the ranch.''

She ignored this veiled reference to the reasons for her own presence here. ''Who are you hiding from?''

''I'm not hiding, exactly. Just laying low for a while.'' At Kaly's quizzical expression, he expanded, ''Just long enough for the red-haired terror of the Circle R to cool down that redheaded temper of hers.''

Kaly's curiosity was piqued at the thought of Jackson's being afraid to face his petite sister-in-law. ''What did you do to set Carrie off?''

''It's more what I didn't do,'' he said. ''I may as well tell you—Carrie will fill you in, anyway. We've been hit by rustlers a couple times lately.''

''Rustlers?'' Kaly knew her mouth was agape, but couldn't prevent her surprise. ''You mean like in the Westerns on TV?''

''I mean like in the 1990s,'' he replied grimly. ''Trucks and thieves stealing my beef. Some neighbors have been hit, too.''

Kaly knew next to nothing about ranching, but she never would have guessed that rustling was a problem in this day and age. ''Are there any clues?''

''A few,'' he answered obliquely. ''Anyway, Carrie found out about it last night, and all hell broke loose because we hadn't told her.'' He frowned impatiently. ''Lord, we were just trying to spare her the stress, but try telling *her* that.''

Kaly rolled her eyes upward. ''Is that line part of the male formula, or what? I used to hear the same thing from my dad whenever he made a decision for me that he knew I wasn't going to like.''

Jackson eyed her with lazy interest. ''Yeah? Like what?''

Kaly started to enumerate on her fingers. ''Like the time he got me dropped from the Little League, like when he called my date's father to warn him of my curfew, and like when he signed me up at the college of his choice.''

Jackson's mouth quirked. ''You played on your brothers' Little League team?''

Kaly gave him an exasperated look. ''Yes, I did, and I was an excellent shortstop, too. Lots of the guys were upset when my dad made me quit.''

''I'll bet. You must have done wonders for the team uniform.''

''Deviate,'' she said loftily. ''I was nine and the best darn shortstop in the league.'' She grinned mischievously at the memory. ''But I paid my dad back by making him coach a girls' team. He claims it was the worst summer of his life. He's never forgiven me for it.''

His amusement lingered. The mental image of Kaly as a pigtailed nine-year-old riding herd on her father was highly entertaining.

''You do owe Carrie an apology, and I suggest you get to it before she gets any madder.''

''We'll see,'' he agreed reluctantly, ''later. If I wait long enough, she and Jeff will be leaving to go to the city to attend a concert. They plan to spend the night, so I figure by tomorrow she'll have cooled down some." He didn't move, continuing to study her intently. "I think you and I have more important things to talk about," he said finally.

Kaly occupied herself by brushing at the grass stains on her jeans. "I don't think so," she answered softly.

"Pretending it didn't happen won't make it go away," Jackson continued unrelentingly. "We want each other, that's obvious." He stopped, but Kaly was pretending extreme interest in her shoes. When it was apparent she was not going to respond, he added, "I think what happened between us last night scared you. Maybe you scared yourself. I'll agree that we need to back off a little, slow down. Get to know each other better."

And then what? Kaly asked herself bitterly. But she knew the answer to that, without even voicing the question. And then Jackson Roberts expected her to join that long line of women in his past who, in the end, gave him exactly what he wanted. Not that the pleasure in such an encounter would be all one-sided. Her body still reacted with excited shivers at the memories his low voice evoked. But whether it was pleasurable or not, she would still be just one of a throng to him, to be used and discarded. She had no illusions about herself; she didn't have the experience to handle a man like him or to hold him once his attention wandered. That knowledge brought an ache to her heart, and when she spoke her voice was haughty.

"I don't want to get any better acquainted with you, thanks anyway."

Jackson pushed away from the tree and approached with a threatening look on his hard features. He caught her by the shoulders when she would have turned away and forced her to look up at him. His face close to hers, he reminded her silkily, "I think we're a little past the getting-acquainted stage, Kaly, don't you?" His gaze swept her body, lingering on her breasts.

She stiffened in embarrassment. "I knew you couldn't resist gloating about last night. I just want to forget it ever happened."

He caught her chin in one big rough hand, turning her face up to his and running a thumb over her lips. "Forget what, Kaly? This?"

Too late she tried to draw back, but he still held her chin, and his warm mouth covered hers before she could pull free. She tried to ignore the rush of warm pleasure that surged through her at his kiss. It was even more difficult than it had been before. Now he kissed her with a slow, confident self-assurance, certain not only of himself, but of her response.

Kaly tried to twist her head away from those mind-drugging lips. But he forestalled the movement, using the opportunity to cradle her nape with his hand. Her palms pressed against his chest, but as one covered his heart, she could feel its accelerated beat, and this evidence of her effect on him was seductive. Slowly she began to give in to his will, accepting the slow thrust of his tongue as he filled her with his taste.

He kissed her with mind-shattering intensity, until he forced a response from her. Then, when she was leaning bonelessly into him, her arms clinging to his shoulders, he slowly lifted his head.

Pure satisfaction was etched on his features as he noted her heavy eyelids and swollen lips. "You can't forget this and neither can I. No use trying. Ignoring it won't change anything."

She pulled back from him, and this time he let her go. In that moment she hated him. Hated him for the ease with which he seemed able to recover from a kiss that still had her reeling. And for the way he had just used her response to him against her. It was pitifully obvious how she reacted each time he touched her, and she wouldn't waste any more time trying to deny it. But she wasn't about to let things go any further, either.

"I'm not going to sleep with you," she said bluntly, forcing herself to look him in the eye. "You may have thought otherwise after last night, but it's not going to happen. Did you really think that all you had to do was come out here and after a few more kisses we'd take up where we left off?"

He couldn't remember wanting so badly to shake a woman whose lips were still wet from his own. "No, that's not what I thought," he said, even as his body assured his mind that it, at least, was willing to do just that. "That subject's closed—for now." He forced down the frustration that welled up inside him. With her it always seemed like one step forward, two steps back. But he had assured himself—last night and again just now—that she was just as attracted to him as he was to her. She needed time, he could understand that, and knowing she responded to him would give him the patience he needed to let her get used to the idea.

But on his terms.

"We need to spend some time together. I'm going to make reservations for us for tonight, and you're going out with me if I have to carry you kicking and screaming."

This stiffened Kaly's spine. She regretted forgetting for a moment, even an instant, how controlling Jack-

son Roberts could be. So it was with quiet satisfaction
that she told him, "I can't go anywhere with you tonight. I have another date."

Jackson's face froze. "You what?"

"I said, I have another date. And if you'll excuse
me, I need to get back to the ranch. Jeff may be looking for me." She tried to brush past him, but he snared
her wrist with two long fingers and pulled her up short.
Her eyes went from her wrist to his face pointedly.

"Break it," he ordered flatly.

"Absolutely not," she said. "You do not give me
commands, tough guy. I'm not one of your hired
hands."

Jackson contemplated her silently for a moment, his
fingers no longer holding her captive. He rubbed them
along her delicate pulse. "I'm not going to let you
conceal your feelings for me with other men," he said
finally. "You're interested in me. No one else. It's
time you faced that."

Kaly tugged free and immediately went to mount
her horse. She couldn't deny the pull she felt for him,
nor the temptation he represented. Becoming further
involved would be disastrous for both of them, of that
she was sure. But she was not so certain about her
ability to withstand him if he didn't stop providing
constant temptations.

"Oh, and Kaly?" He waited until she turned after
mounting Misty before continuing. "You will sleep
with me. But it won't be because I seduce you. When
I take you to bed it will be your decision. Because you
will finally admit to yourself that you want me as
much as I want you. Think about that on your date
tonight."

His provocative remarks made her skin pale, then

redden in a furious blush. Without replying she wheeled the mare around and rode away.

Jackson watched her departing figure. Damned if he knew how to get through to her. He'd been accused of having an indomitable spirit, but she had a strong will of her own, and she couldn't be pushed.

He considered what she had said to him and a slow smile crossed his face. Kaly might think she'd had the last word, but there was more than one way for this evening to end. He'd show her that.

Jackson narrowed his eyes as he entered the crowded, dimly lighted interior of Los Pueblos's one dining and dancing establishment. He scanned the restaurant quickly until he spotted Kaly and her companion, and then slipped into a booth in a corner where he could see their table.

A waitress walked over and took his order, lingering for small talk. But when he didn't respond to her attempts at conversation, she finally moved away. He wasn't in the mood for chatting with a stranger, even one sending blatant invitations with her eyes. What he was most in the mood for, he thought darkly, was to haul a certain bullheaded research assistant out of here, over his shoulder, if need be.

Earlier that day, his plan had been simple. He would just wait until Kaly left with her date and follow them. It had been easy to justify that decision to himself. After all, there wasn't any use letting some other guy think he had a chance with Kaly. Not when Jackson knew otherwise. The way he had it figured, he was doing the poor sucker a favor.

But he had mistakenly assumed her date would be

Paul Whitfield. When he had seen Kaly get in that fancy truck of Larry Scott's, his blood had run cold.

Nick had nosed around and found that Larry hadn't been home the night the rustlers had hit the Whitfield ranch. Jackson hadn't had to consider any longer. He'd called Roy and given him all the information he'd gathered that pointed to Larry's being involved in the rustling. They'd both decided it would be best to keep the investigation quiet. It would do no good to scare Larry off before they had the proof they needed linking him to the crime. A deputy would be assigned to watch his movements when he wasn't working, and when he made his next move, they'd nail him.

Jackson damned that decision now. It would have been unpleasant to watch Whitfield charm Kaly all night. But to have to sit by and watch her enjoy an evening with a suspected cattle thief was going to be torture.

The waitress brought Jackson a beer, hesitated, then scurried away at the threatening look on his dark features. He barely noticed her as he watched the table across the room. Larry was leaning toward Kaly, talking, and she was laughing.

Jackson groaned as the blond cowboy led her to the small dance floor. She had dressed casually tonight, in a turquoise blouse and white jeans, and she still looked fantastic. Her hair was pulled back into its customary braid, of which Jackson was fiercely glad. He didn't want to think about any fingers but his own tangled in that thick mane. His hand gripped the beer bottle tighter as she moved into Larry's arms.

Kaly felt more relaxed than she had in weeks. She smiled as Larry attempted to teach her, with more enthusiasm than skill, the steps to a line dance. They were out of breath as the music came to an end, and that was when she looked across the dance floor and straight into Jackson's eyes. She stumbled slightly as she met his burning gaze, her movements suddenly uncoordinated.

Jackson smiled slowly at Kaly, taking in her reaction at the sight of him. He saluted her with his bottle, then sipped from it without breaking eye contact.

Kaly felt her hard-won calm flee. Just a glimpse of Jackson's hard, still features had brought that mixture of excitement and anguish she was coming to recognize as inseparable from his presence. Excitement because, God help her, her response to him was as immediate as it was involuntary. And anguish because she was miserably certain that a relationship with him would bring her more pain than she'd ever had to bear.

She and Larry returned to their table. Jackson immediately came over, ostensibly to say hello.

Larry greeted him in surprise. "Well, hey, boss, don't usually see you in here."

"I didn't expect to see you tonight, either," Jackson answered blandly. They talked about ranch matters for a few minutes before he asked, "Mind if I join you?"

Larry looked dismayed. "Well, uh..." His eyes swung to Kaly.

She started firmly, "I don't think..."

The rest of her sentence trailed away as Jackson pulled up a chair and sat down next to her. Immediately she felt suffocated by his proximity. The tables were small, and the chairs necessarily close together. Jackson's large build dwarfed her, the contrast of steely-muscled strength and her softer, slighter frame impossible to ignore. She felt her breathing quicken at his side and strove to keep from revealing her response.

He moved his dark head closer to be heard over the music. "How was the meal?"

"Real good." Larry grinned as he looked at Kaly admiringly. "'Course my appetite is always better when I'm sitting across from a beautiful woman."

Kaly smiled slightly at the compliment but was too discomfited by Jackson's closeness to respond. She allowed the two men to carry on the majority of the conversation, contributing little. Jackson propped one forearm on the table and stretched the other arm behind Kaly to rest it on the back of her chair. She stiffened, not trusting his actions. She sat, rigid and silent while they discussed the day's work. Her breath hissed and she turned her head sharply to glare at him when she felt his thumb rhythmically stroking her shoulder blade. She felt anger take precedence in the welter of her feelings. He was determined to ruin this evening for her! The gentle brushing continued, even when she pulled forward, pretending to change position. No expression showed on Jackson's face. He appeared totally involved in a discussion with Larry about an expectant cow they were watching. Just wait till she got him alone, Kaly vowed. She'd break every bone in his big body!

She attempted to inch her chair away from him until she was wedged next to a table leg, yet still not far enough from that caressing thumb. Not wishing to call attention to herself, she was forced to endure it for several more minutes, her backbone getting straighter with each passing second. When his fingers skated up her vertebrae to the sensitive skin at her nape, she jumped as though she had been scalded. Her sudden movement sent the glass in front of her teetering wildly, and only Jackson's quick reflexes saved it from upsetting completely.

He made a show of righting the glass and turned his face inquiringly to hers. In a purposefully loud voice he asked, "Is that your charming way of letting us know you've been ignored long enough?"

Mortified heat flooded Kaly's cheeks. She couldn't very well respond that she wanted him to keep his hands to himself without making a scene. The taunting gleam in his eyes told her he knew it, as well. Larry was eyeing the two of them quizzically, so Kaly responded weakly, "Not at all. I guess I'm just clumsy tonight."

A corner of his mouth lifted, and Larry immediately denounced her claim. "Don't let her kid you. She's already a pro at line dancing. Even kept up with a klutzy cowboy like me." The evening deteriorated even more from that point. The men continued talking about ranch matters, and Kaly purposefully remained silent. She didn't trust herself to speak when she felt like ripping Jackson's tongue out.

"How about a dance, Kaly?" Kaly's eyes jerked to Jackson in astonishment. He turned to Larry and asked, "Do you mind, Larry?"

It was obvious that Larry did mind, but he wasn't about to say so to his boss. "I guess not," he muttered.

Kaly waited till they got on the dance floor to lay into Jackson. "I suppose you have a very good explanation for your behavior tonight," she snapped as he led her in a Texas two-step.

"Almost sounds like you aren't happy to see me this evening, Kaly. I'm hurt."

"There is no way I'm going to believe your presence here is coincidence," she stated firmly. "Did you come here to play dog in the manger?"

Jackson whirled her around the corner of the dance floor, using the movement to press her closer to him. "Not at all. That would suggest I didn't want you. I'm here because I'm jealous as hell and to prevent you from spending time alone with Larry."

Kaly was speechless at the bland way he made his incredible pronouncement. "You are the limit!" she whispered in amazement. "I can't believe you admit to that."

"I'm not lying to myself like you are," Jackson shot back. "You're hiding your head in the sand, refusing to face what's between us. Well, I'm going to make sure you do face it. I'm not going to let you lead some other poor sap on, feeling the way you do about me."

Kaly would have broken away then, but Jackson was holding her much too firmly. He looked down into her face and allowed grimly, "Be honest with me, Kaly. Be honest with yourself. I don't understand this pull between us, and it scares the hell out of me. But I'm willing to follow it and see where it leads us. I'm not a coward, and neither are you. I can't sleep at night, and I'm not real efficient at work these days. Something's got to change, and fast."

Kaly blinked away tears. She should have been overjoyed at his confession, but it so closely paralleled her own confusion she felt even worse. It was easy for him to choose to follow his feelings, since she doubted they ran very deep. But she was coming to the aching realization that she would not emerge from this relationship unscathed. He might be able to enter into a physical involvement and keep a part of himself detached, but she knew from bitter past experience she didn't have that ability. Jackson was right—she was afraid to show her vulnerability, but it had taken so long to recover from Philip she didn't know if she could risk getting hurt again.

But she wanted to. Oh, she wanted to. She shook with the intensity of her longing for him. However, she knew exactly what to expect from him. He hadn't made a secret of his intentions. A short-term physical involvement was all he had to offer her, while she ached for an emotional, lasting relationship.

A Bruce Springsteen ballad came on next, and Jackson's fingers tightened on hers as he recognized the words that so aptly summed up the agony he'd been going through since Kaly had come into his life. Their bodies slowed, swaying to the haunting refrain.

Kaly stared, mesmerized, into Jackson's eyes. She felt his accelerated heartbeat, and her rapid pulse was just as apparent. It was as though the song was sung by someone who could look into her heart, who saw her restless sleep and put the chaos to words.

Jackson muttered hoarsely, "That's how I feel, Kaly. After I do finally get to sleep I wake up sweating and shaking from wanting you. Do you enjoy doing that to a man? Tying him into little knots so that he doesn't even know himself anymore?"

She swallowed and answered huskily, "You know that isn't true. I don't play games. I'm not responsible for the way you feel."

Jackson's face was taut, as if he was holding on to his control by one frazzled thread. "The hell you aren't. It's you I want to taste again, your name on my lips when I wake from another dream about you.

You're responsible for the way I feel, because you feel the same damn way, but you're too immature to admit it.''

Kaly kept a stranglehold on her last ounce of self-preservation to reply shakily, ''What would be immature is to blindly follow this...this...attraction between us, without any regard to consequences, without any thought to the future.'' She raised her face to his, pleading with him to understand. ''I just can't be casual about it.''

Jackson's features were like granite. He wished he could force some sense into that too-logical brain of hers. He didn't know what else to say, but was damned if he was going to beg. And he was perilously close to begging, he admitted to himself savagely. Kaly Scott wreaked havoc with his normally deliberate pursuit of a woman. His control had withstood all the punishment it could take tonight. If he held her like this much longer, the other patrons were going to get an X-rated floor show.

His voice was laced with all his pent-up frustration when he put her away from him and told her bitingly, ''Maybe you should find someone who will play your high-school games with you. When you're ready for a real man, let me know.'' He stalked away from her. He'd have to trust the deputy Roy had assigned to Larry to keep Kaly from harm tonight. Jackson had run fresh out of patience.

Kaly wended her way back to the table self-consciously, still inwardly reeling from their argument. Larry sat at their table looking glum. When he saw Kaly his eyes looked behind her, then swung back to her. ''Where's Jackson?''

She slipped into her chair. ''He left.''

Larry turned and looked around the restaurant, then turned back to her, his face more cheerful. "Great! We can be alone again." Then he looked more closely at her. "You look a little pale, Kaly. Are you all right?"

She smiled wanly. "I'm fine, Larry. Just a headache. It's sort of warm in here."

"Did you have words with Jackson?" he asked bluntly. Kaly's head shot up. He saw the answer on her face and apologized profusely. "I never should have let him sit with us, Kaly. I'm sorry as heck."

"We just don't get along very well," Kaly remarked as casually as she could. That was an understatement, she thought with bitter irony. Either they were verbally tearing each other up or they were wrapped in a cloak of intimacy that threatened her very sanity each time it ended.

Larry was perceptive enough to drop the subject and offer to take her home. Kaly agreed gratefully.

They took it slow going back to the ranch, and both had their windows down to catch the invigorating night breeze. "If we'd ridden my motorcycle we'd be able to really cool off tonight," Larry said. He glanced at her. "I didn't think you'd want to arrive at the restaurant all windblown, so I brought the truck instead."

Kaly asked delightedly, "You have a motorcycle? I'd love to go for a ride sometime. My brother had one, and I enjoyed riding with him."

"I'd be glad to take you sometime."

The brisk air did help rid Kaly of the dull throbbing in her head, if not her heart. She and Larry talked about their plans for the future. "What I really want is to get my own place," he told her. "It won't be near the size of the Circle R, of course. Just a small place, so I can raise my own cattle and work for myself." He shot her a glance. "Probably doesn't sound too exciting to you, but I've hired on at ranches since I was about fifteen. I'm getting ready to be my own boss."

"I think that's wonderful," Kaly said sincerely. "And I understand the need to go your own way, believe me."

"Well, I've got some saving to do before I'll even have enough for a down payment," he responded. "It takes some major money before a bank will take you seriously."

As they drew near the ranch house, they noticed blazing lights and activity at the barn. Larry frowned. "Maybe you should go in, Kaly. I'd better go over and see what's going on."

Kaly refused. "I'll go with you," she said. "I'd like to see for myself. Maybe there's something I can do."

The two hurried over and encountered frenzied excitement. Men were going off in twos and threes on horseback or in pickups, all carrying flashlights or lanterns.

Nick was giving orders in a terse voice, and when he caught sight of Larry and Kaly he lost no time greeting them. "Larry, go help Rod. We need to take an inventory on the head in the pastures and check all the fences."

Larry looked bewildered. "That'll take days," he objected.

Nick ignored his protest. "You and Rod can go in his pickup. He knows what to do. He'll explain everything to you on the way."

Larry turned to Kaly. "Sorry to leave you like this. Something must be up."

Kaly waved his apology aside. "It's all right. I can make it to the house by myself. You go ahead." Larry nodded and disappeared with the other cowboy.

Kaly stood for a moment, scanning the confusion. Jackson was nowhere in sight. She frowned in consternation. Surely he wasn't still out for the evening. She chewed her lower lip, observing in silence for a while. But when she still failed to see him, she felt cold fear begin to congeal in the pit of her stomach. He had left the restaurant at least an hour and a half ago. He should have been home by now. The mood he'd been in when he'd left her was too dangerous for him to have gone elsewhere. She couldn't imagine his not being in the thick of things here, giving orders and conferring with Nick.

"Nick, where's Jackson?" she asked worriedly.

Nick spared her barely a glance as he answered briefly, "He should be in the office talking to the sheriff." He turned away for a moment to shout instructions at the last men to depart. Then he looked back at her. "He took a blow to the head, but he's probably all right."

Kaly's feeling of dread intensified. "A blow to the head! What happened to him?" She grasped the foreman's arm and shook it slightly. "Nick, what's wrong? Is Jackson seriously hurt?"

The man sighed and took off his dusty hat, running his hand through his dark hair. "I guess he took a walk before turning in tonight and ran into someone who didn't belong here. Jackson was hit from behind. There was no one in sight when he came to."

All Kaly's anger and confusion about her feelings for Jackson were buried as alarm for his well-being flooded her. "Came to? He was knocked unconscious?

Why isn't he on his way to the hospital? He could have a concussion!''

Nick looked at her with amused tolerance. ''I wouldn't know about that. Jackson Roberts sure isn't going to let on to me how much his head hurts or if he's feeling a little dizzy. He raised Cain getting the men out to the pastures, and then when the sheriff came they holed up in the office.''

''He still could be seriously hurt,'' Kaly maintained stubbornly.

The foreman shrugged. ''Go see for yourself, then.''

Kaly hurried away. ''Maybe I can convince him to go to the hospital,'' she said over her shoulder.

Nick shook his head at her optimism. ''Good luck,'' he muttered.

Kaly reached the office door just as it swung open and almost collided with the large, balding man coming out.

''Whoa, there, miss, didn't mean to run you down,'' Sheriff Dumont boomed out as he caught her by the shoulders.

''Where's Jackson?'' Kaly blurted. The sheriff gestured with his thumb, and Kaly saw Jackson standing in the middle of the room, holding a washcloth to the back of his head. The relief she felt at the sight of him standing, apparently healthy, was overwhelming. She ignored the scowl he directed at her and stepped into the room. ''I'm Kaly Scott, Sheriff—Jeff's research assistant.''

The sheriff followed her back into the room. ''Figured who you was—heard Jeff had a pretty young filly working for him.'' He seemed unaware of the narrowed look his words brought to Kaly's face and went on, "Jackson can fill you in on the ruckus. I'm heading back to town."

He replaced his hat on his head and addressed the rancher. "We'll be back first thing in the morning, Jack, to look around." He winked at Kaly as he walked out. "You may want to convince him to see a doctor, miss—he's got a goose egg on the back of his head and the temperament of a grizzly with a sore paw." He continued out the door, still talking. "'Course, the doctor can't do nothing about the temper, no sir, that's Jackson, with or without a sore head." He left, chuckling at his own wit, and Kaly hurried over to Jackson.

"Let me see," she ordered as she pried his hand away from the back of his head. The ice-wrapped cloth he'd been holding to the wound was smeared with blood, and Kaly's stomach turned over.

"Get away," he groused. "I don't need some half-baked Florence Nightingale fluttering over me."

Kaly paid him no heed as she pushed him onto the couch. "Sit down and shut up," she ordered. "I want to see if you need to go to a doctor."

"Get real," Jackson scoffed. "I'm not about to go to a doctor for a tap on the head."

Kaly peered closely at his injury and was relieved to see that the wound was not as serious as she had feared. "Looks like your hard head came in handy this time. Do you feel dizzy or nauseated?"

Jackson pulled away from her touch, irritated. "I've had enough damn concussions to know that I don't have one now," he snarled. "Dumont already checked my pupils. I'm fine. I was only out a minute, if that."

Kaly stood next to him uncertainly. She knew him well enough by now to know she wouldn't be able to convince him to see a doctor in his present frame of mind.

Jackson stood and confirmed her judgment. "I don't need a hospital or a doctor. All I want is a stiff drink, more aspirin and a long soak in the Jacuzzi." He cocked an eyebrow at her. "Think you can help me out with that, honey?"

"Sure," Kaly agreed, ignoring his caustic tone. She was relieved to note that he wasn't swaying on his feet, and his color looked good. She could check on him during the night and call the doctor then, if need be.

Jackson walked past her and headed for the stairs. "Bring everything to my bedroom. I'll be waiting for you."

Chapter 9

Kaly kicked off her sandals and made her way barefoot up the stairs, balancing the tray she'd prepared. She walked carefully to Jackson's room and tapped on the door with her toe. When no answer was forthcoming, she went in, crossed to the nightstand and put down the tray. She turned and went to knock on his bathroom door.

Jackson called for her to enter and she started to, but halted to ask warily, "Are you decent?" An inelegant snort was her only answer. She peeked in to see him seated on the side of the hot tub, minus his shirt and boots. He had started the jets in the Jacuzzi.

With great self-discipline Kaly kept her eyes from lingering on his massive torso. "I brought some sandwiches, too. Are you hungry?"

Jackson started to shake his head, but winced at the pain the movement brought on. "No. Just bring me the aspirin with a glass of Kentucky's finest, will you?''

Kaly eyed him doubtfully. ''I don't think you should be drinking with a possible concussion.''

He closed his eyes for a moment, striving for patience. ''I do not have a concussion,'' he said in measured tones.

''You don't know that for sure,'' she maintained. ''And even if you don't, whiskey isn't going to cure that headache.''

''It can't hurt,'' he answered dourly. When she still didn't move, he snapped, ''Well, do you have any more advice, Clara Barton, or are you going to help me out here?''

Kaly shrugged and left the bathroom, obediently returning with a glass of whiskey and a couple of tablets. Once inside the door she stopped short. Jackson's blue jeans were lying on the floor next to his shirt and boots. White cotton briefs lay starkly on top of the pile of clothes. Kaly's eyes traveled slowly to the hot tub, skittered away and then were pulled back against her will. Jackson's bare chest was partially submerged in the frothing water, and he'd leaned his head back against the edge of the tub, eyes closed.

''Jackson?'' Kaly said in a faint, questioning tone.

His eyes opened immediately and he sighed mightily when he saw her. ''Great. Bring it over here, will you?''

She made her way over to the tub, keeping her eyes carefully on his face. ''Are you sure you should have more aspirin so soon?'' she asked, worried, as he took the glass and pills from her grasp.

''Yes, Mama,'' he mocked, swallowing the aspirin

with a slug of whiskey. He again leaned back and closed his eyes.

Kaly's protests subsided. He was a big man; he'd probably need a greater dose than most. Her eyes wandered over his heavily muscled physique. The strenuous work he did daily showed in his deep chest and wide shoulders. His biceps were thick and heavily corded. She felt her breathing grow shallow as her gaze lowered to the dark mat of hair covering his chest. With great discipline she pulled her recalcitrant eyes back up and mentally shook herself.

Schooling her voice to a matter-of-fact tone, she said, "You'll need to wash the blood out of your hair."

Jackson didn't even bother to open his eyes this time. "All right, but don't use soap. It ruins the Jacuzzi."

Kaly felt her mouth fall open at his assumption that she would be willing to perform the task for him. The man's colossal nerve never failed to astound her. Then she reconsidered. She could only imagine the pain he'd experienced tonight. It wouldn't kill her to help him.

She got a washcloth and soaked it thoroughly. Kneeling beside the tub, she wet his hair, careful to keep her eyes only on his head. When his hair was completely wet and glistening, she dabbed tenderly at the injured area, until she was sure the last trace of blood was removed, then wet the cloth again. As she rinsed his hair, she could feel him relax and sink his head deeper into her palms.

The temptation was too strong to deny. She dropped the rag and massaged his scalp, keeping up a steady rhythm with her fingers. She continued the hypnotic

movement for long minutes, entranced by the sensuous
feeling of the wet strands gliding through her slippery
hands. Finally, reluctantly, she pulled her hands away.
She picked up a towel and lightly rubbed at his wet
hair, soaking up some of its dampness. He thwarted
her efforts by raking one hand through it, slicking it
back carelessly.

Kaly busied herself putting his wet and dirty clothes
in a pile. She reached for the wet cloth and her wrist
was captured. She raised startled eyes questioningly;
Jackson was surveying her solemnly.

He brought her wrist to his lips and dropped a soft
kiss on the inside, where the delicate blue veins
showed beneath her skin. "Thanks, Kaly." His unexpected sweetness, so at odds with his earlier brusque
manner, made her heart turn over. His eyes had lost
the dullness from the pain and looked deeply into hers.
She managed a smile and slipped her hand away.

"I still need to put something on your head. Do you
have any antiseptic?"

Jackson indicated the medicine cabinet. "You'll
probably find something in there."

As Kaly rummaged through his shelves, she heard
the sound of the jets turning off and of him heaving
himself out of the tub. "Jackson!" she scolded, as she
felt her cheeks flush.

"You'll never make a good nurse if you're embarrassed by the sight of a naked man. I'm decent now,
anyway. You can do your worst."

She snuck a look at him and couldn't get her breath.
What he termed decent was barely that. Clad only in
a towel wrapped around his narrow hips, he was seated
on the side of the tub, looking a model of patience.
The white terry cloth contrasted sharply with the

bronzed skin above it. Kaly's eyes traveled downward, despite herself. His legs were as strongly muscled as the rest of him and covered with a lighter dusting of hair. She actually smiled when her gaze hit his feet. Totally without any tan, they were white, long and bony. The incongruous sight helped her regain some of her equilibrium.

"Did anyone ever tell you that you could win an ugly-feet contest?" she inquired as she crossed to him with a cloth and antiseptic.

Jackson looked hurt. "Is this part of your bedside manner, insulting your patient? The rest of my Adonis-like physique cancels out the feet, though, don't you think?"

Kaly rolled her eyes. "I try *not* to think around you. Turn your head." She wet the cloth thoroughly with the medicine and dabbed at his wound.

"Youch!" He ducked his head and tried to pull out of her range. "What are you trying to do—burn me? I may as well go back out and let that guy finish the job."

"Don't be such a wimp," Kaly scolded him. "Hold still. Try to live up to your he-man image."

"You'll see my he-man image before you're through," Jackson threatened. "That's enough!" He grabbed the bottle out of her hand and strode to the counter to put the lid back on it. Then he threw it in the trash.

Kaly preceded him out of the bathroom. "Like I said," she flung over her shoulder, "a wimp."

"Well, you must have a thing for wimps, then," he answered wickedly. "Because you sure do spend a lot of time kissing me."

She cast him an exasperated look. His gratitude

hadn't lasted long. He had already reverted to trying to embarrass her. "I should have let you go into a coma."

Jackson's lips quirked at her exaggeration. "Then you could have given me mouth-to-mouth."

Kaly shook her head. "Some thanks I get for tending to you."

"I'll be glad to thank you properly, if you want to step over here."

She eyed him, askance. "No thanks," she drawled. "I'm not stupid."

He chuckled and she continued warningly, "Either you put some clothes on or I'm leaving. Don't you have pajamas or something?"

Jackson looked at her wickedly. "I never wear pajamas, but I'm eager to please. If you don't like the towel, I can always take it off." His hand went to the knot securing it to his hip.

Kaly crossed to his bureau and opened three drawers before finding one containing clean jeans. She pulled out a pair and threw them to him. "Put these on," she ordered, while she turned her back to him. Her senses became excruciatingly acute, and she was aware of the exact moment his towel hit the floor. Her ears tingled at the sound of denim being pulled up long, lean legs. The sound of the zipper being raised sent heat throughout her body. Her fertile imagination supplied her mind with details of the reverse striptease taking place behind her, and Kaly felt her body warm in accordance with her thoughts.

"All done."

His voice startled her and she jumped guiltily, aware of where her thoughts were leading her. She whirled around and her eyes went immediately, involuntarily, to his zipper. He hadn't buttoned the pants, and a fascinating line of hair arrowed enticingly toward the waistband of his jeans and disappeared below.

Jackson noted Kaly's heightened color and wondered at its cause. "Are you all right?"

Her eyes bounced back toward him. "I'm fine... fine." She forced her eyes away from him and, noticing a set of French doors on one wall said, "Oh, I didn't know you had a terrace off your room." She could have bitten off her tongue when Jackson gave her a quizzical look.

He gestured for her to precede him and they stepped through the doors. The terrace was on the back side of the house and overlooked several of Peg's prize rose gardens. Though the flowers were shrouded in darkness now, their fragrance wafted gently toward them on the cool night breeze.

"Shouldn't you call Jeff and Carrie and tell them about this latest development?" she asked.

"No sense disturbing them this late. I'll tell them when they come back tomorrow."

Kaly turned to face him. "If you're not in the hospital by then," she reminded him. "I'm still not convinced you don't need to see a doctor."

"I'm fine. The headache's about gone," he replied dismissively.

She subsided. It was difficult to make conversation when her mind refused to work. Every sense, every nerve, was attuned to Jackson's nearness. Even the air seemed endowed with current, quietly humming, the growing tension impossible to disregard. She moved uneasily, seeking a return to a more prosaic footing between them, but she was suddenly as tongue-tied as a teenager.

Jackson was aware of her unease. It mirrored his own unrest and magnified it. His large hands clenched the railing, as the strain on his tenuous control increased. Her shallow breathing tautened him, drawing a like response. He wished mightily for a cigarette. Never had his body gotten into such a state merely from a woman's nearness. He didn't understand it, didn't welcome it, but this heightened awareness had been an aspect of their relationship since he'd first seen her. Trying to deny himself the touch and taste of her was playing hell with his libido.

He turned his head to study her. There was just enough moonlight to highlight her features; much of her body was left in mysterious shadow. God, she was lovely. Those eyes shocked him anew each time they met his, their green depths mystical, challenging. He watched the tip of her tongue come out to moisten her lips and wondered if he was making her nervous with his intent perusal.

This is a mistake, his mind whispered, no, shouted at him. The thin veneer of civility didn't run very deeply in him at the best of times, and the events of the night had combined to strip away his last vestiges of acceptable behavior. He needed time and solitude to replace the cool control he normally exuded. He knew he was going to get neither.

"Did you have a good time with Scott tonight?" he asked abruptly.

Kaly blinked at his sudden change of topic. "Yes, I did. Larry's very nice," she answered defensively. She seized on his conversation, welcomed it. Even an argument would be better than this unending tension sizzling between them.

He snorted. "No man wants to be known as 'nice.'"

"I'm sure you'll never have to worry about it," said Kaly dryly. "You fit a lot of adjectives, but that isn't one that springs immediately to mind."

"Good." His low voice sounded satisfied. "I'd hate to have to settle for it. 'Nice' doesn't describe a man who can make a woman burn with desire." He moved closer to her, taking both her elbows loosely in his hands. Her head fell back and she looked up at him, and Jackson bent toward her as he whispered raspily, "Was it 'nice' dancing with me tonight?"

Kaly's gaze was unwavering. "No," she whispered, remembering the heat, the excitement they'd shared on the dance floor earlier.

"How about the way you feel when I touch you?" he continued huskily. "Would you call that 'nice'?"

Kaly shook her head mutely, her gaze still entwined with his. Hot. Passionate. Desirable. Sexy. All those words described the way she felt every time Jackson touched her. He demanded strong emotions from people; he was not an easy man to be around. The force of his personality was too strong, his sexuality too apparent for that.

Jackson brought his lips so close to hers that they touched as he spoke. "And I'll bet there will be nothing 'nice' about this, either." His lips brushed hers, once, twice, before settling firmly. He pressed her lips apart and she met him in an openmouthed kiss that quickly ignited their hunger.

One taste of her. That's all it took to fan the ever-present embers of passion to a raging inferno inside him. He tilted back a little, putting her off balance, so that she was forced to lean into him. Kaly wound her arms around him, one hand on his shoulder and the other twined in his damp hair. He cupped her derriere with one large palm and pulled her closer, pressing her against his rapidly swelling desire.

Fire. Kaly felt a scorching ball whirl crazily in her abdomen, before shooting upward and exploding in her heart. Tiny shards of flame were flung haphazardly within, spreading rapidly to the core of her femininity. She should have been shocked at his physical reaction to her, disgusted at his blatancy, but she reveled in the proof of her effect on him. Unconsciously she moved nearer, delighting in the feel of his body against hers.

Hunger, barely leashed and insatiable, taunted Jackson into asking for more, indulging a bit longer. An ache, long denied and always present, sprang quickly from dormancy and threatened to engulf him. He made a rough sound deep in his throat as he felt the edges of reason fade away, as the world narrowed until it contained only him and the woman in his arms. He pressed kiss after intoxicating kiss against her sweet mouth and felt himself drawn even tighter as she reciprocated.

Kaly gasped as his avid mouth moved to the sensitive spot beneath her ear. It was happening again, the dark magic that so easily entrapped them, propelling them quickly to passion. She felt helpless beneath the onslaught of emotion brought on by his nearness, fueled by his kisses. She shuddered as he nipped, then soothed the area with his tongue. Impatient, she pulled him back to her lips, not caring that he chuckled silently at her eagerness. She wanted to make him feel the same way she did. She wanted him shaking, wanting, just as she was. Kaly embarked on a sensuous journey with her mouth, instinctively remembering what made him lose control. Her tongue skated along the ridges of his teeth, probing beyond them shyly. She flicked the sensitive roof of his mouth and sucked delicately at his tongue.

Jackson shuddered at her sensuous assault. She felt too good in his arms. He knew he was rapidly approaching the end of his control. He pulled his head away, avoiding her mouth as it followed his movement. "No, Kaly," he said, his voice a guttural rasp. "Listen. I'm not going to stop this time." He waited until her eyes fluttered open and comprehension slowly returned to them. His body screamed in protest as he continued inexorably, "I want to make love with you. So if you're going to run, do it now. I can't guarantee you a second chance."

Rational thought returned fully to Kaly, although desire continued to thrum through her veins. She almost mourned the return to reason, forcing her to make a conscious decision. But she had to respect him for leaving the choice to her.

She studied him silently, her body quaking anew at the sight of him. He was so much man. The force of her hunger for him was frightening, even as the sight of him thrilled her. He awaited her answer impassively; she would almost be fooled into thinking he was disinterested, except that she was close enough to see the sheen of perspiration on his face and the ripples of desire that still shook him. She knew in that moment that she was no more able to resist him now than she would have been had he not stopped. She quivered inwardly at the thought of being vulnerable to this man, of allowing him close enough to hurt her. But she was certain that the last thing she wanted to do right now was leave him.

Jackson waited for Kaly's answer, his whole body tense. She looked fragile, with her huge eyes staring up at him solemnly. She was mute so long that he thought he read her answer in her silence. He started to move away, not trusting himself to remain near her and not touch. Her voice stopped him.

"I'm not running."

Jackson swung his disbelieving gaze back to her. Kaly stood with her head held high, her gaze direct. Relief soughed through him, even as he warned, "I'm through playing games with you, Kaly. I'm not going to stop and I can't promise it's going to be 'nice.'"

He broke off as she slowly approached him and wrapped her arms around his neck, rising on tiptoe to look into his eyes. "I don't want 'nice,'" she answered huskily.

Jackson stood frozen, unable to believe what she was telling him, both with her words and her actions. His arms crept to her waist and he pulled her to him. He asked huskily, "What do you want?"

"You."

At her answer his fingers tightened convulsively on her waist. He consciously untensed them, caressing the taut skin apologetically. "Then we're even, honey, 'cause I know I want you." He pulled her against him, not caring that she could feel his trembling. He buried his face in her throat, before sweeping her up in his arms and carrying her inside. He stood her by the huge bed and touched a light switch. All the lights were doused except for the dim lamp on the bedside table. He watched Kaly's nervous gaze flicker to the lamp and away, and discerned the direction of her thoughts.

"I want to see you," he murmured, coming back to her and caressing her face in both hands.

She was still worried. He could feel it. "I don't think—"

"That's right, sweetheart—" his tongue traced its way around the pouty outline of her lips "—don't think." His mouth covered hers fully and Kaly forgot her apprehensions about the light. She returned his kiss, eager to return to that pinnacle of passion they had reached so easily. He nuzzled her ear, her throat, dropping kisses in random patterns on her smooth skin.

Jackson pulled away from her, his hands going to her braid. Slowly he unfastened the ribbon she'd used to hold the end. It fluttered silently to the carpet.

Kaly focused on his expression as he slowly unbraided her hair, a look of absorbed concentration on his face. She felt his hands working in the thick mass, until her hair was loose and his fingers combed through it hypnotically, bringing it forward and fanning it over her shoulders.

Jackson was making himself move slowly, trying not to frighten her with his excitement. He buried his face in the sweet scent of her hair. God, she'd run away screaming if she knew just how close he was to losing control, to giving in to the carnal longing welled up inside him.

"It's gorgeous," he said thickly. "Like honey. Why don't you wear it down more often?"

Kaly swallowed. He had made the simple act of untwining her hair so sensuous she was unable to concentrate on his words, much less respond to them. "It's...easier...to keep it back. Then it doesn't—" she broke off to receive the soft kiss he pressed at the corner of her mouth "—get in my way."

She watched Jackson as he let strands of it run

through his fingers. He brought forward a handful and rubbed his face in it. Kaly felt desire radiate throughout her body at his action. Something deep in the pit of her stomach unfolded at the sight of him taking such seductive pleasure in her blond tresses.

Jackson couldn't believe the difference Kaly's unbound hair made in her appearance. With it loose, as it was now, she looked...seductive. Wild. The answer to every man's most secret dream. He played with it for a moment longer, pressing back fantasies of the thick mass spread out on his chest, his belly and lower. He firmly corralled his rampaging, lustful thoughts and returned to wooing her. He felt a measure of control return. Being certain that this interlude would end in the most pleasurable way possible made him capable of restraint. He suspected that she wasn't very experienced, and he wanted to make this good for her.

He kissed her softly, gentling her to relax again, and soon her arms went around his waist as she returned his kiss with all the emotion he could desire. Jackson's hands moved slowly up to cup her breasts, his fingers tracing around them. His kiss changed, becoming deeper, more passionate. While he explored her mouth, he slowly slipped each button on her blouse free. When he finished he looked down to admire the picture she made. The sides of the blouse framed her slender torso. Her breasts were lovingly cupped in a lacy demi-bra, the tops rippling enticingly.

Jackson swallowed hard at the sensual display and moved with agonizing care. One finger traced her breasts where they met that seductive piece of lace. Then, fingers splayed at the side of each breast, he pushed them up with his thumbs and used his tongue to delve into the sexy crevice. Jackson's head raised at Kaly's involuntary gasp. His eyes locked with hers as he brushed her blouse from her shoulders. Neither watched it pool in a turquoise puddle at her feet. His hands went back to her waist, lightly stroking as he tortured himself with anticipation. Finally, with aching slowness he reached around her and unfastened her bra. She trembled in his arms as he removed the scanty scrap and it joined her blouse on the floor.

Jackson groaned audibly at the sight of her, bared to the waist. Her breasts were high and firm, rising proudly above a waist that he could nearly span with his two hands. Feeling his temperature rise as he looked at her, he endeavored to recapture control. Her peach-colored nipples were beaded impudently, begging for his attention. Lowering his head, he flicked a nipple with his tongue, wetting it, teasing it to a tighter point. With a low sound that was almost a growl, he took it into his mouth, suckling deeply, causing Kaly to moan. Her hands went to his shoulders, hanging on to his strength as her world tilted madly. Jackson's free hand stroked her other satiny breast, kneading it gently as his thumb rasped its nipple. She was wildly responsive, and he took his time pleasuring one breast, before switching his attention to its twin. He wet the nipple generously with his tongue and then blew gently on it, making it bead even more tautly. At Kaly's silent urging he lowered his head to it and drew it into his mouth.

Kaly's knees were weak and she leaned heavily into him. She'd had no idea that her breasts could be so sensitive. She felt each pull of his mouth deep in her womb, setting off a chain reaction of passion signals all over her body. He did not let up on his sensual ministrations, one hand going to the button on her pants. He unfastened it, sliding the zipper down slowly. His hand eased in and stroked her satiny stomach, which quivered in response. He moved lower then, brushing over her silk-covered mound seductively.

She caressed Jackson's shoulders and back wildly. She wanted to return the sensual explorations that threatened to drive her wild, but she lacked the control and the experience to reciprocate. Every flick of his tongue set her nerve endings on fire. She squirmed sensuously against him, eager for every feeling he evoked from her. Jackson lifted his lips to hers and bestowed upon her a devouring kiss. He pushed her jeans down and followed their trail along her silky thighs with his hands. Lowering Kaly back onto the bed, he dispensed with her jeans, leaving her clad only in silky bikini panties.

He gazed at her lying in the center of his bed, looking seductive and quintessentially female, and he could feel the hunger in him begin to throb painfully. The sight of her filled him with exultant masculine satisfaction and raging passion. She moved restlessly beneath his regard, and he lowered himself beside her, leaning half over her. Their lips met again as he pressed his chest gently to hers and rubbed himself against her breasts.

Kaly gasped at the unfamiliar pleasure. ''Jackson, please,'' she murmured, and mindlessly arched her back, eager for a firmer pressure. His rougher torso rasped her softer, more sensitive skin delightfully, but soon that wasn't enough. She needed to touch him, explore his body as he did hers. Her hands slid up his sides and moved between them. He obligingly lifted away a bit, and she caressed his chest shyly. At his hiss of indrawn breath she grew bolder, stroking him, smoothing her hands over his bulging pectorals. With one finger she touched the arrow of hair descending toward his jeans and followed the trail, slipping daringly into the unfastened waistband. He caught her hand and brought it to his lips, pressing a kiss into it.

Kaly opened her eyes and looked uncomprehendingly at him and he answered her unasked question huskily. "I love your hands on me, honey, but not this time. I'm too close to exploding as it is. If you keep teasing me like that I won't last any longer than a teenager."

Kaly blushed deeply at his frank admission, but something within her swelled with womanly pride that she could wring that kind of raw desire from a man of his experience. He evoked such churning, unfamiliar passion in her she was fiercely glad she could wreak similar feelings in him. She tested her newfound power by moving her lips to his chest, her tongue flicking daringly at the button of his nipple.

Jackson foiled her teasing by rolling over, pulling her on top of him. He lifted her above him so that her breasts swayed temptingly close to his lips, and once again he closed his mouth around a nipple, batting at it playfully with his tongue. Kaly closed her eyes slumberously and pressed demandingly closer to his mouth. He obeyed her unspoken request and his cheeks flexed, as he suckled her strongly.

Kaly almost sobbed as the pleasure mounted in her, and she moved unconsciously on top of him, squirming and rubbing against his bigger, harder body. Her movements were sending him into orbit, and Jackson's hand went to her silk-clad bottom, pressing it still. His fingers delved beneath the stretchy elastic to the smooth skin beneath. He fondled her firm bottom and impatiently pulled the panties off so there would be no impediment to his play.

He rolled over again, landing Kaly partially beneath him. She trembled with anticipation and the beginning curls of trepidation as his avid gaze devoured her in all her nude splendor. His hand lay on her silky stomach, gentling her trembling. One finger twirled teasingly in her navel before his fingers moved slowly down to curl in the honey-colored thicket of her womanhood. With his lips just above hers, their gazes locked, his thumb found the bud of her desire, and Kaly jerked helplessly. Jackson leaned down to kiss her and her arms came up to his chest to knead the muscular expanse.

Their kiss became deeper, wilder, even as Jackson moved one finger along her moist heat and barely entered her, keeping up the pressure with his thumb. Kaly bucked beneath him, on fire, and whimpers came from far back in her throat. He slowly eased one long finger inside, stroking and probing her tight moistness until she was sobbing, her fingers clenched painfully on his hard biceps.

Sweat broke out on Jackson's face, and every muscle in him tightened as he watched the sweet anguish twist Kaly's countenance. He felt the edges of passion crowd closer, threatening to take him over, and he rolled off her to stand next to the bed.

Her eyes opened and she watched as he peeled his jeans over lean masculine hips; her breath caught in her throat. All he'd been wearing were the jeans, and the rigid proof of his desire was instantly, achingly exposed. Kaly trembled at the sight of Jackson's nudity. She'd known he was a big man, but unclothed he seemed almost overpowering. The broad shoulders, deep chest and huge biceps were echoed in the long, muscular legs and throbbing manhood. For the first time, she felt panic begin to well in her. She sat up on the bed, uncertainty clouding the passion in her face.

Jackson recognized the brief flare of alarm in her wide eyes and moved next to her, soothing her in his embrace. "I won't hurt you," he whispered hoarsely. He lifted her chin with one finger, forcing her to meet his eyes. "Nothing will happen until you're ready. Do you trust me?"

Kaly's eyes were locked with his and her mind didn't register the strangeness of his question. She didn't think he could help but hurt her emotionally when their relationship ended, as it surely would. But she didn't believe he would use his strength against her. In this instant, under these circumstances, she knew she trusted him completely to take the greatest care of her, and she nodded mutely.

Jackson let out the breath he hadn't realized he'd been holding. He felt an unfamiliar tenderness for this woman and set out to assure her that she was safe in his arms. She was aroused, but he wanted her mindless with desire, until his presence was all she could focus on. He wanted to wipe out the memory of any man who had come before him and fill her senses, her mind, her body, with him. He used all his expertise, not thinking of it as such, intent only on bringing the most exquisite pleasure to her.

Kaly writhed slowly on the bed, under the tutelage of his hands. Callused fingertips moved pleasurably over her softer skin. His knowing hands were everywhere, stroking the skin in back of her knees, kneading the bottoms of her feet, caressing her breasts. He touched her intimately, with more knowledge of her body than she had herself. He took her lower lip between his teeth, even as one hand moved to her womanhood. The tender dual assault left Kaly unable to do more than respond. Liquid heat spread through her as Jackson began a rhythmic stroking. Her heels ground into the bed as the torturous pleasure mounted.

He wanted their love play to last forever. But the look of anguished passion on Kaly's face and her body twisting sweetly under his combined to snatch away the remnants of reason. He could feel his control fleeing and moved to protect her while he was still capable. Divining his intent, she touched his arm. "No." Her whisper stopped him. "It's all right. You don't have to."

He moved back to her. "Sure?" he murmured, his lips brushing hers.

"Very sure," she sighed, her eyes fluttering closed again.

Jackson knelt between Kaly's thighs, letting her feel his pulsating presence. He held her mouth in deep kisses as he rasped his chest across her tender breasts. His hand inched between their bodies, finding unerringly the heart of her desire, and Kaly whimpered, feeling a coil of tension draw unbearably tighter at the delicious sensations. The delight became almost unbearable, and her body twisted against his, her head tossing mindlessly on his pillow. Only then did he carefully flex his taut buttocks and push slowly into her, stopping when he heard her surprised gasp.

Kaly's eyes fluttered open at his possession. It had been a long time for her, and her body tensed slightly at the feel of his pulsing desire. Her fingers clenched tightly on his shoulders. She wanted him, needed the feel of him inside her. He loomed over her, his massive torso blocking out the dim light. His face filled her world as their gazes meshed and he watched her take him.

"It's all right," he murmured. "Let yourself relax. I'm not going to hurt you. You trust me, remember?" He held himself above her on his elbows, his face a taut mask of passion, and struggled to keep himself from taking her in a long, deep thrust that would end his torment. He felt Kaly relax a little against him and inched farther inside her, before stopping again to let her body adjust to his intimate invasion. He gritted his teeth as he felt her delicate inner quivering to accommodate him. He pressed inch by agonizing inch into her, until finally he was buried inside her, as deeply as he'd dreamed of. Waves of ecstasy threatened to overtake him as he struggled to remain still. He could feel with every fiber of his being, the tight, moist sheath cradling him so intimately.

Ripples of pleasure were flooding Kaly's being, making it impossible to focus on anything else. Her world narrowed to Jackson and the feelings his body wrung from her. Control slipped away, leaving only scorching passion in its wake. She writhed beneath him, sobbing, reaching for that ultimate pleasure that seemed just out of reach. He was so…oh…it was…

Jackson waited until Kaly's hips rocked him, signaling her unconscious desire. He pulled almost completely out and sank into her again. A cry emanated from Kaly at the rapturous feelings overtaking her. Strong hands gripped her hips as Jackson set a rhythm that she was helpless not to follow. He thrust into her over and over, and she whimpered involuntarily as desire carried her up over its edge. Her whole body tightened as she bucked frantically beneath him, and then her world exploded; shattering colors swam before her eyes, and she was flung over the edge, crying his name.

Feeling her satisfaction, Jackson reached even more frantically for his own, lunging into her with ever-increasing power until he, too, shouted hoarsely, caught up in the maelstrom of his own release.

Chapter 10

Kaly held him for a long time as their breathing gradually returned to normal. When Jackson raised his head and looked down at her, she forced herself to meet his gaze, although she had never felt more open, more vulnerable, in her life. She read with disheartening certainty the male satisfaction stamped on his face, but also a softness, an almost tender look she'd never seen there before.

He studied her silently, pushing her heavy, tousled mane gently away from her face, tracing her delicate features with one finger. She looked fragile beneath him, the exhaustion he read in her countenance tempered with the content look of a well-loved woman.

"You're on the pill?" he asked.

She nodded, her eyes dropping diffidently. "The doctor thought it would...I was so irregular..."

He nodded. A more urgent question was eating him, though, had been burned into his brain when he'd entered her. His passion eased, it again teased his mind and he asked it bluntly.

"You haven't had much experience, have you?"

Kaly stiffened and turned her face away. She pushed at his shoulders, intent on rolling away from his intent regard. Jackson resisted her attempts to free herself from his scrutiny, and waited for her reply. Unable to get away, to hide from that experienced voice, she answered in brittle tones, "Sorry I wasn't up to your usual standards."

He frowned, and forced her chin up with one long finger. When she finally looked at him he growled softly, "That wasn't what I meant, and you know it. It's just that you're so...so small. I could tell that you don't..." He searched for an expression that wasn't as coarse as the one that sprang to his mind. "You haven't...been with many men." He brushed his lips against her nose, her cheek, her forehead. "Have you?"

Kaly avoided his eyes but gave a slight shake of her head.

A surge of exultation coursed through Jackson at her admission, though he was incapable of explaining the source of the feeling. He knew he was being crude, but that didn't stop him from pressing her further. For some reason, it seemed imperative for him to know.

"Two?" he guessed.

He read his answer in the faintly indignant look on Kaly's face, but scarcely dared to believe it. "Only one?"

She refused to meet his gaze, but he knew he'd guessed accurately. His arms tightened protectively around her before he became belatedly aware that his weight held her pinned to the bed. He rolled over and cradled her head against his chest.

His eyes stared unseeingly at the ceiling. A primordial instinct he had never felt before had flooded through him at her disclosure. He had never been a possessive man. That made this euphoria he was feeling even more inexplicable.

He'd known Kaly wasn't like most of the women he'd dated, those who knew the score and were willing to engage in an encounter with a man without expecting more from it than mutual pleasure. But he had expected that such a lovely, intelligent woman as Kaly would have had many admirers. It was exhilarating to find out that he wasn't one of many, and he was struggling against an arrogant male impulse to make sure no other man ever trespassed again.

Kaly was appalled at his blunt questioning, and with her innate modesty she was still reeling from what she had just revealed to him. But in the aftermath of desire, which Jackson had satisfied, in the middle of his bed, still lying close to his hard body, she was strangely helpless to deny him anything, even something as intimate as her past. She felt his eyes on her, and it took all the courage she could summon to meet that navy gaze.

Jackson's rough hand massaged her spine soothingly, and Kaly unconsciously relaxed against him. "Tell me about him," he requested quietly.

She enjoyed his rhythmic caress for long moments before beginning softly, "We had plans to marry after graduate school." Kaly stopped here for a moment. She snuggled against him, not relishing having to rehash the past. Both his hands had joined in the soothing motion along her back. She arched slightly into him as one large hand rubbed the base of her spine. The hypnotic movement was making her drowsy.

"Midway through our programs," she continued, "Philip lost his scholarship. He started to press me to marry him right away. He wanted me to quit, get a job and put him through school." She paused, before adding reflectively, "I think the worst thing about it was thinking I knew him so well and finding out how poor my judgment actually was."

They were silent for long minutes as Jackson reflected on the man who had been fool enough to toss this woman away. "His loss," Jackson pronounced finally, rolling her half over and rising on an elbow above her. He bent his head to hers, his intent plainly written on his face.

Kaly's eyes opened wider and flickered down his body involuntarily. "More?" she asked ingenuously.

Amusement showed on his dark features. "Much more," he promised. He rained kisses on her face as he drew her under him and began to weave his spell once again. She gave herself up to his compelling caress, and they moved together again in the language of love.

Bright streamers of sunlight painted the room when Kaly finally awoke the next day. She was disoriented, looking about confusedly for long moments before the happenings of the night came flooding back to her. She sank into the pillow, biting her lip. Jackson had obviously risen and dressed long ago. It was his habit to rise early, and from the direction of the sun, Kaly guessed that it was close to noon.

She rose and began to pull on her clothes hurriedly, wincing as her movements reminded her of tender muscles. He had made love to her over and over last night, arousing her after she thought she was deplete of energy and then starting again. Jackson had shocked her with his need for her. She had shocked herself with her answering need. Her cheeks grew pink at the memories. His reputation as a lover was well deserved. Her experience couldn't match his, but she was darn sure she didn't like waking up in an empty bed the next morning.

She glanced quickly around the room to see if she had forgotten anything. Her eye caught sight of a rose lying near the pillow she had slept on. She walked slowly over, bending to pick up the fragile bloom. One of Peg's long-stemmed beauties, it was the palest blush of pink and tightly budded, just beginning to open. All the thorns had been carefully cut off.

Kaly brought it to her nose and inhaled the gentle fragrance. A tiny smile crossed her lips at Jackson's unexpected thoughtfulness. She shouldn't read too much into the gesture; he'd probably done this for countless other women. But she couldn't help the warmth his consideration caused. He must have known she would focus on this rose now, instead of on her awkwardness in rising from his bed.

After placing the rose in a vase on her desk, Kaly worked for several hours that afternoon, determined to finish everything before Jeff returned. She progressed steadily, turning down Peg's invitation of breaking for a late lunch. Instead, she sipped a diet soda as she typed, ignoring the housekeeper's dire predictions of what skipping a meal would do to her system. She was so engrossed that she failed to notice she had a visitor until he was standing right in front of her desk.

"So, it's just as I thought. You *are* a prisoner here slaving away for Jeff Roberts."

Kaly had to smile at Paul Whitfield's theatrical tone. She pushed her chair back and greeted him warmly. "Paul, what a pleasant surprise. I didn't know you were expected today."

Paul seated himself on the corner of her desk, his expensively shod feet crossed at the ankle. He shrugged in response to her comment. "I'm not. I wanted to see you. I figured it would be weeks before Jeff let you get away from the office again, so I thought I'd drop in and see how you were doing." He lowered his voice and leaned toward her. "You look even prettier than I remember."

Kaly smiled wryly. She could well imagine what she looked like after working all afternoon with very little sleep the previous night. Paul managed to look just as polished in jeans and a dress shirt as he had in his suit the other night. His engaging grin was toothpaste-ad bright.

Despite Jackson's dour predictions about Paul and his morals, she had enjoyed his company at his party. Now the two of them talked for some time before Paul revealed the purpose of his visit.

"I came over to see if you could get away long enough to go for a drive."

She shook her head regretfully and motioned to the computer. "I really have a lot of work to do before Jeff returns today. I need to get caught up."

"How about this evening?" Paul suggested. "We could drive into Albuquerque. God knows, it's not exactly a cosmopolitan city, but it beats anything around this backwater." He smiled winningly and added, "I know Jackson has a more or less standing date with

Gwen on Sunday nights. We could ask them along, if that would make you more comfortable.''

"Gwen?" Kaly managed.

"Surely you met her—the redhead at my party?"

Kaly remembered her all too well. She had to be the woman who'd been dancing with Jackson when Kaly had first caught sight of him. And she'd acted as if she knew him very well indeed. Kaly's stomach plummeted in direct correlation to her thoughts. Despite all her earlier reservations, she had allowed herself to become one of Jackson's string of women. The magic of last night was immediately tarnished.

Paul studied her closely before going on, seeming to choose his words carefully. "He hasn't made a move in your direction, has he?" At Kaly's startled look, he expanded. "The only reason I ask is that he's hell on women. No lady is safe from him."

Kaly managed to keep her voice surprisingly light as she answered him. "Why would you ask that? I'm hardly his type."

"A woman like you is any man's type," Paul responded smoothly. "And Jackson is known around these parts for his appetite for beautiful women." Paul's handsome face was full of concern as he added softly, "I wouldn't want to see you get hurt."

Kaly busied herself with straightening sheaves of typed pages on her desk. "I can take care of myself." Her tone prohibited further prying.

"Well," Paul urged her, "if you don't feel like driving to the city tonight, come home with me. I'm not much of a cook, but I can toss a couple of steaks on the grill and open a bottle of French wine. What do you say?"

They were interrupted before Kaly could form an answer.

"She says no."

Jackson's voice brooked no argument as he came in the door. He'd observed the cozy picture they made with Paul perched on the corner of her desk. Nothing would give him greater pleasure than to smash the man in his too-perfect nose. He was unaccustomed to the pure possessiveness he felt. And illogical as it was, he resented Kaly's friendliness with Paul. Last night gave him rights, dammit. It was time she admitted to them.

"I'm perfectly capable of answering for myself, thank you," Kaly said tartly.

"You obviously aren't capable of remembering that Jeff comes home today, and he made it plain he wanted to work this evening." Jackson told the lie without batting an eyelash. He didn't care what he had to do to rid them of this unwanted guest.

Kaly gazed at him defiantly as he uttered the blatant untruth. Jeff had announced no such intention. She was unsure what Jackson was getting at, but she was not going to endure his obdurate attitude.

"The sheriff called and is coming out again, too," Jackson continued. "Things are going to be busy around here."

"What's Dumont coming out for?" Paul asked. "Have you been hit by rustlers again?"

"I surprised a trespasser on the property last night," Jackson informed him. "I heard something, but before I turned around, he slugged me from behind."

"Slugged!" Paul exclaimed. "Did you see a doctor?"

"There was no need," Jackson said dismissively. "Seems I scared the person off before he could do any damage. But I'd advise you to take count of your herd. No telling if he went somewhere else after he left here."

"You were pretty close," Paul observed. "Are you sure you didn't hear or see anything that'd help wrap this whole thing up?"

Jackson hesitated, then shook his head. "It was dark, and like I said, I never had a chance to turn around."

"Well, Kaly, looks like we'll have to put our plans on hold. After what happened to Jack last night, it wouldn't hurt for me to go home and take inventory of the stock." He smiled and lowered his voice intimately. "But I will insist on a rain check on my invitation."

Under Jackson's impassive stare, Kaly said goodbye and Paul made his exit.

The front door slammed and Kaly faced the computer screen again. Determinedly she restarted her interrupted work—until Jackson came over and turned off the monitor. She sighed as his hand remained on the button, making it impossible for her to work. "What's on your mind?" she asked.

Jackson settled down on the corner of her desk, the spot Paul had recently vacated. "You weren't seriously considering going out with him, I hope."

"No more than you were considering going ahead with your standing date with Gwen," she said, hurt entering her voice, despite her best efforts.

Jackson leaned forward and spoke sincerely. "I wasn't. You can't possibly think I'd spend the night with you and then turn to someone else." He saw her hesitation and cursed profusely. "You did think that. Dammit! You really think I'm a bastard, don't you?"

He pushed away from her desk and took several paces before turning back and asking furiously, ''Why the hell did you go to bed with me if you don't trust me, huh?''

Kaly stared at him in silence. His sudden anger at her lack of faith in him took her aback. How could she explain to him that, while she had every confidence in herself intellectually and professionally, she didn't have much in regard to her womanhood? Her failure with Philip had destroyed that. She struggled to make him understand her confusion.

''Paul told me that you and Gwen usually went out on Sunday nights,'' she said.

Jackson gaped at her. ''You'd believe Paul, a man you met a week ago, but you don't trust me, the man whose arms you slept in last night?''

She dropped her gaze then and whispered, ''I didn't know what last night would mean to you.''

Kaly's quiet voice arrested Jackson's anger. He'd been so caught up in the territorial feelings roused by seeing her with Paul that he hadn't considered what Kaly might be feeling. He studied her now and his irritation drained away. She looked as vulnerable as she had after they'd made love. Although he could understand how she might think the worst after all she'd probably heard about his past, he felt strangely hurt that she didn't have more faith in him. He mentally shrugged the feeling away. He'd have to work to build that loyalty with her. Last night she'd admitted that she trusted him, physically at least, and he would take that and build on it. It might have happened too soon, but he was not above using their physical relationship to bind her to him. He mentally cursed Whitfield for his untimely appearance. He couldn't allow

Kaly to build any emotional barriers between them now, either real or imagined.

He felt fresh anger course through him as he remembered the easy way the man had addressed Kaly. Paul was slick, and Jackson was damned if he'd allow him to get close to her again. He came over and squatted down in front of her, forcing her to look at him.

"Last night was special for me, too," he said huskily. "I don't know what it means, but I do know that something like this doesn't come along very often."

Kaly caught her breath. Was he describing his feelings, or was he talking only about the physical attraction between them? Her eyes shifted restlessly away from his navy ones, so knowing and seeking.

"I don't know how to handle this," she complained, and he almost smiled. Her capable mind was used to dealing with the most complex academic matters, and she was impatient with herself when she couldn't as easily analyze the emotional ones. He rose, pulling her to her feet and into his arms. He embraced her stiff body and lowered his lips to her ear. "What do you say we just follow this through, see where it leads us? I don't have any more idea about what's in store for us than you do, but I'm willing to give it a shot." He planted a warm kiss below her ear. "In fact," he growled, "I insist on it."

Kaly found her knees weakening alarmingly. Her mind became annoyingly fuzzy when he touched her. She sighed with inward trepidation. "All right," she agreed, her voice quiet. She couldn't resist him, so why pretend otherwise? But she needed to clarify some matters between them. He needn't think he was going to have things all his own way.

His head came up at her response, and he studied her soberly. "All right?"

"Yes, I'll agree to see where this...relationship leads us," she said. "Under one condition."

Jackson's brows lowered as he anticipated another roadblock. "No conditions," he asserted. He was not a patient man in the best of situations. His need of her was immediate, and he resented any further obstacles in their path.

"One," she insisted. "At least for now." Her gaze slid away from his as she named it. "I don't want any one else to know about us, not even Jeff and Carrie."

With magnificent control Jackson managed to avoid shouting at her. He growled through clenched teeth, "Would you mind telling me why not?"

Kaly broke away from him. She needed to place some distance between them if she was to think clearly. "I don't know, I just feel uneasy about it. It doesn't look very professional for me to be living in your house working for Jeff, and be...involved with you." She turned to look at him pleadingly. "Please, Jackson, agree with me on this."

His face remained implacable at her entreaty. "No."

At this inflexible response Kaly's eyes widened in amazement. "Why not? I don't think it's asking too much for us to be discreet."

Jackson was coming very close to throwing something. "Discreet, no, but you're not asking for me to be discreet, are you?" he said furiously. "You already know I'm not about to go out and announce it to the world. What you really want is for us to hide our involvement, to pretend it doesn't exist. I won't do that. I've told you before, Kaly, I don't share what's mine.

Our relationship will be exclusive. I'm sure as hell not going to sit idly by and watch a stream of men fall all over themselves to date you.''

Kaly could feel her own temper rising. ''As if I'd be involved with more than one man at a time!''

Jackson forced his rage down. Nothing would be served by their yelling at each other. ''I told you last night, I'm not interested in playing games. We either have an adult relationship or we have nothing.''

She tried to make him understand. ''I'm not trying to hide anything, Jackson. I just don't want everyone to know that I, that we're…'' She broke off nervously.

Jackson gazed intently at her, understanding dawning slowly. Kaly wasn't playing coy; she didn't want to play the field. She was shy about revealing the fact that they were sleeping together. He mentally berated himself for his obtuseness. What she hadn't realized, and what he was at a loss to explain to her, was that everyone would assume they were lovers after they were seen together a couple of times. His reputation, while not totally earned, had enough truth to it that most people assumed he was having an intimate relationship with every woman he dated. He was unable to think of a way to shield her from that attitude and grimly acknowledged he wouldn't even try. The understanding that she was his would keep other men at bay. It seemed as if he'd been tripping over her admirers lately, and he was selfish enough to want to clear the way for himself.

He took her hand as he endeavored to reassure her. ''I don't notch bedposts and I'm not about to flaunt our private lives.'' Kaly slowly lifted her eyes to mesh with his. ''I won't go out and proclaim that we're lovers, but don't ask me to hide the way I feel. I want to take you out in public, so people are going to see us together. I'm not responsible for the conclusions they draw, but I promise I'll try to act…discreetly in public.'' It was as much as he was willing to allow her.

Kaly sighed. She supposed she was being foolish. He was such a stud that of course people were going to think what they wanted when she was seen with him. She'd have to brave it out. But she was perilously close to losing her head over him. She could feel herself being drawn closer to Jackson, and she was afraid she wouldn't be able to walk away. She was frightened of the time when he tired of her.

He sensed her weakening resolve and drew her close again. ''You think I'm stupid,'' Kaly mumbled against his shirtfront.

He chuckled. ''Honey, you're the furthest thing from stupid I've ever seen. I have a hell of a time keeping up with that mind of yours.''

She squirmed restlessly against him. ''I must seem miserably naive compared to all your other women.''

Jackson was surprised to feel a warmth envelop his heart. She was as different from the other women he'd known as it was possible to be. That was partly what fascinated him about her. ''I wouldn't compare you to any other woman,'' he replied honestly. ''I've never met anyone like you before. In some ways you're as naive as a schoolgirl. In others, you're more woman than I've ever known.''

She peeked up at him through her lashes flirtatiously, amazed at how naturally the gesture came to her.

He caught the look and gave her a hard kiss. His lips lingered, and when she would have moved away he prevented it by capturing her lower lip gently in his teeth. He nipped lightly, before releasing it to rub his shadowy cheek lightly against her silky one.

The rasp of his midday beard was erotic against her soft skin, and Kaly turned her head to his chin, dragging her lips against his whiskers. The abrasion against the tenderness of her lips was maddeningly arousing, and she used her tongue to bathe the area before capturing it in her teeth.

Jackson's breath was coming faster as he shuddered and nuzzled her neck. His voice was husky as he asked, "What should we do tonight? Do you want to go into the city, have dinner, maybe a movie? Or would you rather stay here and... What? What's the matter?" he demanded as he noticed her shaking her head.

"Jackson, I wasn't merely putting Paul off when I told him how much work I have to get through tonight. I have to finish this up for Jeff so we'll be ready to start fresh tomorrow. And I really need to put in several hours on my dissertation. I'm falling behind."

But Jackson attended only to the first part of her comments. "So what you're saying is that you would have gone out with Paul if you'd had your work done, is that it? Your turning him down had nothing to do with me, it was only because you were too busy?"

Kaly could not believe how easily his temper ignited. "That's not what I meant at all. I'm just saying that I do have a lot to do tonight. And you said that Sheriff Dumont was coming out later. Or was that another lie to get rid of Paul?"

"What do you mean, another lie?"

"I mean," Kaly reminded him testily, "that you told him I had plans to work with Jeff tonight, when you knew that wasn't true. Next time I'll thank you to let me speak for myself. I've been doing it for a long time—I think I can manage.''

Jackson pushed away from her. ''Well, my apologies, Miss Scott.'' His tone was icy. ''I was just trying to help you out of a sticky situation.''

Kaly snorted. ''You weren't trying to help me—you were trying to control me. And I won't tolerate that, Jackson. I make my own decisions.''

Jackson's voice rose as he lost his tenuous grip on his temper. ''You want to make your own decisions? Great. Just don't expect me to stand meekly by if you decide to see another man. I won't be led around on a leash.''

''Fine!'' she fairly shouted at him.

''Fine,'' he growled in return.

They stood glaring at each other for a long moment before they heard the sound of a throat being cleared from the doorway. Jeff addressed his wife innocently. ''See, Carrie, I told you they'd get along swell in our absence. Look at them. I think they're really starting to like each other.''

Kaly whirled around at the sound of Jeff's voice and flushed guiltily at the sight of Carrie and Jeff's bemused looks. She backed up several steps.

Jackson's mouth tightened at her retreat, but when he answered his brother his voice was mild. ''Glad to see you back. We were afraid you'd like it so well in the city you'd take up permanent residence there.''

''Good thing we didn't,'' Jeff answered as he and his wife strolled into the room, still staring curiously at them. ''Looks like if we'd left you two alone here much longer, you'd have torn each other apart.''

Jackson glanced at Kaly, an amused light in his

eyes. *Don't you dare!* her eyes seemed to warn him. He quirked an eyebrow at her, but answered his brother innocently enough. "You couldn't be further from the truth, actually. I was just asking Kaly for a date."

Carrie looked delighted, Jeff skeptical. Jeff responded tongue in cheek, "Oh, is that what you were doing, asking for a date? You must be losing it, Jackson." In an aside to Carrie he added, "And to think I once admired his technique with women."

Quickly tiring of being the center of attention, Kaly changed the subject. "Jackson had some trouble here last night. He was waiting for you to come home to tell you about it." She succeeded in diverting the couple's focus from her, but Jackson looked unenthusiastic about her selection of topic.

Jeff and Carrie's voices rose in concern, and confusion reigned for the next few moments as all four talked at once. When Jackson was finally able to briefly explain, he purposely downplayed his injury.

Carrie, however, pounced on that piece of information. "He hit you from behind? Oh, Jackson, were you hurt?"

"Only my ego, but according to Kaly, it could use a little deflating," Jackson responded dryly.

Carrie looked at Kaly sympathetically. "I'll bet he wouldn't let you take him to the doctor, either, would he?"

"How'd you guess?"

"Years of experience with the pigheaded men in this family," Carrie answered airily. "They prefer to be waited on at home rather than getting medical care."

"She made an excellent nurse," Jackson said wickedly, with a sidelong glance at Kaly. "She responded to my every...need."

If Kaly could have, she'd have thrown something at his arrogant head. Since she couldn't, she did the next best thing—escaped. "Why don't I go out and fix some lemonade for us all?" she offered, and quickly left the room, with Carrie tagging along to help.

Jackson watched her go, humor alight in his eyes. The little coward, he thought. He knew he shouldn't tease her like that, but it was so easy to bring that color to her cheeks. How long had it been since he'd seen a woman blush? Had he ever? She was a mass of contradictions—so sure of herself, with a sharp tongue and ready wit, and yet so shy in some ways. When he turned to look at his brother, Jeff was watching him solemnly.

"Sounds like you had an exciting day while we were gone. Did anything else happen I should know about?"

Jackson shook his head. "The sheriff's coming back out today to look around. We'll know more then."

Jeff hesitated, unsure of the reception of his next words. "I hope you're not riding roughshod over Kaly, Jackson. She's a damn fine assistant, and I can't afford to lose her. I won't stand by and let you make her life miserable while she's here."

Jackson laughed grimly. "I can't imagine Kaly Scott allowing anyone to ride roughshod over her. Maybe you haven't noticed, Jeff, but Kaly does a whale of a job defending herself. Besides, I already told you. I was just asking Kaly to go out with me."

Jeff looked disbelieving. "Didn't sound like your usual suave invitation to me, but what do I know? Do you get pretty good results from women, shouting at them like that?''

Much to Jeff's interest, Jackson looked distinctly uncomfortable. ''We, uh, got off the subject, I guess. She's already agreed to…go out with me. We were just discussing the time and place.''

Jeff looked serious. ''Don't hurt her, Jackson.'' Jackson's head swiveled as he locked gazes with his brother. ''She's not your usual type. She obviously hasn't been around. Maybe you'd both be better off if you'd just steer clear of her.''

Jackson was silent. Hadn't he told himself the same thing over and over? But it was a hell of a lot simpler to think it than to stick with it. Kaly and he had already made their decision, and it wasn't Jeff's business, or anyone else's, what their relationship was. He respected his brother's opinion as much as he did anybody's, but he would not let Jeff dictate his behavior. His voice was terse when he answered his brother. ''I'd say that was up to Kaly and me, wouldn't you?''

The two women returned to the room just then, interrupting them. ''Looks like the sheriff's coming up the front walk,'' Carrie announced. ''Kaly, would you mind getting another glass?''

Kaly set the tray down and willingly returned to the kitchen. When she reentered the office, Sheriff Dumont was already seated. She greeted him cordially, handing him a glass of the icy drink.

''Sure is nice to see you again, Miss Scott,'' he told Kaly jovially as he accepted the glass. ''Not every day I get to visit with two such pretty gals as you and Mrs. Roberts here.''

Kaly sneaked a furtive look at Carrie, who rolled

her eyes. She smiled. The man was sincere, even though his type of gallantry quickly wore thin.

The sheriff took a healthy swig from the glass he was holding as though unaware of the ill-concealed impatience on Jackson's face. "Sure does hit the spot on a hot day," he said, smiling expansively at the women. "My compliments."

"What can you tell us, Roy?" Jackson came right to the point. "Did you find anything when you went out to look around?"

"Well, it just so happens I did find something interesting, Jackson," Roy replied. "Found a clear trail of what looks like motorcycle-tire tracks. 'Pears you were right when you said last night you thought you heard a bike roaring off."

Kaly looked at Jackson in surprise. "You never said anything last night about hearing that."

Jackson was still gazing pensively at the sheriff. "Because I wasn't sure I had. I was pretty dazed for a couple of minutes, and it didn't make much sense at the time."

Jeff was frowning in puzzlement. "It still doesn't make sense. A motorcycle? I know you found tire tracks at the Blanes after their stock was stolen. But what could anyone do on a motorcycle?"

"Wait, there's more." The sheriff pulled a copy of a bill of sale out of his pocket and held it out to Jackson. "Bad news, I'm afraid. Seems some of your missing cattle have been sold over in Alberdeen. A small buyer bought them before receiving our notice to be on the lookout. Went back and checked the brands again." He pointed to the signature on the bill.

"Robert Rowe," Jackson read grimly.

He shot a look at the sheriff, who shook his head.

"Already had it checked out. The name's a fake, same as the address and phone."

Jackson cursed. "That's a three-hour drive from here." He raked his hand angrily through his hair.

"We probably ought to start sending notices out even farther," Roy mused. "Looks like the thieves are a little lazier than we first thought. Didn't even bother to change the brands on the cattle. They're willing to drive far enough that your brand won't be recognized."

The mood of the group grew grim. It was almost impossible to catch rustlers unless they were caught in the act. Once they had the cattle, it was a fairly simple process to drive out of state and sell them to a buyer, using a fictitious name.

"Did the buyer remember anything about the guy at all?" Jackson asked, without much hope.

"All he remembered was that he was wearing a black leather jacket with a bunch of chains hanging all over it. Said he remembered it because he wasn't dressed really like a rancher," the sheriff told him. "Of course we're checking that out."

Roy didn't need much urging to stay for supper that evening. As he lingered longer and longer into the evening, Kaly excused herself to go work in her room. She labored with total concentration over her paper for some time before wearily readying for bed. She had barely slipped between the cool sheets before her mind emptied and exhaustion overcame her.

Chapter 11

"Loafing on the job?" Jackson's voice jolted Kaly in mid-yawn as she was leaning back in her desk chair. Eyebrows raised, he strolled into the office and over to her desk, *tsk*ing at her inactivity. "It's so hard to hire good help these days."

Kaly smiled at the glint in his eyes and met his lowering head halfway to return his welcoming kiss. "I think you'd find the help you want in the employment columns, under *S* for slave," she retorted huskily.

He moved slowly away and pretended to mull over her response. "I do like the sound of that. Especially if you were the slave and I the master. I can think of several interesting scenarios."

Kaly shook her head in mock sadness. "Your fantasy life really borders on the unhealthy, do you know that?"

"What's unhealthy is the way I feel after the past

four days with little more than a stolen kiss from you,'' murmured Jackson as he picked up one of her hands and played with her fingers. ''But I think the planning sessions with the sheriff and ranchers are over.'' He continued, his voice lower, ''I have an appointment I can't get out of this afternoon, but I'll make it back in time to take you to dinner. We can drive to Albuquerque for a meal and dancing.''

At Kaly's silence, Jackson lifted her hand to his mouth and pressed his lips to her palm. ''You promised me a date. Remember?''

Kaly thought with real longing of spending an evening with Jackson. They hadn't been alone in the four days since Carrie and Jeff had come home. All of Jackson's free time had been spent in meetings, discussing the investigation. Seeing Jackson and talking with him only on the most casual basis had been difficult for her, too. She felt the most intense craving to be alone with him. He was getting to be an addiction, and she needed her fix.

Jackson lowered his face till it was level with hers. ''What do you say, Kaly? Want to go out for a little while with me? I made reservations for eight o'clock tonight.''

She raised her eyebrows. ''Pretty sure of yourself, weren't you?''

''The only thing I was sure of was that I had to get you out of here before I attacked you in full view of my brother and sister-in-law,'' Jackson asserted, only half joking. ''Unless you want to take the chance of being ravished on this desktop—'' he slapped the said piece ''—you'll take pity on me and say yes.''

Kaly's eyes swept the desktop before she consciously reined in her rampant imagination to answer him. Her gaze was trapped by the hungry look in his eyes. She answered throatily, "For the sake of the order of my desk, I guess I have to agree."

"I guess you do. I have one condition, though…"

"I thought you didn't like conditions."

"Only the ones I make," he joked, before turning serious. "I want you to wear your hair down like you did at the party."

Kaly didn't answer right away. She was remembering his fixation with her hair the night they'd made love, the way he'd unbound it and played with it. She felt desire begin to hum through her veins at the memory, until his voice jarred her from her reverie.

"Will you?"

Kaly silently nodded.

"Good." Jackson took both her hands in his, pulling her to her feet and into his embrace for a brief, but thorough kiss. He lifted his head to whisper rawly, "I'd better get out of here while I'm still able. We'll leave about seven, okay?" He brushed one more kiss across her mouth before putting her away from him deliberately and heading for the door. A heavy sigh escaped him. It seemed a hell of a long time until seven o'clock.

"This is lovely, Jackson," Kaly exclaimed after the hostess had seated them. The back wall of the restaurant was solid glass, and their table was placed where they could gaze out at the stunning skyline. The setting sun gilded the city in a stunning orange-pink glow.

"Yes, it is," he murmured, his eyes not moving from the vision in front of him. She'd done as he'd requested, leaving her hair unbound, held away from her face with a headband of hammered brass. Her sundress and matching jacket were almost demure, but that didn't alleviate the desire that had been sizzling in him all the way over here. He shifted uncomfortably. Not even the arrival of the white-jacketed waiter with their steaming entrées disturbed the sexual tension that was growing more palpable by the second.

Jackson watched, his eyes alight with interest as Kaly tasted her crab dipped in hot butter, her eyes closing as she savored the treat. As she delicately licked the shiny butter from her lips, she opened her eyes to find Jackson's fixed on her, hot and avid.

A tiny drop of butter remained, caught in the corner of her pink lips. He leaned slowly across the table, and Kaly sat motionless under his heated gaze, mesmerized. Jackson slowly wiped the drop off with one finger, tracing a trail across her lips.

When he sat back in his chair, she made a conscious effort to calm her labored breathing. Her hand trembled slightly as she reached for her glass. It became increasingly difficult for her to concentrate on her meal. Each time she looked at Jackson, the hunger in his eyes made her forget what she was saying or thinking.

Kaly became intensely aware of the flavor and texture of each bite she tasted, her senses almost unbearably heightened. The slippery sensation of the butter on her lips, the act of tearing the crabmeat from its shell, were almost erotic. Lifting her fork to her mouth, she locked gazes with Jackson, who watched hypnotically as she parted her lips and took the morsel between her white teeth. Candlelight flickered as they became totally immersed in each other.

The interruption of the waiter jolted both of them.

"May I bring you anything else?" he inquired politely.

Jackson shook his head and signed the bill. He leaned across the table to growl in Kaly's ear, "Let's go to the lounge for a dance."

She shuddered at the low timbre of his voice. She remembered with clarity that it got lower the more aroused he became, until it was a raw guttural rasp. They rose, and when he closed his hand on her elbow shivers shot across her already sensitive skin.

Jackson murmured, "Are you cold?"

Kaly looked up at him and almost forgot to answer. His pupils were dilated, his nostrils flared, signs of his rising passion. She could only manage to shake her head mutely to his question. A hard smile tilted the edges of his firm lips as he accurately guessed the reason for her nonverbal response.

They found a table in a shadowy corner and listened for a time to the mellow jazz tunes. Without a word, Jackson stood up, his hand extended to Kaly. For the first time that evening she slipped off her dress jacket, hanging it over the back of her chair, before stepping toward him and allowing him to bring her to his side. As they walked the short distance to the dance floor, the hand at Kaly's waist slid up and touched the bare expanse of her back. Jackson reacted as if he had been scalded.

"God almighty, woman, what do you have on?" he muttered before dropping behind a step to gaze at the backless dress. The jacket had successfully hidden the garment's cut, and his heated look directly affected the strength in Kaly's limbs.

He pulled her into his arms and they moved slowly to the music. Jackson's hand caressed her bare back before moving to her derriere, pulling her closer to him. His mouth touched her hair, her ear, her neck. Kaly felt lethargic and fluid as they moved, leaning heavily into him. The band played one song after another for over an hour, and Jackson and Kaly never drew apart. So engrossed were they in each other that it took them a moment to notice when the music stopped. The musicians were going on break.

"Ready to go?" Jackson asked.

Kaly looked up at him. His eyes were glittering sapphire slits, his desire easy to read. She nodded mutely. Almost since they'd entered the restaurant, the sexual tension had been building until she felt as tautly strung as a wire. They retrieved her jacket, which she threw over her arm as they headed toward the door.

Inside the car, Kaly felt uncomfortable separated from Jackson. She reached over to rest her hand lightly on his upper arm. She felt the tautness of his rigid muscles before he turned to her and leaned over to press a hard kiss on her mouth. They reached blindly for each other, desire fanned instantly. But after only a moment, Jackson pulled reluctantly away. Determinedly, he turned the key in the ignition and started the drive back to the ranch.

The ride home was quiet, but the awareness between them seemed to grow with each mile. Jackson was not silent by choice. It took all his willpower to keep his mind on the road, rather than on the woman at his side. He clenched his teeth tightly to rein in the thrill he felt as her hand caressed his arm. Never had he felt this way with a woman. The anticipation made the final culmination of desire even more satisfying, he knew, but he'd never felt as though he would explode at a mere touch. His much touted control was nil, his fuse shorter and his hunger wilder.

He glanced at her briefly and saw that she had fallen asleep. Her lips were parted slightly, and Jackson shifted uncomfortably, arousal riding him hard. He briefly contemplated pulling over to a private spot, but forced himself to continue driving. He didn't want to take Kaly in the front seat of his car, dodging the gearshift and steering wheel. He wanted to be able to spend all the time she needed to feel comfortable and to respond in the way he knew she could. He'd manage to wait till they got home. Somehow.

It seemed only minutes to Kaly before Jackson was lightly shaking her.

"Wake up, honey. We're home." He pressed a light kiss on her sleep-softened mouth. Still somewhere between sleep and consciousness, she responded completely, her lips parting, and Jackson could not prevent himself from giving her a deep, passionate kiss. Kaly made a sound of pleasure and moved closer to him, coming completely awake under the expert tutelage of his mouth. Her hands reached for him and framed his face caressingly, stroking his hard cheeks as she sought to get closer and closer to his lips. This was what she had dreamed of since they'd made love. Kissing him, touching him, wanting him.

Loving him.

The acknowledgment of her feelings brought a bittersweet joy along with the pain that came from knowing there was no future for them. Her attraction for him was only physical, she knew. He wasn't heartless; she was sure he would feel guilty if he knew how emotionally involved she was. She'd been aware from the beginning that she lacked the capability of protecting a part of her inner self from him, even as she gave him her body. Loving, for her, involved the whole person, and she didn't know how to keep one part separate from another. Jackson, on the other hand, was an expert at that. He wouldn't want her love; he was obviously wary of entanglements. But she had been unable to deny herself the time she could have with him, even knowing how it would end. For the first time in her life she had departed from her carefully planned future, and she couldn't bring herself to care. She would deal with the pain later, when Jackson turned his masculine intentions to another. But for now, she would grab all the moments she could, to be hoarded miserly for the time when memories were all she had left of him.

The answering sweetness of her lips was mind-drugging. Jackson broke away with difficulty, his breathing ragged. "God, sweetheart, you go to my head faster than any wine," he gasped, laying his forehead against hers as they both struggled to control their breathing. He pressed small kisses next to her eyes. "Kaly." He waited until her eyes opened and looked at him. "Come with me. I want you in my bed. I can't wait any longer."

Kaly was shaken by the depth of the emotion in his voice, which was echoed in her own heart. "Yes," she whispered, barely getting the word out before he captured her mouth with his once more.

Jackson came around the car and opened her door, helping her out. Kaly was grateful for his support. Her knees felt wobbly and she wasn't sure at first they would hold her.

The darkened house seemed oddly still as they entered, and to Kaly their footsteps up the stairs echoed loudly. Jackson led her past her bedroom door and down the hallway to his own. When they reached it he looked down at her once, kissed her softly and guided her into his room. Then he closed the door and pulled her into his arms. His head came down and he claimed her mouth with the passion that had been building in him all evening. He allowed his desire full rein, able to fully indulge them both for the first time in days. His tongue went in search of hers, sucking at it, enticing it to return his play. They stabbed at each other with their tongues, using them as sensual weapons in a war of delight. When Jackson felt Kaly melt totally against him, he tore his mouth away.

He pushed her jacket to the floor and deftly unzipped her dress, pushing it down her thighs. He looked at her and his breath caught in his throat. She was completely bare except for a tiny scrap of panties, little more than lace and elastic, and her sandals. His hands swept hungrily up her waist to her breasts, which he cupped with both hands. His breath soughed out roughly at the exquisite pleasure of kneading her softness in his big hands. He was perilously close to the edge already, and Kaly's actions didn't help his control. She was impatiently pulling at his tie, in an effort to open his shirt. Jackson shrugged his jacket away, his hands and Kaly's fumbling greedily, trying to undress him so they could feel each other totally.

Jackson began to chuckle at Kaly's frustrated attempts to disrobe him. He was minus his suit jacket, but the tie was only loosened, the buttons on his shirt partly undone. He grabbed her hands in both of his, bringing them to his chest.

"Slow down, honey, we've got all night." He was speaking as much for his own benefit as hers.

"C'mere, I've got an idea." He swept her up in his arms and strode to the bathroom off his room, pulling her sandals off on the way. He set her on her feet in front of the Jacuzzi, reaching down to turn on the jets. Kaly turned doubtful eyes to his. He leaned down to drop a kiss on the tip of her nose. "Just try it, please? For me?"

Kaly felt a strange mixture of shyness and daring, standing partially nude under his avid gaze. "One of us is a trifle overdressed for this party, wouldn't you say?"

Jackson grinned, delighted at her playfulness. He spread his arms wide, indicating surrender. "Go ahead, honey. I'm all yours."

Kaly was battling her own inherent modesty. But she longed to see him, just once, lose that iron control that was so much a part of him before she lost her own. While they maintained eye contact, she swayed closer to him. She reached for his tie and, without taking her eyes from his, very slowly pulled the tie from its loop. She smoothed the edges of it down the front of his chest before leisurely pulling it, inch by inch, from his shirt.

Jackson's eyes narrowed intently as he recognized the game she was playing. He felt his temperature sky-rocket at her deliberately sensual moves.

Kaly took his tie and placed it around her own neck, letting the ends trail provocatively over her breasts. His eyes were fixed on the tie, as she meant them to be. Her hands reached for him again, trailing down his shirtfront, before moving with agonizing slowness to his remaining buttons. She unbuttoned each languidly, pausing to press a kiss to each new inch of skin she bared. When the shirt was completely undone, she smoothed the sides away to bare his powerful torso. She bent and moved her lips softly to him, exploring the broad expanse with meticulous precision.

Jackson's eyes slitted shut and his big fists clenched. His chest was taut with the iron will he was exerting, and Kaly nipped a hard muscle daringly. When she looked up at him, he appeared like a man on the edge of exquisite agony. The skin was pulled tightly across his cheekbones and his mouth was taut. A sheen of perspiration shone on his tanned face.

Kaly pushed the shirt over his thick shoulders, down over the hair-roughened forearms, and let it flutter to the floor. Her hands passed back up his skin in a reverse journey, over his arms, up to his biceps, which she squeezed testingly. She moved up to his powerful shoulders and kneaded soothingly, before moving her hands down his chest and circling each nipple with a forefinger. Kaly pressed her face to his chest and nuzzled the soft dark hair that grew there, like a cat wishing to be stroked. Her hands continued their erotic exploration, descending his torso with deliberate slowness. She reached the waistband of his pants, her fingers splayed on either side of the button. She caressingly ran her thumbs up and down either side of his zipper.

A throaty growl emanated from Jackson's throat, and Kaly glanced up to catch him watching her in the predatory way a wild animal eyed its prey. Her fingers trembled on the button on his waistband, and she almost tore it off in the clumsiness brought on by his heated gaze. She pulled the zipper tab down a fraction at a time. A muscle jerked in his cheek at her actions; otherwise he was motionless. Her hand shook as she lowered the tab, her knuckles brushing the hard proof of his desire. She completed the zipper's descent, revealing a sliver of black cotton briefs, and Kaly felt her nerve almost desert her. She tried to garner her flagging resolve and pressed a kiss into the dimple of his navel, before using her tongue to stab the indention bravely.

This last act of precious torture broke Jackson's control, and he grabbed her by the shoulders almost bruisingly, pulling her up his body and kissing her with fierce intensity. Kaly reveled in this sign of his passion. He broke the kiss to mutter, "You enjoy tormenting me, don't you?"

Kaly was feeling a newfound confidence, assured of her own powers. Jackson might be able to bring her to mindless passion and earthshaking, rapturous releases. But she had found that she, too, could affect his big body mightily, and the knowledge was heady.

"I expected you to be able to last longer than that, Jackson," she purred tauntingly. "I barely got started."

He grinned wickedly. "We'll see who can outlast whom, honey. You want to lay odds?"

He quickly bent and removed his shoes and socks. He stripped the dress pants off and tossed them carelessly out of the way. Kaly's breath literally stopped. The briefs were not capable of hiding his straining manhood, and it sprang forth easily as he removed them. Nestled against a thatch of dark hair, it was mute testament to the passion she'd unleashed in him.

"Now who's overdressed?" he asked. He wrapped an arm around her back and brought her close to him, flattening her breasts against his powerful chest.

Kaly's head dropped back over his arm as she arched further into his caress. She sighed delightedly at the rapturous feeling of hair-roughened muscle tickling the tender tips of her nipples. Jackson removed her panties with one sweep of his hand before turning away to step into the frothing water. He took her hand to help her in and he sat, pulling her onto his lap.

The hot bubbly water was almost too much for Kaly's already sensitized skin. Jackson's manhood was pressed intimately against her hip, and she shuddered delightedly at the combined pleasure of the frothing bubbles and the solid mass of his body. He bent his head to kiss her repeatedly, his tongue pleasuring her mouth even as his hands began to roam her body. His hands cupped her breasts, fingers playing lightly with her nipples, rolling them between thumb and forefinger, stroking and kneading lightly.

Kaly moved gently in his lap, buoyed by the water and rocked by the sensations he was causing in her. His touch was torching her nerve endings, once again causing her response to flare out of control. His mouth explored her jaw, her neck and shoulders, making her shudder with desire. She moved closer against him, and Jackson groaned at the sweet pressure against his throbbing length. He turned her so that she faced him and took her mouth demandingly, pausing only to change the slant of their kiss.

Kaly already felt light-headed, and she moved fiercely against him, needing a release from this sweet agony. Jackson felt her desperation and lifted her, so that her breasts were even with his mouth. He took his time, caressing each before drawing one puckered nipple into his mouth and suckling strongly.

A tremor shook her as she felt each pull of his mouth deep in her womb, and she rocked against him, unconsciously seeking more. He paused to switch to her other breast and Kaly gasped. She was beyond words, a writhing mass of sensitized flesh that sought relief from the unbearable sweetness. Callused fingertips found the slippery folds of her femininity, and he stroked gently before sliding one long finger inside her. She sobbed as she felt the tight bar of passion in her abdomen draw even tighter. She pressed her breast closer to his mouth, encouraging a firmer caress. Her hand crept down and she touched him, velvet and steel, and as her hand closed around him, Jackson's mouth released her, unable to contain the hiss of his breath between clenched teeth.

He buried his face in her breasts, nuzzling, turning his head to kiss first one, then the other. "Kaly—" his voice was thick with need "—I can't wait anymore. Are you ready?" He positioned her hips above his, deftly easing into her a little, before leaning back against the tub.

She hesitated in the unfamiliar position, sensing that he was giving her control this time, not trusting himself not to hurt her. But her own raging desire didn't allow for shyness to stop her for long. She experimentally slid her hips down, and his gasp mingled with hers. She watched him through half-lidded eyes as she moved to take more and more of him. His eyes were tightly closed; perspiration dotted his forehead and upper lip. Kaly sensed he had almost exhausted his restraint.

She began to move, slowly at first, then harder and quicker as her own passion began to take over. The tight knot in her abdomen grew tauter until she was sobbing with need, Jackson's fingers hard on her hips. Each movement drew the knot tighter. Jackson pulled her hips closer to his as his own control burst, and he lunged upward, lost in the quest for fulfillment. Kaly clung to his shoulders, shaking with need, until a forceful thrust sent her spinning into space, and her body seemed to explode in a kaleidoscope of colors, waves of ecstasy shimmering to the outreaches of her body.

Jackson continued to thrust wildly until he groaned, his big hands clamped tightly to her hips as his own need exploded and his body shuddered blissfully.

They held each other close, limp and exhausted. Long minutes later, Jackson roused himself enough to remember where they were. The hot water was draining the little strength they had left.

Reluctantly they separated and climbed out of the tub. He rubbed Kaly gently with a large bath towel, before wrapping her in it. He knotted another towel carelessly around his hips before scooping her up in his arms and striding to the bed. He laid her on it and turned off the lights, then dropped his towel and got in beside her.

Kaly was still feeling the aftershocks of their lovemaking, but she was dazedly aware of his intentions. "Jackson," she said, avoiding his mouth as he pulled her closer to him in the big bed, "my clothes? I can't stay here tonight."

He easily kept her captive in his arms, subduing her feeble attempts to sit up. "Relax." He pressed a soft kiss below her ear and she shuddered wildly. "I'll take you back to your room before dawn. I want to sleep with you in my arms tonight."

Kaly felt herself responding to the sweet spell he so easily wove around her. She was astounded that she was capable of passion again so soon. There was nothing she would like as much as sleeping with him all night again, with one big arm keeping her close to his chest. But still she was apprehensive. She didn't want anyone to suspect where she had spent the night. She tore her mouth away from his and he continued down her throat, finding the hollow at its base where her pulse paced quickly and kissing it gently.

"I'm not sure...I don't..." She broke off weakly as he filled his hands with long tresses of her hair and rubbed his face sensuously in them.

"You always smell so damn good," he muttered. "Even your hair smells wonderful."

Kaly's protests subsided as she felt herself being pulled in by the undercurrents of his recurring passion.

He found the knot in her towel with one hand and loosened it, pulling the sides open to reveal her nude form to him. He rolled her under him, and Kaly's eyes fluttered closed as he moved against her once again in a compelling caress.

Kaly hummed to herself as she slid the last of the volumes back into place in the bookcase in the office. She'd been using them to research some facts for Jeff's book. Things were going well on the manuscript. So well, in fact, that Jeff planned to take the day off to drive Carrie to the city.

The thought of how close she was to finishing her collaboration with Jeff brought a slight frown to Kaly's face. She longed for every extra day she could get with Jackson. They had been spending all their free time together, going out to eat and to movies, and horseback riding. She smiled as she remembered one particular picnic at Cherry Stream. He'd managed to talk her out of all her inhibitions, and her clothes, and into skinny-dipping with him. The memory still had the power to send heat through her body in remembered pleasure.

Each moment she spent with him found her more in love than ever. And sometimes the depth of her emotions terrified her. She wondered how long she could keep her feelings a secret from him. For she knew it would take just a hint of them to send him running for the hills. She had no doubts about how Jackson felt about her. He had told her things when they were in bed together. He had said that he wanted her, that he needed her. Just remembering the guttural rasp with which he had delivered those words brought a delicate shiver. But he had been depressingly reticent about anything more personal.

Which meant only one thing, of course. She had known what she was in for with Jackson Roberts, and the knowledge hadn't deterred her. She had been warned about his reputation many times. She had warned herself. But she had been unable to withstand the temptation he held for her, and she had no one but herself to blame for her situation.

She loved him in a way she had never dreamed possible. But she knew that nothing had changed for him. A woman had hurt him, and a part of him would always remain scarred and bitter from the experience. He would not allow himself to trust a woman again, much less settle down with one. It was this certainty that kept her from voicing her love for him. It was becoming increasingly difficult to keep from telling him when they were straining together for passion's release, or afterward, when the tenderness she felt almost made her weep.

Engrossed in these dismal thoughts, she was startled

to feel arms wrap around her from behind. Jackson hugged her close to him and kissed her neck.

"Mmm. I've been waiting to do that all day. It gets harder and harder to take you back to your room every morning." Suddenly he seemed to realize how stiffly she was standing, and he turned her around in his grasp, tilting her face up to his. His gaze was perplexed.

"Kaly? Is something the matter?"

She shook her head, but broke away from him. Moving over to her desk, she busied herself with straightening its surface.

Jackson watched her silently for a moment. Every instinct told him she was hiding something from him, even in bed. Hell, especially in bed. Their lovemaking grew more fantastic every time, though he always thought that would be impossible. But she seemed to try to close a part of herself off from him, to hold a piece of herself separate. It puzzled and infuriated him. Sometimes the desire to take her completely was so strong he was afraid he'd hurt her with the strength of his passion. Always her response was everything he could desire. Yet still that niggling feeling remained.

He was getting that same feeling now, and he was quiet as he attempted to puzzle it out. Kaly, distracted by his extended silence, glanced at him. "What's wrong?"

"That's what I'm wondering," he responded slowly.

"What brings you in the house in the afternoon?" she inquired with forced normalcy.

"A cute little green-eyed blond about this high." He gestured to his shoulder. "You know her?"

Kaly shook her head, her earlier morose thoughts

fading. When she was close to him, all her fears disappeared. "'Fraid not," she teased.

"Too bad," he sighed in mock disappointment. "She's lured me away from my work by refusing to stay out of my mind. I figured since she was such a distraction, anyway, I'd take the afternoon off and spend it with her. But since she's not here—" he stalked her toward her desk purposefully "—I think you'll do nicely."

She shrieked as he reached out to bring her close to him. "You are filthy," she said as he tried to rub his dusty cheek against hers. "You're in desperate need of a bath."

"Is that an invitation?" Jackson asked interestedly. "'Cause if it is, I'll let you scrub my back for me. And anything else you feel like scrubbing, too."

"Fat chance."

Jackson heaved a long-suffering sigh. "Just like a woman. Issue an invitation, get a guy all heated up, then welsh out."

Kaly choked. "That wasn't an invitation. And it seems to me it doesn't take a whole lot to get you all heated up, either."

"It doesn't take much from you," Jackson affirmed. "Especially since I have vivid memories of how well you do in a hot tub." He nibbled at the sensitive cord on her neck. "Can I at least interest you in spending the rest of the afternoon with me? I'll let you pick what to do."

A sudden thought struck Kaly. "I think I'll take you up on that offer, cowboy. How soon can you get cleaned up?"

"It wouldn't take much time at all if an extra pair of hands wanted to help me," he said persuasively.

But Kaly only reached up and dropped a light kiss on his chin. She ducked under his arm and headed for the office door. "I'll meet you back here in exactly thirty minutes," she told him.

Chapter 12

Kaly hurried back downstairs. The thirty minutes she had given Jackson were almost up, and she and Peg had managed to spend them fruitfully. A basket was packed, and a quick phone call to the barn had ensured that their mounts would be saddled and waiting. Thinking of her plans for the day lightened her step.

She entered the office expectantly, but Jackson wasn't there. Kaly sighed impatiently. And men were always complaining about how long women took to get ready! She crossed to the window and peered out toward the barn, wondering if Jackson had gone outside already. Then steps sounded in the room. Before she could turn around, two large hands grasped her waist from behind.

"Waiting for me?" a gravelly voice asked, before a kiss was pressed to the sensitive area below her earlobe.

"That depends," she said, not turning, "on just who you are."

The hands at her waist moved down to caress her flanks, then up again. "Let's see if I can refresh your memory," he responded teasingly, and then proceeded to whisper in her ear.

Kaly giggled at the extravagant descriptions of himself that he was painting in that husky undertone. "Now do you remember me?" he finished.

"Um-m-m, I think so," she pretended to guess. "Fred Flintstone?"

The hands tightened on her waist and spun her around to face him. Her eyes widened in mock amazement. "Why, it's Jackson Roberts! From your description, I expected someone much more apelike."

Jackson's face lowered threateningly to hers. "Apelike?"

"I'm kidding, I'm kidding," she replied placatingly. "I swear, I rarely think of primates anymore when I think of you." She waited a heartbeat, then added, "But 'Neanderthal' now, that's a word you do still occasionally bring to mind." Kaly shrieked as he picked her up, threw her over his shoulder and headed out the front door.

They passed Jeff and Carrie on the porch steps, who watched them in amusement. "He must be asking her for another date," Jeff surmised. He shook his head sorrowfully. "He definitely seems to have lost that impressive smoothness he once had."

Kaly was giggling so hard she could hardly talk. "Jackson! Where are you taking me?"

Jackson continued striding. "The last man who called me a name landed in the horse trough," he explained matter-of-factly as he continued toward the barn.

"But surely you could make an exception," Kaly hastened to appeal to him. "Besides, you didn't let me finish detailing what a sterling example of masculinity you are."

He stopped but didn't put her down. "Continue," he demanded.

She searched for outlandish descriptions to appease him. "Well, you're a shining example to gentlemen everywhere. A real prince among men. Not at all the kind of person to, let's say, throw me in a horse trough."

Jackson let her slide partway down his chest, until her face was level with his. "Yes," he informed her, "I am." He pretended to reconsider. "However, there is one way you could talk me out of it."

Kaly watched him warily. "There is?"

He nodded. "You could spend the day *and* the evening with me."

Kaly pretended to weigh the options. "Either spend all day with you or take a bath in the smelly, slimy water that horses put their mouths in? Okay, okay," she answered quickly when he started to lift her up again. "I guess I'd rather spend more time with you."

Jackson lowered her until her feet touched the ground and rubbed noses with her. "You've had a very narrow escape," he told her.

"I know."

"You'll have to have something very special planned to make it up to me."

"I do." Kaly's voice was smug.

His face was alight with interest. "You do, huh? Do I get a hint or do I..." His voice trailed off as his eyes took in the scene over Kaly's shoulder. "What the hell?" he muttered.

Kaly turned to see what he was talking about. Three men were grouped around another coming out of the barn. "Is someone hurt?" Kaly's voice was alarmed as she hurried to keep up with Jackson's long strides.

"Looks like Nick," Jackson affirmed grimly.

As they neared the men, one of them spoke. "Boss, someone's going to have to run Nick in to the doc in town."

Nick contradicted the man testily. "I don't need a damn—darn doctor," he said, amending his words when he caught sight of Kaly. "It's just a scratch."

"Where have I heard that before?" Kaly murmured with a meaningful look at Jackson. Not for the first time, she was struck by the strong similarity between Nick and Jackson. It seemed they also shared an aversion to medical personnel.

"Let's have a look," Jackson ordered, and unwrapped the bloody cloth around Nick's arm. Kaly gasped when she saw the wound. "Hell, yes, you need a doctor." He quickly rewound the cloth. "Looks mighty deep to me. What happened?"

"Cow was shoving me around and I caught my arm on a loose nail," Nick muttered, shrugging away from the others.

Jackson's mouth flattened. "Tom, you drive Nick into town," he ordered tersely. "When you come back see to it that he goes home for the rest of the day." He ignored Nick's protests at his words. "Rod," he said, his gaze spearing another man standing near, "you and Larry get a couple of hammers and go through those barns. I don't ever want to see an accident like this again.''

The men went off to do his bidding, and Jackson looked at Kaly. "I'm going to have to make a phone call, honey. I had an appointment this afternoon I was going to have Nick take care of. I'll call and try to postpone it."

But Kaly could tell by the look on his face as he spoke into the phone a few minutes later that their plans for the afternoon were thwarted. The receiver was banged back in the cradle with a crash, and the scowl on his face when he turned to her would have been comical if she hadn't been so disappointed herself.

She managed a slight smile. "No go, huh?"

"Afraid not. Whitfield is adamant that it has to be today." He heaved a sigh. "I'm sorry about this, sweetheart," he told her as he reached an arm around her waist to pull her close. "But he called a week ago for some information on our breeding operation. I think he's ready to do business with us."

"I understand," Kaly answered, leaning her head against his shoulder. And she did. She knew how hard Jackson had been working in recent years to establish the ranch as a purebred breeding operation and how much the prospect of a client meant.

"Damn Whitfield, anyway," Jackson grumbled. "If I didn't know better I'd think he knew exactly how we'd planned to spend the day, and is only insisting on this meeting to ruin it for us."

"I doubt it," she answered with a smile. She had never said anything to Paul about her relationship with Jackson, but when his calls and visits had come to an abrupt halt, she'd assumed he'd heard that they were seeing each other.

Jackson brought his other arm round her to capture her in a loose embrace. His head lowered and he pressed a kiss to her forehead. "I'll try to get away as soon as I can. Maybe we can salvage the evening." They kissed lingeringly before he tore himself away and Kaly made her way back to the house.

Kaly worked on her paper for the rest of the afternoon. Jackson called before supper and said he wouldn't be back until later that evening. She couldn't help feeling a bit miffed at the way the day was going, especially since she'd had such high hopes for it earlier. At loose ends after dinner, she watched television for a while, flipping through the channels desultorily. *This is ridiculous,* she finally decided when she found herself watching an old sitcom. *I can certainly manage to entertain myself better than this!*

She wandered out to the barn, intent on saddling Misty for a ride. As she approached it, she met Larry Scott wheeling his motorcycle around the corner.

"Hey, are you up for that ride I promised you?" he called.

Kaly eyed the cycle longingly. She adored speed, loved the wind whipping her face. It had been years since she'd ridden with her brother. "I'd love to," she said, smiling sunnily at him. "Just let me tell Carrie where I'm going, okay?"

Minutes later they were roaring down the ribbon of road away from the ranch. Larry shouted back at her once, promising to keep off the gravel, and she nodded. Conversation was impossible over the sound of the cycle and the wind, combined with the noise-muffling helmets. Contentedly, Kaly watched the scenery, aglow with the setting sun, whiz by.

It was nearly dusk by the time they turned back toward the ranch. On the way Kaly noted lights ahead. As they approached a small bar on the side of the road, Larry slowed to a stop. "Would you like to go in for a drink?"

Kaly eyed the building dubiously. It was a bit dilapidated, the sign proclaiming it as Pete's faded by the weather. A dozen motorcycles were lined up outside and she could hear music coming from inside.

"It's not as bad as it seems." Larry read her hesitation correctly. "It can get a little wild on Saturday nights, but other than that it's all right. By the looks of it tonight there's not too many people. How about it? Are you game?"

Kaly shrugged and nodded. It wasn't the sort of place she usually frequented, but she wasn't a snob, either. Larry had been kind to offer her this ride, and it had succeeded in taking her mind off her frustrated plans for the day. It couldn't do any harm to spend some more time talking to him over a drink.

They entered the bar, and Kaly was relieved to note it was not in the least threatening. Her eyes narrowed at the dimness. Smoke hung in the air, with stale cigarettes and beer the overpowering odors. A jukebox sat in one corner, and a song of lost love wailed from it. The dance floor was occupied by a few couples, but most of the people sat at the bar or at scattered tables. No one paid them the slightest attention.

Larry guided her to a table, where a lethargic-looking waitress took their order. Then they passed an enjoyable hour or so just talking. Kaly laughed often. Larry's good-natured wit was highly entertaining.

The door opened then, and a large group of people, obviously bikers, came in. Larry glanced up and his eyes widened in alarm. "Uh-oh," he muttered, watching the group carefully as its members filled the small bar.

Kaly looked at him curiously. "What's the matter?"

"Some rough characters just came in. I think this place is about to get rowdy. Maybe we should leave."

Kaly shrugged. "Whatever you think."

Larry stood up. "I'm going to the washroom first. Wait right here until I get back."

Kaly nodded bemusedly as he walked away. He certainly seemed worried, but she failed to see why. The noise level had risen since the group of bikers had walked in, but the place still seemed pretty normal, with the dance floor now crowded, and others grouped around a pool table. She rose from her chair and made her way back to the ladies' room.

She noticed with interest as she passed through the crowd that many of the people sported tattoos, including some of the women. She caught sight of Larry as she walked toward the back of the bar and watched with some surprise when he paused to speak to a burly, bearded man in a leather jacket covered in chains. Larry dug in his pocket and handed the man something before brushing by him to go into the men's room. The biker walked up to the pay telephone on the wall next to the door Larry had passed through.

The ladies' room had a line of women waiting to get into it, which put Kaly directly in back of the biker. She watched him curiously as he punched in a phone number with one huge hand. On the back of that hand he sported a tattoo with a large eagle carrying a snake in its mouth.

She grimaced. Not very appealing. Larry was right, some of these people did look rough. She was beginning to feel glad that they would be leaving in a few minutes. She turned her eyes ahead again and sighed impatiently as it appeared that the line in front of her hadn't moved at all.

"Yeah, where the hell have you been?" Scraps of the biker's phone conversation drifted to her. "The boss said to call you, that's why. He's planning another job. Are you in or not?"

Kaly glanced back at the man quickly and wondered what he was talking about. Whatever it was, it didn't sound pleasant. His tone and demeanor were menacing enough to give her chills. Her eyes moved over him, and she suddenly recalled how the sheriff had described the man who had sold some of the stolen Circle R cattle. A lot of people wore black leather jackets, but how many draped chains all over it?

She watched the man consideringly for another moment, before shaking her head at her flight of fancy. After all, what were the odds she would happen into this place and run into someone involved in the rustling?

She inched ahead as the line shortened. The man on the phone raised his voice. "You think you done all the work? Who the hell you think sold the..." Kaly's head snapped back toward him, straining to hear the rest of the sentence. Had he said "cattle"? The increasingly loud conversations of the women in front of her made it impossible to pick up more than a few of his words.

"Forget it." A loud burst of laughter from in front

of her made Kaly grit her teeth, and she strained harder to hear what the bearded man was saying.

"I said forget it. Tell him yourself." More loud talking from some women coming out of the washroom and others going in. Larry walked out of the men's room, saw Kaly and frowned, then moved toward the bar area. The line in front of her was getting shorter, which meant she had to move farther from the man on the phone.

"I'll give it to you. You can call and tell him yourself if you got the guts. I'm…" Whatever else the man said was lost in the noise. Kaly watched surreptitiously as he pulled a piece of paper from his pocket. It sounded as if he was reading a number, but Kaly couldn't be sure. As the man hung up the phone, he ripped up the small paper and dropped the pieces on the floor.

Kaly eyed the pieces speculatively. She glanced again at the biker, but the man's back was turned as he began to walk away. Without another thought she knelt down and began to pick up the pieces he had dropped on the floor. She snatched her hand back quickly, narrowly avoiding having a spiked heel grind into the back of it. The remaining pieces were scattered as people moved back and forth through the area, kicking the minuscule scraps aside. Mentally cursing, she crawled farther on the floor, reaching for another of the minute pieces.

"What the hell do you think you're doing?" Two hard hands grabbed Kaly's shoulders and yanked her to her feet. She looked up into the biker's face and swallowed. His long hair was pulled back with a leather thong. His belly hung over his studded belt, but he looked tough. And mean. Kaly gulped again, her mind racing. She sent a wild gaze to their table, but Larry wasn't looking in her direction. She decided to brazen it out.

She twisted her shoulders out of his grasp and sent him a cool look. "I lost a contact, do you mind?"

"Yeah, and what were you doin' with that paper?"

Kaly held a tiny piece up and said in what she hoped was a bored voice, "I'm going to put my contact on it if I can find it—to keep it safe until I can put it back in." Over the biker's shoulder she saw that Larry had at last noticed the confrontation and was hurrying toward them. The bearded man looked suspiciously at her and said slowly, "Hey, you was watching me when I was on the phone, too."

Kaly tried to appear calm, despite her rising panic. "You've got an interesting tattoo," she indicated his hand. "I was admiring it."

The biker seemed to lose some of his surliness. "Yeah? Well, I got a lot more than a tattoo for you to admire. Why don't you and me go somewhere private?"

Kaly quaked inwardly. "Sorry," she said as lackadaisically as she could manage. "I've already got a date."

The biker moved closer, pressing Kaly's back against the wall, his fetid breath bouncing off her cheek. "So lose him," he ordered.

"I don't think you understand," crooned a dangerous voice from behind the biker's shoulder. "I'm this lady's date. And I don't want to be lost." Kaly's eyes widened in horror as she looked over the biker's shoulder. Where Larry had stood a moment ago, Jackson now towered, his face a mask of menace.

The biker turned slowly and eyed Jackson. "Butt

out, pal,'' he said contemptuously. "Me and the lady are gonna get to know each other better.''

Jackson reached one arm out, and Kaly hurried over to him. He pushed her behind him, where Larry grabbed her and tried to drag her to the door. Kaly dug in her heels, determined not to leave without Jackson.

The huge man moved toward Jackson. "You've got an awful big mouth. Let's see if you can back it up.'' He whipped an ugly-looking switchblade from his pocket and waved it in front of him.

Kaly was terrified. She was only half-aware of the people nearest them moving tables and chairs to get out of the way. The knife flashing dangerously close to Jackson was a wicked-looking weapon, and Jackson was empty-handed. Gazing wildly about the bar, she darted toward a nearby table, grabbed a beer bottle and put it in Jackson's hand.

Jackson didn't take his eyes off the biker. His fingers closed around the bottle and he hefted it, before slamming it against the edge of a table. He raised the jagged edge to the biker. "C'mon,'' he coaxed, making little circles with the weapon. "C'mon.''

The two men circled each other before the biker lunged toward Jackson, his knife slicing downward. Jackson leapt to the side, keeping his back away from the wall so he couldn't be pinned against it. Again the biker lunged, but this time as Jackson leapt aside, he kicked up with one booted foot and caught the man squarely in the chin. The biker's head snapped back, and he stood for a moment, weaving dizzily. Then he crumpled slowly to the ground.

Jackson dropped his weapon and grabbed Kaly, who was looking at the downed man in disbelief. He literally dragged her from the bar, with Larry trailing them. The fresh air felt wonderful to Kaly, but she was given no time to enjoy it. Jackson hauled her across the road, opened the pickup door and practically threw her in.

He turned to fix Larry with a hard stare. "I'll see you back at the ranch shortly." His terse tone promised that the scene would not be pleasant. Larry nodded dejectedly.

Kaly watched from the corner of the cab as Jackson turned on the ignition, threw the truck into gear and roared away. His jaw was tight and a telltale muscle jerked spasmodically. Hoping that silence would calm him, she said nothing for several minutes. But when he turned off the highway onto a gravel road, she was surprised into blurting out, "Where are we going?"

"Someplace where I can teach you a lesson," Jackson growled.

Kaly's eyes widened in shock. "I beg your pardon?" she said icily, unable to believe how chauvinistic he sounded.

Jackson pulled the truck onto the shoulder and turned off the lights. Then he turned off the ignition and pressed the button that locked both doors. He sat rigidly in his seat, both hands clenching and unclenching on the steering wheel.

"Do you even know," he asked softly, almost conversationally, "can you even imagine the danger you were in back there?"

Kaly recognized that tone. Its deceptive softness masked churning fury. But she was not in the mood to find some way to defuse it. She hadn't done anything wrong, and she was not about to let him chastise her as though she was a child.

"I wasn't in any real danger," she said.

He turned his narrowed gaze slowly to pin her with eyes that looked as glacial as the North Atlantic. "I see." His tone was measured, as if he couldn't trust his voice not to betray the rage seething in him.

Kaly searched his face warily, looking for a sign that his anger was abating. She did not find any. Despite her irritation, she found herself offering an explanation. "Larry and I just went out riding for a while. The place was nearly empty when we stopped there. When the last bunch came in we decided to leave."

Jackson nodded politely, still disguising his wrath. "And the animal in the bar? The one you were in no danger from?" He mimicked her mockingly. "Is he a new friend of yours?"

Kaly's own eyes narrowed. She didn't care for his tone. Not at all. "I don't know who he is, but he *was* wearing a leather jacket like the one Roy described, wasn't he? I decided to keep my ears and eyes open, that's all. I didn't think he'd notice me."

Jackson's face was incredulous. "You saw one leather jacket out of the dozens in that bar and decided to ask that bozo, 'Excuse me, are you by any chance one of the rustlers?'"

"Quit trying to make me sound stupid!" she hissed. "I was only trying to help you!"

"You were trying to get raped or killed!" he thundered, losing the iron grip he'd had on his temper. He reached out and pulled her over, lowering his face to hers as he continued shouting at her. "You don't need me to make you look stupid, Kaly. You do an excellent job of that yourself!"

Kaly stiffened as her own anger started to match

his. "You bad-tempered ingrate," she seethed. "You're right, I shouldn't have tried to help. Because you're not worth it! As far as I'm concerned, you and your damned cows can rot in hell!" She pulled away from him and scooted back across the seat. She tried unsuccessfully for several moments to unlock her door before turning to face him furiously.

Jackson, his eyes half-closed, was leaning against his door indolently, watching her struggle.

"Open this door now," she demanded between gritted teeth.

He cocked an eyebrow. "Or what?"

Kaly clenched her fists so tightly she could feel her nails biting into her palms. "You are, without a doubt, the most irritating, infantile man I have ever had the misfortune to meet. And I wish that biker had clobbered you!"

He bared his teeth at her. "Bloodthirsty, aren't you? But you aren't going anywhere, because I'm not letting you out of my sight again." And that was the God's honest truth, he assured himself grimly. The woman attracted trouble like a magnet, and he still felt ice in his veins from the scene he'd witnessed in the bar. He had tried to play this her way; he knew she didn't like to be pushed, but he was tired of dancing around her feelings. The only way he could keep her safe was if she did exactly as she was told. "Stay away from Larry Scott," he ordered tersely.

Her eyebrows shot up at his audacity. "I am in no mood for your King Kong imitation. You don't tell me what to do, big man!"

He lowered his face so that the sparks in their eyes clashed. "Yes," he informed her, "I do. And you'll do it, too, if I have to tie you to my side."

Kaly glared at him furiously. "For the last time, I wasn't going to get hurt tonight. Even if that guy was involved in the rustling, I still could have gotten rid of him myself, and if I didn't, Larry would have helped me."

Her naive trust made him grind his teeth in frustration. "You were in more danger than you realize, sweetheart," he told her caustically. "You walked into the place with the man suspected of masterminding the rustling."

She blinked at him in amazement. "What are you talking about? I went there with Larry." At his curt nod, her mouth fell open. "Larry? You suspect Larry Scott? That's crazy!"

"Think so? Well, the sheriff doesn't agree, and neither do I. We don't have positive proof, but there are sure enough things pointing to his involvement."

"I don't believe it. If Roy is so convinced, why hasn't he arrested him?"

"Because, like I said, we aren't a hundred percent sure yet. It seemed better to put a watch on him and maybe catch him red-handed than to question him and scare him off before we have the evidence we need."

"You have someone watching him?"

He nodded. "How do you think I knew where to find you? The deputy trailing him radioed the sheriff, who called to let me know who you were with and where you both were." When Roy had warned him that Kaly was with Larry, he had gone rigid, his muscles shaking with rage, as well as fear that she was in danger. Then he had walked in on that scene in the bar, and found her in danger of another kind.

"I still think you're wasting your time," she maintained stubbornly, interrupting his thoughts. "If you really want to follow up on a lead, you should have someone check out that biker you left unconscious on the floor. I overheard a conversation of his that sounded suspicious.'' She proceeded to repeat what she had heard.

''Did you hear him say cattle?'' Jackson demanded, when she was done.

''Well, no,'' she admitted reluctantly. ''I couldn't hear everything he said. I might not have noticed him at all, except I was so surprised to see Larry talking to someone like that...'' Her voice trailed off. Jackson's eyes were alight with interest.

''You saw Larry and this guy talking?''

Kaly wished she had thought before blurting that out. Now it looked even worse for the ranch hand. ''They only spoke for a second. Then Larry gave him something before he went into the men's room.''

She could tell from Jackson's face that this last bit of information just made Larry more suspicious in his eyes. She couldn't help but wonder herself what the two men had had to say to each other, but she wasn't going to assume that Larry was guilty, not until they had much more than circumstantial evidence to go on.

''You still don't realize how lucky you were tonight,'' Jackson muttered, raking one hand through his dark hair.

Kaly was growing tired of the whole argument. ''You almost missed us,'' she informed him. ''We were on our way out.''

He cocked an eyebrow at her, silently reminding her that she had been nowhere near the door and in no position to leave when he'd found her. Kaly correctly read the sardonic expression on his face. ''We were leaving,'' she stressed. ''But we'd gone to the washrooms, and I saw that man's jacket…'' She shrugged. ''He was on the phone right by me, and at the end it sounded like he was reading a number off a paper, so when he ripped it up and threw it on the floor, I tried to retrieve the pieces.''

Jackson stared at her in horror. ''You picked it up? God almighty, Kaly, no wonder he went after you. Of all the damn fool things to—'' He bit off the rest of his statement at her pointed look.

''I fobbed him off with some excuse about losing a contact lens, and he believed me. By the time you came up to us, he had forgotten all about the paper.''

He closed his eyes for a moment. He could imagine too well what had taken the man's thoughts off the pieces of paper. He folded her to him and whispered, ''God, Kaly, what the hell were you thinking of? Anything could have happened to you in there. Anything. You could have disappeared and never been heard from again, did you ever think of that?''

Kaly struggled, but it was quickly apparent she couldn't escape from his grasp, and she discovered that she really didn't want to. At his tortured words, the last incident of the fight in the bar came rushing back to her, and she began to shake as she relived it. Jackson could have been badly hurt, even killed. She wedged her hands between their bodies and tried to feel for any injuries he 'may have sustained in the brawl.

''He didn't hurt you anywhere, did he?'' she asked worriedly.

Jackson loosened his grip on her, enjoying the feeling of those small hands moving slowly, exploringly, over his torso. She was feeling for wounds, he knew, but her touch was causing a heat to build, and it spread quickly through his body.

"No, the only blow I took tonight was to my pride," he said huskily.

She stopped her search and leaned into him, resting her head on his shoulder. "It could withstand a few more," she murmured. "You've probably been riding roughshod over people since you were a toddler."

Jackson shook his head, ignoring her comment. "That bar is pure trouble and no one but punks hang out there. Larry had no business putting you in danger like that." His arms tightened involuntarily as he closed his eyes in gratitude that he'd found her when he had. He couldn't trust anyone else to take care of Kaly the way he could. If he'd been ten minutes later... He shut the thoughts off. He'd found her. She was all right. He lifted her face with one hand on her delicate jawline and fixed his mouth to hers, first gently, then with more fervor, as if to prove that fact to himself.

Kaly responded by rubbing her lips against his, opening her mouth to close it over his lips. Their tongues dueled intimately before Jackson sent his deep into her mouth, an indication of his intentions. Jackson could feel the womanly curve of her hip pressed tightly against the hard ridge straining against his jeans. Kaly unbuttoned his shirt quickly, clumsily spreading kisses randomly across his chest. He hissed in a breath. He wanted her, had to have her—now. He moved her so that she sat astride him.

Kaly moved her head and whispered, "What?" but he sealed her lips fiercely. The memories of the night, the could-have-beens, rolled over him and he was suddenly frantic to bond with her, proving to himself that she was all right. He pushed her top above her breasts and released the front catch on her bra. He pulled a nipple into his mouth with frenzied arousal, making her gasp at first at his fierceness, before giving a low moan and arching into him. He unzipped her jeans and pulled them off in one fluid motion, then dispensed with her panties. With one hand he parted her womanly folds and sent an exploring finger inside her.

Kaly sobbed at the almost unbearable speed that her arousal had come upon her. She rocked against him, against the tongue and lips working magic on her breast and against his hand practicing the same witchcraft on her femininity. She began to cry out in earnest now, desperate for release.

Jackson unfastened his pants and freed his throbbing sex. He had barely enough control to protect her before he lifted her up, positioning her carefully. He eased her down, his breath escaping in a long groan. As he bent to take her other breast in his mouth, Kaly moved faster and faster, frantic to have all of him. Jackson grasped her hips firmly and thrust up fiercely. Kaly screamed softly and he repeated the action, over and over, blind to everything but release of his desire. At his peak, he shouted her name hoarsely, then leaned his damp forehead against hers, their ragged breathing mingling.

He held her afterward, his hard arms keeping her trapped against his body. He was oddly reluctant to let her go. Eyes wide and unseeing, he stared out at the night sky. And tried to shake the fear he still felt from her brush with danger.

Chapter 13

Jackson tipped up her chin and sealed her mouth with his once more, reassuring himself again that she was safe. Their seeking mouths pulled away reluctantly, and Kaly nestled her head into the niche beneath his chin, marveling at how perfectly she fit there.

"I never realized pickup trucks could be so erotic," she murmured, rubbing her face against his shoulder.

Jackson's breath soughed out of him in choked laughter. "This one never has been before." He turned her face up to him. "It must be you." He hadn't made love in the front seat of a pickup since the randy days of his youth, when he'd had more hormones than sense. But since he'd met Kaly, good sense seemed to be a thing of the past.

His lips brushed hers again, feather-light. Part of him was bewildered at the myriad emotions he experienced when he was with her. But he was damn certain he liked it. He pressed her head gently against his chest and rhythmically stroked her heavy fall of hair. His hard mouth tilted slightly. Their relationship had been tempestuous since the beginning. They were both too stubborn for it to be otherwise. But his was a forceful personality. It took a woman with Kaly's inner strength to stand up to him. She didn't quake before his temper—she gave him hell right back. She might make him mad on a regular basis, but she sure never bored him. His arms tightened around her.

They held each other, enjoying the afterglow for a time, before Jackson sighed into her hair. "I forgot all about Jeff and Carrie. They must be wondering where we are."

"I suppose we should go home," Kaly whispered languorously, but made no move.

"Mm-hmm," he agreed, but it was several more minutes before they moved apart and straightened their clothing.

When they arrived at the ranch, Jeff and Carrie met them at the door, flinging it open before they could reach it.

"What happened?" Carrie demanded. "I never expected you to be gone so long, Kaly."

"I didn't expect to be—" started Kaly, but Jeff interrupted her.

"If you two hadn't shown up soon, I'd have come looking for you."

A blush spread up Kaly's neck to her cheeks. Just thinking what Jeff would have seen had he found them made her skin heat. She could feel Jackson's eyes on her, amused probably, darn him, and refused to look his way.

Jeff explained to Jackson, "Larry came by about an hour ago and said you two were fine but that you'd had a run-in at the bar?'' At Jackson's nod, he turned to Kaly. ''What in Sam Hill was Larry thinking of? He had no business taking you to a place like that. And you never should have gone with him. He's...'' With a look at Jackson, then at his wife, he subsided.

''It wasn't Larry's fault,'' Kaly defended him. ''It looked like it would be a pretty tame night there. That's the only reason he stopped.''

Jackson herded them all into the office. ''What did Larry say when he was here?'' he queried as he sat on the couch and pulled Kaly down next to him.

''Just that you'd arrived in time to get Kaly out of a jam and got in a tussle with a lunatic,'' Jeff responded with feigned indifference.

Jackson's mouth flattened. It sounded as if he had one more thing to take up with Larry Scott. He promised himself savagely that when the net closed around the hired man for good, Larry would pay for putting Kaly in danger tonight. One of the hardest things Jackson had ever done was to let him walk out the door of the bar, instead of making sure he'd have to be carried out.

''Larry told us you said you'd be home shortly.'' Jeff took an exaggerated stare at his watch. ''Of course, he didn't give us your definition of 'shortly.' Maybe it's different from ours.''

''We stopped somewhere so Kaly could...explain what happened tonight,'' Jackson responded with uncustomary diplomacy. ''Where's Larry now?''

''He volunteered to relieve Rod in the barn, staying up with the cow that's about to deliver.''

Privately Jackson thought Larry was probably trying to atone for his mistake tonight by pulling the extra duty. Aloud he said, ''I'll let Kaly tell you what happened tonight." He nodded at her and invited, "Go ahead."

She addressed Jeff firmly. "Well, first of all, nobody should blame Larry. He didn't put me in danger. We were leaving when Jackson got there."

The two men exchanged a look. "Stopping at Pete's is just one in a long line of things we blame Larry for," Jeff muttered. Carrie gave her husband a puzzled look.

"He never should have stopped there in the first place," Jackson said tersely. "He goes to Pete's enough—he knows damn well what it can be like."

"He thought it would be harmless tonight, since it wasn't a Saturday. And he was very protective. We got up to go when it started to get more crowded."

"Maybe he had reasons to be in that bar tonight," Jeff surmised, glancing at his brother. "Reasons that had nothing to do with Kaly."

"Don't try to tell her that," Jackson responded. "She thinks he's ready for sainthood." Kaly eyed them both with exasperation.

"Okay, time out," Carrie interrupted. All eyes went to her. "Why am I getting the feeling that everyone in this room knows something I don't?"

Kaly appeared smug at the looks that crossed both men's faces. Jeff appeared almost comically dismayed, and Jackson was noticeably wary.

"Well?" Carrie asked, when several moments passed and no one answered. "Fill me in, since you've obviously been back to playing your macho 'Let's protect the little ladies from all this unpleasantness' routine."

"It wasn't like that at all," Jeff finally said uncomfortably. "We have reason to believe Larry might be tied up in this rustling."

Carrie's eyes widened. "Larry? And Kaly went with him tonight?" Her eyes swung to the other woman's. "Oh, Kaly!"

"Carrie!" Kaly returned. "There must not be any real proof that he's involved, or he wouldn't be walking around free."

"On the contrary," Jackson said, "after tonight there's more to point to Larry than ever." He relayed what Kaly had told him about the events of the night to the other two.

Carrie shuddered. "I can't believe that animal actually had his hands on you, Kaly. You could have been seriously hurt."

Jackson slanted a glance toward her. "Exactly," he murmured, his voice full of meaning.

To circumvent the lecture she could feel coming, Kaly opened the zippered compartment of her purse and carefully removed the scraps of paper she had recovered from the bar floor. She laid them on the table in front of her.

"I think it might be a phone number," she proposed as she tried to arrange the pieces into some kind of order. "I couldn't be sure, but it did sound as if the biker was reading off a number. 'Call him yourself'— that's what he said. He might have been talking about the person in charge of the rustling."

"I don't know," Jeff said slowly. "He could have been talking about almost anything."

Jackson was leaning over Kaly's shoulder, trying to make sense of the pieces of paper. "Maybe, maybe not," he answered distractedly. "The jacket he was wearing was similar to the one the buyer remembers on the man who sold him our stolen cattle.'' He looked up from the table to his brother. ''Jeff, why don't you call the sheriff and tell him what went on tonight? Roy better see if he can pick up that biker for questioning before he takes off for parts unknown. He can come and get these bits of paper later. Maybe he'll be able to figure them out.''

Jeff strode to the office phone and placed the call. As he spoke in a low tone to the sheriff, Jackson studied the pieces spread before him. He finally threaded his hand through his dark hair impatiently. ''I give up. Too many pieces are missing.''

Kaly had been studying the jagged portions and reached over to move one. ''But you can tell that the last number is a seven, see? The edges show it has to be the end piece. And we know this is the first piece.'' She indicated another with a similar edge. ''Three. That's the first digit in your phone number.''

''Yeah, ours and about three million other Americans,'' Jackson said with a snort.

Kaly stared at him for an instant as she probed her memory. ''But he wasn't making a long-distance call,'' she said slowly. Excitement was in her voice as the puzzle started to unravel for her. ''I was close enough to see that he wasn't placing more money in the slot.''

''It could have been a collect call,'' Carrie suggested.

''Even if he was talking to someone who lived around here, that still doesn't necessarily link him with the rustlers,'' Jackson cautioned her. ''But Roy does suspect that the rustlers have been staying in the vicinity. The whole thing sounds like a good job for the sheriff. He'll be able to run checks on a list of numbers with three for the first digit and seven for the last, starting with the numbers around this area. It's a possible lead." He rubbed the back of his head reflectively. "I'll tell you one thing, though," he said in grim remembrance, "if that biker is the one who slugged me out in the pasture, I'm just sorry I didn't hit him harder tonight."

Jeff hung up the phone and heaved a sigh. "Well, Roy seems to think we might be on to something here. The deputy will continue following Larry when he's not here working." He looked at Kaly. "I'm just glad you got back safely tonight."

"Ahem." Carrie cleared her throat and looked at Kaly. "Do you suppose," she asked sweetly, "that it occurs to either of these thickheaded men that you would have been more than safe tonight if either had had the sense to tell us about Larry earlier?"

They exchanged a meaningful look, then both swung pointed gazes to Jeff and Jackson.

Jeff rose quickly and changed the subject. "Well, I think the little one's had enough excitement for the night. What do you say we put him to bed?" he asked, patting the round mound of Carrie's stomach.

Carrie nodded agreeably. "Yes, I think *she* is ready to call it a night," she said. They left the room amid good-natured predictions about the gender of the next addition to the Robertses' clan.

Kaly and Jackson watched them go, then he stretched tiredly. "Bed sounds like a good idea. But first we better put these away." He nodded to the pieces of paper, still on the table. "Can you find me an envelope?" She rummaged through her desk drawers and finally came up with one which she handed to him. She smiled slightly as she watched his big fingers handling the tiny bits. He dropped each slip in and sealed the envelope, then locked it in his desk.

Jackson glanced back at her. His look sharpened as he noted the tilt to her lips, and he wondered what she was thinking. His eyes dropped to half-mast as they lingered on her mouth.

Kaly could feel herself begin to tremble. It was heady, this excitement that throbbed through the air between them, springing to life with just an exchange of glances, but it was frightening, too. It was always a little scary for her to feel so out of control, so willing to disregard what her mind told her and to follow her heart.

Right now she was inclined to do just that. Arousal was easy to read on his face. The skin had tautened over his cheekbones, and his eyes were sapphire slits. "Come to bed with me." Jackson's voice was a husky murmur.

Kaly moved silently toward him, and one hard arm tucked her to his side. She was anxious to recapture the magic that had enveloped them earlier and so was Jackson, as evidenced by his hasty retreat to his room. They undressed quickly, silently and came together on his bed. Kaly shuddered at the spiraling emotion brought on by his nearness. She rubbed her breasts against his chest experimentally and was rewarded by his immediate response. He gripped her hips and stopped her play by bringing her completely against him, so they were touching from lips to toes.

"I don't know how you do this to me," he rasped. "I can't seem to get enough. One look, one smile are all it takes to make me want you beneath me again."

Her neck arched under his ardent mouth. "Fireworks," she whispered shakily.

"Yeah, fireworks," he agreed as he moved his lips to the sensitive spot beneath her ear. "Hot, sizzling, then the explosion." He raised himself above her and pressed himself to her core. Then he proceeded to prove the truth of their words.

Fireworks.

Kaly dozed lightly off and on, largely content to remain awake and enjoy lying in Jackson's heavy grasp. He lay on his side facing her, one arm cradling her close to his hard body. She watched him as he slept, noting the exhaustion with which he slumbered. She loved watching him in such unguarded moments. His face was less fierce in sleep, but not much softer. One dark lock of hair fell boyishly across his forehead, and as she pushed it back lightly she felt an aching tenderness for this tough man.

Kaly shuddered as she thought back to the events of the night. She could have lost Jackson so easily tonight; all it would have taken was one slip of that knife.... She snuggled closer to him. Even so, she was glad he hadn't had to use that bottle she'd put in his hand. Although the biker might not agree, she was grateful there'd been no bloodshed.

She wouldn't have had to take any action at all, she reflected, if Larry had moved to help Jackson. She despised herself for the notion. Everybody's suspicions about the hired man frustrated her. Jackson had shared no real evidence that linked him to the rustling, and she didn't believe anything that had happened tonight incriminated him. Still, she couldn't help but wonder about Larry's strange behavior in the bar. She'd seen him exchange words with the biker earlier.

Whatever would he have to say to a hairy monster like that?

Kaly lay there for a long time, but slumber remained elusive. Her mind stubbornly remained completely alert. She peered at the luminous glow of the clock radio on the nightstand and grimaced. Obviously sleep was out of the question, at least for now.

She recalled that Jeff had said Larry was going to be up all night with a cow, and she abruptly decided to join him for a time. He probably dreaded facing Jackson the next day. Remembering Jackson's biting tone when he'd spoken to Larry, she told herself she definitely needed to run interference for the hired man. She would speak to Jackson again tomorrow, to try once again to convince him of the man's innocence in the cattle rustling. Despite Jackson's suspicions, he must not have enough to accuse Larry, or the man would be in jail by now.

She slowly inched out from under Jackson's arm. He clutched her more tightly at first; she held her breath as she watched carefully to see if she'd awakened him. He needed his sleep; he'd probably been up for twenty hours. She watched carefully, but the frown soon smoothed from Jackson's brow and she was able to slip from the bed. She donned her clothes soundlessly and tiptoed to the door.

Minutes later, Kaly closed the front door noiselessly behind her and ambled up the path toward the buildings. All were dark save for the first of the cattle barns. Dim light spilled from beneath its closed doors. The night was black, with not even a star visible, making her progress halting. Kaly cursed softly as she tripped and almost fell. It was with a sigh of relief that she reached the barn and tugged at the heavy door to let herself in. The cavernous structure was positively spooky at night, and she hurried toward the pale glow coming from the back of the barn. She heard faint noises from some of the stalls she passed, animal sounds, but saw no sign of Larry.

She ventured to the last stall, where a brighter light was shining, and poked her head through the entrance. "Larry?" she called tentatively. Kaly didn't find him there, but she was disarmed at the sight before her. A cow was lying on the straw with what was obviously a newborn next to her. The calf still shone wetly from its recent entrance into the world, and Kaly watched enrapt as it struggled to get to its feet. Finally, after several attempts, the calf rose to stand spindle-legged, each leg splayed in a different direction. She laughed delightedly at the sight, before the calf, exhausted from its exertions, tumbled gracelessly to the straw again.

"What are you doing here this time of night?" a gruff voice said behind her, and Kaly jerked around in surprise.

"Larry!" she exclaimed weakly, sinking back against the stall door. "You frightened me to death!"

He finished wiping his hands on the cloth he was holding before he redirected his original question to her. "What are you doing? Haven't you had enough excitement for one night?"

Kaly studied him, biting her lower lip uncertainly. He didn't sound exactly welcoming. Of course, he'd probably spent the past several hours anticipating Jackson's wrath. She gestured toward the stall. "Is this what you've been doing tonight, helping deliver her baby?"

Larry's face lightened a little at Kaly's ingenuous

way of speaking of the cow in human terms. "She didn't need much help. I was just here in case something went wrong. Jackson is mighty particular about the cows he's breeding with that fancy new bull of his. He wants to get the breeding part of the business off to the right start, so we try to bring the cows into the barn when they're ready to drop, so we can help if they need it."

Kaly relaxed under his explanation. As he spoke, Larry began to seem his old self again, instead of the stern stranger of a moment ago. She impulsively laid her hand on his arm and said, "I hope you didn't spend the night worrying about what happened earlier. I've explained to Jackson and Jeff that it wasn't your fault."

His arm, which had stiffened at first, relaxed at her earnestness. "I knew I was in trouble as soon as I saw that last group of bikers come in." He gave her a crooked grin. "I just hope that guy wore Jackson out enough to make his right jab a little less lethal by tomorrow." He rubbed his jaw. "Although I'd be satisfied to still have a job when he's done with me."

"You will," Kaly said with more assurance than she felt. She would have her work cut out for her in the morning, but somehow, she would convince Jackson and the sheriff that they were wasting their time. She just couldn't believe that Larry was capable of stealing from anyone. Once they followed up on that phone number she'd found, she hoped they would find the real culprits. "I don't think you have anything to be anxious about. You didn't do anything wrong and Jackson knows that." At least he would before he confronted Larry, Kaly vowed. She'd make certain of that.

The ranch hand surveyed her intently for a moment

before responding. "I hope you're right. I like working here. Jackson's a tough boss, but he's fair. It would be rough to have to start over again."

"You won't have to," Kaly said firmly. She tilted her face up to his. "Feel better now?"

Larry nodded slowly, then said, "Let's give Mama and baby a chance to get some rest." He turned on a lantern-style flashlight that was sitting in the straw and snapped off the extension light he'd been using. The two moved out of the stall, and Larry reached behind Kaly to latch the door. He flipped a switch on the wall and the barn fell into darkness, save for the beam from the lantern he was holding.

Kaly eyed the silent man beside her and wondered if she would rile him if she asked him some of the questions that had plagued her earlier. "There's just one thing about tonight that puzzles me," she ventured cautiously. She stopped and looked up at him. "What were you and that biker talking about before you went into the men's room?"

"He asked me for a quarter to make a phone call." Larry shrugged. "I wasn't going to argue with a character like that. I gave it to him."

"He didn't say anything else?"

"Not to me. But I sure had a scare after I came out and saw him reach for you. What the heck were you doing there, anyway? You could have gotten hurt tangling with someone like that," Larry said with remembered anxiety.

"I was only going to use the washroom before we left," she responded. "I no more wanted to get into a conversation with that creature than you did." They had reached the front of the barn and stood before the half-open door.

"Well, I'm glad you're okay, anyway." Larry moved his shoulders back and forth wearily, working out the knots in his tired muscles. "I'm heading home. I can't wait to get cleaned up and grab a little sleep, not necessarily in that order." He grinned crookedly at Kaly. "I'm going to need all my senses about me to stand up to Jackson tomorrow. C'mon. I'll walk you back up to the house."

But Kaly shook her head. She was more wired now than ever. "It's no use. I'm not going to be able to sleep yet. Do you think I could go back and look in on the new calf one more time?" she asked.

"I don't see why not," Larry replied. "But you'd better take this flashlight with you." He handed her the one he was carrying.

"But what will you use?" Kaly asked. "You'll need something to find your way to your bike. There's no moon or stars out tonight. I nearly fell on the way out here."

"My bike's parked close by, and I've got cat's eyes. Always could see well in the dark."

Kaly accepted the light from him and shifted it to her other hand as he started away. "See you tomorrow."

Larry touched the brim of his hat, turned and disappeared into the darkness.

Kaly made her way quickly toward the back of the barn. Intent on her own thoughts, she was startled by a noise to her right. She shone her light in that direction and almost screamed at the sight of the eyes staring at her. She clapped a hand to her mouth. Jackson's purebred bull gazed impassively back at her. Kaly went weak with relief. As she studied the huge animal, she was nervously grateful for the stout door separating them. She'd never seen the bull up close before, and she wondered at the men's ability to control the giant animal.

She hurried on. The beam from her light swept the last stall containing the new calf. She watched in amusement as the calf suckled energetically from its tired mama. There was something very sweet about its fuzzy face. Hard to believe that it would grow into an ugly creature like its sire, Kaly mused. She watched for a time, feeling the tension of the past several hours seep away as she observed the picture of nature at work. After a time, Kaly felt her eyelids grow heavy. She turned away from the stall, intent on going back to the house.

The ray from her flashlight bounced over the barn phone on the back wall. She fixed the light on it, marveling at the intricate system Jackson had, linking lines to all the buildings and the house. A large sheet was tacked next to the phone, and she idly played the beam over it. It was a list of all the hired men's phone numbers, at least those who didn't live in the bunkhouse full-time. She examined it more closely. All had the same first three digits—345—indicating that the men lived in the area surrounding the ranch. Kaly thought back to the paper she had found tonight and was more convinced than ever that the man in the bar was somehow involved in the rustling. She just had to persuade Jackson to give more credence to her theory.

As another yawn overtook her, Kaly started to turn away, when something in her subconscious stopped her. Puzzled, she spun back to rapidly scan the list again, seeking that which had bothered her. Her flashlight moved down the list of numbers, then bounced back to the center of the paper to a phone number that ended with a seven. Kaly's rounded eyes followed the number across the paper to match it with its owner.

Larry Scott.

Kaly's stomach did a slow roll. She looked more carefully at each number on the sheet, but his was the only one that ended in a seven. She turned away, shaken.

As Jackson had said, the number could belong to any one of three million people. She started toward the door of the barn, still mentally berating herself for her wild imagination. She was abashed at the immediate suspicion that had sprung to her mind. Larry had never been less than a friend to her. But one circumstantial piece of evidence, and she had quickly joined everyone else in suspecting him, if only for a second.

But an irksome voice inside Kaly slyly reminded her of the way Larry had explained away his conversation with the biker. He had admitted he'd been to that bar before. He'd certainly have had the opportunity to establish contacts there. Whoever was in charge of this operation surely wasn't acting alone, or without inside information on when and where to hit.

Kaly's mind whirled from her inner debate, before she shook her head firmly. She must really be exhausted even to consider that good-natured Larry Scott could be behind the rustling. She had determined to help clear his name, not to add to the trouble he was already in.

The heavy barn door squeaked as she pushed it shut. Still mentally castigating herself, she walked past the corner of the barn in the direction of the house. The night was still cloudy, and she was glad of the flashlight.

A faint noise reached Kaly's ears and she spun

about nervously. She played the beam of her light over the area, but she was unable to detect anything out of the ordinary. *You really are in a fanciful mood tonight,* she told herself derisively. She stood still for a moment longer, trying to calm her racing heart. She listened intently, but heard nothing further. She hurried on until the breeze brought a strange odor to her nose, which brought her up short again. She sniffed disbelievingly. It smelled like…gasoline.

Kaly stood uncertainly, biting her lip. This was too weird. She was hesitant to wake Jackson for what would probably turn out to be nothing, but she couldn't shake the eerie feeling she was getting. He could go back to bed later if they didn't find anything, but right now she was going back to the barn to call the house and get him out here. Most likely her sense that something wasn't right was a product of the night's adventures. Nevertheless…

She used the flashlight to guide her way back to the barn. Her footsteps seemed to echo loudly in the shadowy building, and she found herself unconsciously tiptoeing. When she was midway down the barn, she heard the telltale squeak of the heavy doors behind her. Without thinking, she slipped into an empty stall to her left, snapped off her light and crouched down, scarcely daring to breathe. She strained to hear. At first all was silent. Then she heard footsteps scuffling lightly in her direction. She held her breath as a beam of light swept across the stall she was in and beyond. The steps echoed to the end of the barn and then back, before fading away. She heard the squeak of the barn door again.

Kaly remained where she was for long minutes, beginning to feel a little foolish. More likely than not, the shadow and flashlight belonged to Nick or one of the other men, coming to check on the noise *she* had made. She inched out of the stall and headed toward the phone. Crazy or not, she was summoning Jackson. She needed to hear his voice, even if he growled at her about her wild imagination. There was still that smell of gasoline she'd noted outside, and she wouldn't feel safe until he checked things out. She reached the phone after what seemed like an eternity, and with shaking hands, turned on her light to determine which button she needed to push to ring the house.

Suddenly everything seemed to happen at once. A weight hit Kaly from behind, then she was pulled backward, jerking her hand off the phone. Her light went flying, landing several feet away and shutting off at its contact with the floor. She was yanked against a body, and a hard arm was across her throat and a hand firmly pressed against her mouth, muffling her terrified screams. She struggled wildly with her assailant, kicking backward and squirming to either side.

"Stop it," the voice of her attacker hissed, and he tightened the arm around her throat. Kaly could feel darkness rushing in as oxygen was cut off. Consciousness receding, she clawed frantically at the punishing arm. Dimly she heard the whispered voice again, this time as if from a distance, tell her, "Stop struggling, and I'll loosen my arm. Keep it up and I'll break your neck." The arm was tightened briefly again as he added, "Understand?"

Kaly nodded, as much as she was able. When the arm was loosened, she went almost limp. Her attacker lowered her to the floor, flipping her over facedown. Her hands were quickly bound behind her back, a gag stuffed into her mouth, and her feet tied together. Next she was dragged to a nearby empty stall and deposited unceremoniously in the straw. After several deep breaths of air, reality came rushing back to her. As her assailant rolled her over, her eyes fluttered open, then widened in shock.

Paul Whitfield stood over her, sneering down at her. "Surprised to see me? Well, the feeling's mutual. After I'd taken care of Scott, I didn't expect to see some-one else sneaking around in here." He rose, dusting off his dark pants. "Really, Kaly, you were awfully easy to outwit. You fell for the oldest trick in the book, thinking the squeak of the door meant someone had left the barn. All I had to do was stay inside the door and wait for you to come out from your hiding place."

She stared up at him, her numb mind having difficulty comprehending. Paul was behind the rustling, he had to be. But she had no idea what he hoped to accomplish in the barn. Very few cattle were kept here in the summer months, only those few having calves and sometimes the purebred bull. Her eyes widened in panic. Was Paul now planning to steal the bull and the cows Jackson had bred to it? That would be demented; there was no way he could hope to remain undetected driving a truck this close to the house. Desperately seeking answers, she tried to speak around the gag, but only muffled sounds emerged.

Paul chuckled at her frustrated attempts to speak. "I don't have time to chat. I have to go out and finish my little job. Don't go away now," he taunted as he strode from the barn.

Kaly lay still only until she was sure he had left the barn; then she worked herself into a sitting position. She bent her knees, pressed her bound feet firmly against the floor and threw her weight forward, attempting to stand. She fell to the floor several times before admitting defeat. The rope tying her ankles was just too tight. Instead, she pulled her knees up, rolled to the side and used her elbows to push herself to a kneeling position. Attaining her objective, she walked on her knees to the gate of the stall.

Paul had not bothered to latch it behind him, obviously thinking she wouldn't be able to escape. She moved unsteadily through it and paused a second, trying to think. There was a second set of double doors immediately to her left, but she knew they were kept locked at night. Her stomach dropped as she faced the disheartening certainty that the only other way out of the barn was the same way Paul would be coming back in—the doors at the front.

Kaly turned carefully and began to knee-walk toward that exit. If she could move fast enough, if Paul's errand took him long enough, she just might make it. She determinedly fought her rising panic and concentrated all her energy into staying upright and moving toward freedom. The barn was shrouded in total darkness, and once her knees hit something lying across the floor, sending her sprawling painfully facedown. Cursing silently, she rolled to her side again and got back onto her knees. Again she moved in the direction of the doors, at a slightly slower pace. As she moved she could feel a sticky substance dripping down her face. Blood, she realized grimly, from her fall.

As long as I'm on my knees, I might as well pray, she thought with black humor. She had a feeling she'd be needing some divine intervention to get out of this mess.

After what seemed like an eternity, she reached the

doors. She stopped for a moment, hoping fervently that Paul had lacked the foresight to bar the door from the outside. Turning sideways, she pressed her shoulder against the heavy door and pushed with all her might. The heavy door swung outward with that telltale squeak, but not far enough for Kaly to wedge her body through. She pushed again. Simultaneously the door was pulled open from the other side. It flew wide, and Kaly landed outside, flat on her face again. The force of her fall winded her for a moment.

Paul rolled her over roughly, and she glared up at him murderously.

"Well, I guess you are as smart as they say, Kaly. Almost made it, too, but you know what the yokels around here say. Close only counts in horseshoes." Quickly he stepped around her and grasped her beneath the shoulders, dragging her back toward the back of the barn. He dumped her into the same stall he'd left her in before. He remained squatting over her, rocking back and forth on his heels in the hay, studying her.

Kaly again attempted to speak, frustrated by her inability to be understood around the gag.

Paul laughed. "You have a very expressive face, you know that?" He ran one finger lightly along her jawline, laughing again as she jerked her face away furiously. "And what spirit. You intrigued me, you know." His face twisted then, spite marring his normally handsome countenance. "Of course, that was before I realized what a gullible little fool you were, falling for Jackson Roberts's obvious line. I never would have figured you a sucker for a backwoods cowboy with no class.

"I really started this rustling operation just to play

with these fool ranchers a bit. Such a rough-tough bunch, and I was stealing them blind right under their noses,'' he bragged. "But it's turned into more than that. Even after paying off those punks I hired, I still have enough money to buy myself a prime stock breeding bull.'' He slapped both palms on his legs. "I've about run through the money my father left me, but I think Jackson hit on a real money-making scheme right here, with this breeding operation. I've had him over at my place several times in the past few months, to pump him for information.'' He laughed shortly. "As a matter of fact, after our session this evening I feel ready to start my own business. Only trouble is, there's not room for two of us in these parts, so Jackson will have to be taken out of the running. While he's still trying to collect the insurance money from this accident I'm planning, I'll be stepping in and taking care of all his clients for him. By the time he gets this business rebuilt, I'll have the established operation. He won't stand a chance against me.''

Kaly was almost frozen with fright. The chilling memory of the unfamiliar odor she'd encountered outside made horrible sense now. It *had* been gasoline. He was planning to burn the place down—with her in it. She couldn't let him get away with this insanity. Her mind racing frantically, she suddenly let her eyes flutter closed and her face turn to the side. She forced her body to relax, hoping he'd assume she fainted. When she heard him mutter in surprise and move closer, she pulled her knees up and kicked out at him with all the force she could muster.

Paul grunted in pain and amazement as he took the brunt of the blow in his chest. He was upon her again before she even had time to roll away. Expecting his rage, Kaly was even more frightened by the twisted smile on his face. ''Full of spirit right to the end, aren't you? Your being here was a mistake, you know. I didn't plan on hurting anybody. But you could be a bonus. What would damage Jackson's reputation more than having his current girlfriend found dead on his property?'' At Kaly's widened eyes he added, ''Don't worry, Kaly. I'll make sure you don't suffer.'' With that he rose and left the stall, securing it behind him.

Kaly was more terrified than she could ever remember being in her life. She moved closer to the door, using her bound feet to kick against it with all her might, but it held strong. She kicked at it again in pure frustration. She could think of no way to get out of the locked stall. For the first time since this nightmare began, she felt hopelessness wash over her.

She thought of Jackson, and tears gathered in her eyes at the thought of never seeing him again, never feeling his touch, fighting or loving with him again. If only she had never left his room! Her damnable curiosity had gotten her into trouble again, trouble she despaired of getting out of.

Her senses warned her that Paul was coming back. The smell of gasoline was almost overpowering now. He hurried into the stall and dragged her toward the back of it. He was panting, out of breath, as he told her, ''I've already lit the gasoline outside the barn. It shouldn't be too much longer. You won't be awake to feel a thing.'' Then he swung the heavy flashlight at her head and Kaly saw bright lights as it cracked against her skull. Then she sunk into dark unconsciousness.

Chapter 14

Jackson moved restlessly in the bed, something teasing at the edges of sleep, a nagging something that refused to let him rest peacefully. Still half dozing, he reached for Kaly with one long arm and met only emptiness. It took his sleep-sodden mind long moments to realize what that void meant. Slowly, his body fighting exhaustion, his eyes flickered open. After another second, they opened with a snap, and he stared hard at the space beside him, the space where Kaly was supposed to be. His mind came alert with alacrity as his big body jackknifed to a sitting position, his eyes already scanning the rest of the dark room.

"Kaly?" he called out, his sleep-roughened voice low. At the continuing silence he leaned over, flicked on a light and climbed out of bed. He padded silently to the bathroom and found that room also empty. He checked the balcony before anger began to simmer inside him. She had probably slipped into her own room already. He usually carried her to her own bed before dawn, insisting she spend the major portion of the night with him.

He pulled on a pair of jeans, not bothering to button them, and strode grimly down the hallway to her room. This sneaking around was going to stop, and now. He had listened long enough to her pleas for discretion, and his patience had just run out. She was his, that was all there was to it, and he didn't give a damn who else knew it. He burst through her door, making no attempt to mask his entrance, but stopped short as the light revealed that Kaly was not there and that the bed showed no signs of having been slept in. Jackson quickly checked the bathroom, but finding it empty, went downstairs to the study. He fully expected to find her there, pleading nerves as an excuse to work, instead of sleep. But the study was dark. A quick check proved she was nowhere downstairs.

Cursing under his breath, he ran lightly up the steps to don shirt, socks and boots before heading outside. Surely she wouldn't have been foolish enough to saddle a horse and ride at night, he fumed silently. He hoped he would find her on the grounds, perhaps taking a mind-clearing walk through Peg's rose garden.

Before Jackson could descend the stairs again, the air was rent with a raucous clanging. It only took a second for him to identify the sound as an alarm from one of the outside buildings. Taking the steps three at a time, he rushed to the front door. The scene awaiting him when he threw open the door was one from hell. In the distance, smoke billowed out from the cattle barn in thick, choking clouds, and flames danced their way merrily along its side. Jackson's booted feet thudded heavily across the oak hallway floor and he burst into the office, rushing to the phone. He rang the bunk-house and the sheriff in quick succession, leaving it up to Roy to alert the fire department. He met Jeff in the hallway, and together they raced across the yard.

Nick was already organizing several hired men into a water brigade. The few animals in the flaming barn were bawling in terror, and Jackson and Nick succinctly conferred on the best way to lead them to safety.

Carrie had followed the men with blankets, and Peg arrived with more. Carrie blithely ignored her husband's outraged demands that she return to the house, promising to stay well out of harm's way.

"Have you seen Kaly?" Jackson called to her. Carrie frowned and shook her head, turning to peer into the darkness. "See if you can find her." He barked terse instructions to Jeff, who in turn charged the men with their duties. Jackson and Nick wet handkerchiefs to tie around their faces and then grabbed several of the blankets, soaked them in water and rushed toward the barn to attempt to rescue the animals.

It wasn't until Jackson entered the barn that he realized the expensive sprinkler system his insurance company had insisted upon was working. The water acted on the blaze inside, not completely dousing it, but slowing the fire's spread. The water turned the flames into hissing clouds of smoke. The heat was intense and he could hear the crackling of the fire as it crawled up the outside walls. Jackson choked on the smoke he was inhaling, narrowing his eyes, trying to see through it. His worry should have been focused on the danger in the flaming barn and rescuing the animals, but all his thoughts and anxiety were elsewhere.

Dammit, where was Kaly? What could have lured her out of his bed in the middle of the night?

It took both men to get the bull outside, where Jackson instructed several men to take it to safety. Stopping to fill his tortured lungs with air, he swept the area with burning eyes, seeking Kaly's familiar figure. He spotted Carrie standing in the shadows with another woman and felt a sudden fierce relief. Kaly. Obviously Carrie had tracked her down. He and Nick went back to the barn, each throwing a wet blanket over the heads of terrified animals before leading them outdoors. Again and again they entered the flaming structure, the heat searing them, blackening their faces, to emerge, coughing and choking, with the cattle.

The last trip in was to bring out the new mother cow and her baby, and it was a rough one. Though the fire hadn't spread a great deal inside, the smoke had increased tenfold. The heat was quickly growing unbearable. Nick simply reached down, lifted the calf in his arms and walked out with it, hoping the cow would follow. The cow, frightened by the heat and flames, was frantic about her offspring. Jackson was kicked as he attempted to cover the animal's face, but eventually he was able to lead her to safety. As he stumbled out the doors and away from the barn, he heaved great breaths of fresh air into his aching lungs.

Jackson looked up, relieved, as sirens screeched and Roy's car pulled into the yard, followed by trucks from the Los Pueblos fire department. Many of the ranchers in the area also served as volunteers, but he didn't spring to help his neighbors as they unwrapped the heavy hoses and endeavored to thwart the hungry conflagration. As the firemen did what they could to save his barn, Jackson's gaze swept the crowd that had gathered looking for Carrie and Kaly. When he spotted Carrie, he strode through the throng to the shadowy area where she was standing, away from the heat and smoke of the fire. But when he reached her she was alone, save for Peg. He could feel his gut clench with a fear that had nothing to do with the fire and everything to do with one small blond woman.

''Where did Kaly go?'' he asked tersely, his voice gravelly from the smoke.

Carrie shrugged helplessly. ''I never found her, Jackson. I've looked everywhere.''

He stared hard at her, time crawling to a halt. ''But I saw you with her,'' he croaked disbelievingly. ''She was standing right here with you.''

His sister-in-law shook her head. ''You must have seen me with Rod's wife. I asked her and Peg to help me look, but we haven't been able to find her.'' Her voice trembled with fear. ''Jack, where could she be?''

He gazed unseeingly at Carrie for another moment, fear clawing in his gut, before swinging his eyes back to flames reaching toward the sky. He turned and ran back toward the barn, shrugging aside those who would have halted his progress, pausing only to repeat his terse question, ''Have you seen Kaly?''

Everyone responded negatively, and Jackson tried to tamp down his alarm, which was threatening to overwhelm him. When he felt a hand on his arm he pulled away impatiently, unwilling to pause and answer one of the multitude of questions being tossed his way. Only the words spoken had the power to stop him.

''Is Kaly safe?'' It was Larry Scott, and Jackson turned in astonishment to find him holding a hand to his head.

The hired man's words hung in the air between them for a second, and then Jackson reached for the man's neck with both hands. "You son of a bitch," he snarled, his fingers pressing hard. "I'll kill you if you've hurt Kaly. What have you done with her?" His face was a mask of murderous fury as he punctuated his threat by squeezing forcibly.

"Jackson, what the hell are you doing?" Jeff grabbed at his brother, but it took several of the nearby men to pull him off the cowboy, who dropped to the ground, gasping for breath.

"Where is she?" Jackson roared at Larry, fighting to get away from those who held him.

"Don't know," Larry choked out. "Trying to tell you. Barn earlier. She…went back…see new calf." He stopped and heaved for more air. "I got hit…left in bushes."

For the first time the gash on Larry's head made its way through the haze of Jackson's panic-fogged mind. Unfamiliar dread twisted through him, freezing his thoughts, his voice, his actions. Kaly had been in the barn earlier—she still might be. He turned to stare in horror at the burning building, where the firemen were fighting what appeared to be a losing battle with the scorching flames. Someone had done this purposely; the fire had not been an accident. His shock began to dissipate at Larry's next words.

"Has anyone looked in the barn for her?" The blond man's frightened countenance met Jackson's frozen one for reassurance. "She couldn't still be in there, could she?"

Good Lord, Jackson thought, sick fear snaking through him. Surely he and Nick hadn't walked right past her in there. To know he'd been close enough to save her, but had been ignorant of her presence...

He sped back toward the barn and grabbed several wet blankets. Tying a cloth over his face and nose, he ran toward the flaming structure.

"Hey, what's he doing? Dammit, stop him, someone!" The call sounded behind him, but when a hand grabbed at his shoulder, he flung it off and kept going. He made it to the entrance, felt the searing heat, before he was forcibly stopped. He twisted violently, but three men dragged him back toward the fire truck.

"What the hell do you think you're doing, Jackson?" the chief shouted. "I can't let you go back in there!"

"I've got to! Kaly may be in there—it's the last anyone saw her." He yanked futilely at the men still holding him. "Dammit, let go of me!"

The chief nodded at the men, who slowly loosened their hold. He spoke adamantly. "If someone is in there, we'll be the ones to go in, not you. We have the gear and materials to enter the building if the fire inside allows it. Do you have any idea whereabouts she might be?"

Jackson tried to push aside his fear enough to think. "The new calf was in the last stall on the west—that's where she was headed."

The chief nodded. "Is there another way into the barn, closer to the back?"

"There are back doors, but they're kept locked at night."

The fireman shouted orders to some of the men, who grabbed axes and hose off the truck and followed Jackson around the barn. Three men stood abreast, slamming their axes against the doors, as others sprayed the face of the building trying to lessen the flames.

Splinters of wood flew through the air, as the axes made gaping holes in the doors. While the men broke them down, two others donned protective masks.

"She can't be in the corridor. We would have seen her when we brought the animals out," Jackson shouted to the chief, who was giving orders to the men. "You'll have to check the stalls."

The chief nodded, and the men entered the building.

Jackson stood watching, unable to be more than a spectator at what he fervently hoped would be Kaly's rescue. Cold sweat beaded his brow, despite the scorching heat from the fire. He closed his eyes against the anguish he felt at the thought of Kaly's being trapped somewhere in that roaring blaze. The crackle of the flames as they licked their way hungrily over the building mixed with the hiss of the steam formed as the water hit them.

His Kaly. He couldn't lose her now, not when she'd become such an important part of his life. He prayed to God, as he hadn't since his father had lain dying of cancer, to spare Kaly, to bring her back to him.

A shout went up, stirring Jackson from his misery. It seemed an eternity since the firemen had gone in, though in reality it had been only a few minutes. The two men came out carrying a...Jackson squinted through the haze as he raced toward them. A body.

Jackson recognized Kaly as he drew nearer. The sight of her unconscious form jolted him, and he felt the cold, tangy taste of fear in his mouth. She was motionless as they carried her away from the burning barn and out of reach of the smoke.

Jackson paced along beside them. They laid her

limp body down some distance away from the excitement, and he fell to his knees next to her. Her still face was blackened, and congealed blood matted her hair. One fireman began giving her first aid. A second later Jackson noted with vast relief the shallow rise and fall of her chest.

"She's alive!" one of the men shouted. "We'll need the emergency helicopter, though." Another went to make the call on the radio.

Jackson stroked her forehead with fingers that visibly trembled. He had to touch her, had to, or go insane. He reached for her hand and froze. In his joy at finding her alive, he had completely overlooked the strangeness of her position. She was bound hand and foot! His gaze swung to the fire chief.

"They found her like this?" His words came out hoarsely.

The man nodded grimly. "She was gagged, too."

Jackson's head whirled. Someone handed him a knife, and he moved her gently to her side and carefully cut away the cords around her. He winced as he saw the raw, scraped wrists. Some bastard had tried to kill Kaly. The thought kept hammering at him, at his disbelieving mind. But why? What possible enemy could she have made since her stay here?

Upon the heels of that question, realization dawned. She had been hurt because of him. Whoever was behind the rustling operation had hurt her in an attempt to get at him. Nausea rose in his throat as he accepted the probability. His fault, his fault, his fault. The thought pounded at his brain. He unclenched his big hands, one of which had still been gripping the knife. Laying it aside, he reached to hold one of Kaly's still hands in his.

"I'll get him, sweetheart," he vowed brokenly. "I'll never let you be hurt again. I promise." As he waited for the helicopter to arrive from the Albuquerque hospital, Jackson wondered bleakly if he'd ever be able to forgive himself for putting her in danger.

The sound of the chopper was heard long before it could be seen in the smoke still billowing from the building. The medical team quickly disembarked and went to work. They lifted her unconscious body onto the stretcher, hooking her to oxygen. Jackson's attempt to follow her aboard was thwarted when a member of the emergency team informed him there was no extra room available. Jackson swallowed hard and nodded before tearing his eyes away from Kaly's immobile form.

Backing away, he turned and ran toward the garage, roaring out with one of the pickups. He slowed when he spied his brother and sister-in-law, and opened the door to explain the situation.

"If you're going to the hospital, I'm coming, too," Jeff said, heading around to the other door.

"Me, too," Carrie piped in.

Jackson glared at them helplessly. "Someone should stay here," he argued.

"Nick can take care of anything that comes up. What are you waiting for?" Jeff demanded.

Jackson lost no more time in debate. The tires squealed as the truck sped away from the ranch. To the hospital. To Kaly.

When her bedroom door pushed open a week later, Kaly looked up eagerly. She was stir-crazy from the monotonous bed rest she'd been prescribed after her release from the hospital, and she welcomed the opportunity to talk to anyone. Jackson appeared at the door carrying a large bouquet of roses, and her face softened into a sweet smile.

Jackson had been like a wild man, a nurse had told Kaly after she'd regained consciousness. He had badgered the staff unmercifully, asking for assurance that her condition had stabilized and insisting she be given special treatment. Kaly had no memory of the scene the nurse described to her, when Jackson had burst through the emergency-room doors, shouting at everyone in sight. She could well imagine him threatening the doctor on duty, who had treated him like a lunatic for the rest of Kaly's stay. She knew only that Jackson had been at her side when she'd first opened her eyes, and the entire time she was hospitalized. Her heart was so full with love at the sight of him she thought it would burst.

Now, Jackson stood in the doorway for a moment, drinking in the picture she made as she sat up in the bed. Her honey-colored locks hung around her shoulders, and dressed in the fancy peignoir set he'd given her, she looked more like a seductive siren than a recovering patient. He stepped into the room and presented the roses with a flourish.

"Something for *mademoiselle*," he said with an atrocious French accent, laying the flowers in her outstretched arms.

Kaly brought the pink blooms to her face, breathing in their fragrance. "They're beautiful, Jackson, but I thought Peg said she'd scalp you and hide all your hats if you cut one more rose from her garden." Her voice was still hoarse from the effects of the smoke, a vivid reminder of the horror she'd endured.

Jackson shrugged as he sat on the side of the bed,

facing her. "I'm not afraid of that old war-horse. Besides, I had these delivered from town."

Kaly giggled, earning herself a mock scowl. "But you didn't order them because you're afraid of Peg," she agreed with mock seriousness.

"I decided you needed some pink flowers in here, and she didn't have any more pink roses in the garden."

Kaly cast a wry look around the room. Every spare space had been cleared to display his offerings. The first dozen bouquets were in vases, but after that Jackson had had to make do with drinking glasses and quart jars. They covered the surfaces of the dressers and tables, and several sat on the floor. She had no idea where this newest addition would go.

Jackson bent over her, his face close to hers. "Don't I even get a thank-you kiss?" he begged huskily, his navy eyes alight with intent. Their lips met, and lingered to taste, tongues sweetly entwining. Jackson's blunt forefinger traced the lace that demurely hid her breasts from his eyes. When their mouths broke away, Jackson's breathing was already choppy. Ever since Kaly had been hurt he had spent almost all his time with her, first by her hospital bed, now in her room at the ranch. He'd insisted on sleeping in her bed each night since she'd come home, holding her while she slept, as if to convince himself that the nightmare was over, that she was indeed safe and in his arms again. But the proximity was wearing down his control, and he was finding that even a simple kiss was enough to make his blood pound.

It seemed like forever since they'd last been able to make love, and he wanted it badly, needed to get as physically close to her as he could. Perhaps then he'd rid himself of this fear of losing her. Inwardly cursing the errant part of his body that insisted on acting like a randy teenager, he moved off the bed to walk toward the window, searching for a subject that would take his mind off his raging hormones.

One came immediately to mind as he abruptly remembered the phone call he'd had from the sheriff earlier that day. He hadn't talked to Kaly about Paul Whitfield since she'd first been able to give them the information they needed at the hospital. He didn't like to think of what the man had almost accomplished, how close Kaly had come to death. But he knew the time had arrived for him to let her know what was going on. He turned back to face her. "I talked to Roy again this morning."

"Oh?"

He studied her face carefully, but was unable to read anything more than interest. He found himself relaxing imperceptibly. If she'd shown any signs of distress whatsoever, he wouldn't have continued. "Whitfield must have left the area as soon as he heard you were alive. He was trailed to California and picked up at LAX. He was buying a ticket to Argentina."

Kaly stiffened. Though she was aware that Jackson was watching her closely, and that he would clam up if he thought she was getting upset, she couldn't prevent the reaction. "Where is he?" she asked, proud that her voice sounded almost normal.

"In jail in Albuquerque," he responded. "Don't worry, Roy thinks the odds are against his making bail. There'll be a good case that he's a flight risk." *Add to that his being charged with attempted murder and arson,* he added silently, feeling familiar rage rise at the thought of Whitfield. Not for the first time, he wished savagely for a return to the justice of the Old West. Nothing would be as satisfying as getting his hands on Whitfield after his attempt on Kaly's life. But he'd have to content himself with making damn sure the man stayed in prison for a long, long time.

"You'll have to testify at the trial," he said abruptly. "I argued with Roy, but he says there's no way to get you out of it. They'll need your testimony."

She looked at him steadily. "It's all right, Jackson. I can do it."

He frowned at her willingness. "I don't want you to have to do it," he said. "I don't want you to have to put yourself through that whole ordeal all over again. To have to face him again."

"I can do it," she repeated firmly.

He strode back to the bed and sank down next to her, picking up one of her hands and holding it in his larger, harder one. She had a spine of steel and more heart than ten men put together. Hell, yes, she could do it, but that wasn't the point. He wanted to protect her from that, from anything that would ever hurt her again. Apparently he wasn't going to have the chance this time. But she wouldn't be alone in that courtroom; he'd be with her every step of the way.

"I still can't believe how stupid I was, telling Paul all about our breeding operation just so he could turn around and try to destroy me." He laughed without amusement. "He played us all the way, right down to planting that phony vehicle description. He described having seen Larry's truck when the rustlers supposedly hit his ranch, and we all swallowed it."

"So that's why you suspected Larry," Kaly said thoughtfully. "You never said."

"Roy picked up the biker you saw in the bar," he continued, "and he spilled all he knew about everyone involved in the operation. None of them ever actually met Paul. He only talked to them on the phone, and the bikers did all the work. They sent the money to a post-office box in Albuquerque. But Paul was real careless when he gave the one guy his phone number."

"Well, at least Larry is cleared," Kaly said. "And he never has to know he was under suspicion, does he?" Jackson looked away. "Does he?" she demanded.

"Yeah, I did let him know it, there at the end," he admitted uncomfortably.

"Jackson!" Her tone was disapproving. "I certainly hope you've apologized to him."

He cocked an eyebrow, glad she didn't know just how much he'd had to apologize to the man for. He'd been out of his head with worry about Kaly, and when he'd thought Larry had something to do with her disappearance, he'd been uncontrollable. "It's been taken care of," he stated finally. The two weeks' extra vacation the man was being given had helped ease some of Larry's dismay at how he had been distrusted. "Now, can we please stop talking about everyone else and talk about us?"

Her eyes widened a little at his impatient tone. "All right," she said quietly, inwardly quaking. He was right, they did need to talk, but a cowardly part of her wanted to put it off. She was too afraid of what he was going to say.

"Do you know that I used to sit next to you and watch you sleep?"

Her eyes flew to his. Whatever she'd expected, that wasn't it. She shook her head silently.

"When you were in the hospital, and even when I brought you back here, I'd sit for hours and watch you. It took me a long time to believe you were going to be okay." Her spirits rose at his expression of concern, but were dashed again at his next words. "I never would have forgiven myself if something had happened to you because of me."

She snatched her hand back from his. The last thing she wanted from him was guilt, or worse, his pity. "Don't blame yourself for this, Jackson," she said stiffly. "I don't."

He frowned down at her, wondering at her sudden change of attitude. "That's not what I—"

A knock sounded at the door. He bit off an imprecation and strode to open it—and came face-to-face with Larry Scott.

"Carrie said it would be all right for me to come up and see Kaly," the younger man explained, eyeing Jackson warily.

"Come in," Kaly called warmly. She noticed the wide berth he gave Jackson as he walked by him and wondered at it. The cowboy came over to the bed and stood uncomfortably, his eyes going between her and a silent Jackson.

"Carrie said you'd been hurt the night of the fire," Kaly said to him. "I hope you're okay."

He shrugged easily. "Just took a few stitches is all. I didn't even know what hit me. Paul nailed me right before I got to my bike. But you're the one who really got hurt. How are you feeling?"

"Fine," she said firmly, "and I'm getting out of bed tomorrow and going back down to work." She fixed Jackson with a glare when he looked as if he might object. "If I stay cooped up in this room much longer, I'll go nuts."

"I suppose it'll be all right," Jackson conceded, as if giving her permission, "but you'll start working only half days. And if you seem to be tiring, it's right back upstairs for you."

"We'll see."

"Yes, we will," he replied imperturbably. She could get her back up all she wanted, but she'd listen to him on this or she'd be back in bed before she knew what hit her.

"Anyway, I'm off on vacation for a couple of weeks," Larry said, interrupting their battle of wills. "I didn't know how much longer you would be staying at the ranch, so I wanted to be sure and say goodbye, in case you're already gone when I come back."

"I'm glad you did," she told him, ignoring the pang that struck her at the reminder of how little time she had left with Jackson. "I wanted to tell you how sorry I was for thinking you could be involved in the rustling, even if it was just momentary."

"Kaly was actually your biggest supporter," Jackson volunteered. "She refused to believe you had anything to do with it."

She made a face. "When I saw your phone number posted on the barn wall, and it ended with the same digit as the number the biker had thrown away, well, I'm afraid my faith in you slipped."

"Don't worry about it," Larry said. "It's all out in the open now."

"No hard feelings?" Kaly offered her hand.

"None," he affirmed, clasping hers in both of his. Jackson watched the scene as long as he could before moving to the bed and glancing pointedly at their hands. Larry hurriedly released her and backed toward the door. "I better be going now. Hope you're well soon, Kaly."

She watched him depart, then looked at Jackson. "He seemed a little cautious around you," she observed.

"Could we please stop talking about Larry?" he asked in frustration. "We have something more important to discuss."

"How's my favorite research assistant today?"

Jeff breezed through the door, and Jackson silently cursed his brother's timing. It seemed as though fate was conspiring against him. He turned and paced to the window again, leaving Kaly and Jeff to their conversation. He wasn't sure how much more of this he could stand. His patience, never his strongest suit, was running dangerously low.

"There you are, Jeff," Carrie said cheerfully as she entered the room. "You're looking great today, Kaly. Maybe I should have Peg serve lunch up here. We could all eat together then."

That was it, Jackson vowed. The last straw. "No," he said flatly. Turning around, he walked purposefully over to his brother and took him by the arm. Ignoring Jeff's bewilderment, he led him over to his wife and guided them both to the door. "You two go have lunch together. Go on a picnic. Go do anything. Just leave us alone for the next couple of hours, would you, please?"

Carrie's eyebrows rose at his inexorable attitude, but Jeff chuckled and walked her out of the room. "Okay, sure, we can take a hint. Not that you know how to give one. More like a bulldozer, isn't he, Carrie?''

Jackson shut the door firmly on them and faced Kaly again. She was watching him in concern.

"What's wrong with you?" she asked faintly.

"What's wrong," he muttered, as he crossed over to sit on the bed next to her, "is that we have about as much privacy around here as in a bus station."

"What do we need privacy for?" she whispered, her answer already apparent as his head descended.

"For this." His mouth met hers with carnal demand, and she was helpless to do other than respond. His arms went around her, pulling her close, crushing the flowers she still held. "I was so afraid I had lost you," he said in a tortured murmur. He took her face in his hands and looked down at her solemnly. "I love you, Kaly. I want us to spend the rest of our lives together. Is that what you want, too?"

Kaly's heart leapt. She smiled dreamily into his taut face, which was stamped with impatience as he waited for her response. "Yes, that's exactly what I want. I love you, too."

His lips covered hers again, and he swept the flowers to the floor as he pressed her back against the pillows. He dragged his lips away from hers reluctantly to demand, "Say it again."

Kaly obeyed willingly. "I love you," she said, her lips moving against his chin. "I feel like I've waited forever to be able to say that."

Jackson frowned slightly. "Why couldn't you tell me before?"

"I wasn't sure how you felt. You never gave me any indication that you might feel the same way."

"Never gave you any indication?" Jackson's tone

was amazed. "What do you call it, then? I made a fool of myself every time you so much as looked at another man. We slept together most every night. You gave yourself to me in the sweetest, wildest ways imaginable, and you never thought I loved you?"

She struggled to put her fears into words. "I didn't know what to expect from you. Everyone was always warning me about your reputation." Her voice dropped so that it was barely audible. "And you made your distrust of women clear."

He tipped up her chin. "It's true that I've kept women at a distance. There's never been anyone before that I couldn't walk away from. But you managed to get closer to me than any woman ever has."

Her eyes misted and warmth filled her heart. "I'm glad." Their kiss was wild, rife with hope and passion before turning tender. Their lips parted, and he rubbed his forehead against hers. "We have a lot of decisions to make, but for right now you need to concentrate on getting well." His voice lowered. "And on keeping your fiancé happy."

"I don't know." She sighed, turning her face to kiss his palm. "He's a very demanding man. I'm not sure I'm up to it."

His navy eyes gleaming with wicked intent, he lowered his mouth to hers and whispered, "Let me give you some pointers." Then lips met and hearts took flight, as they temporarily dropped plans for the future to celebrate the present.

* * * * *

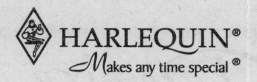

HARLEQUIN®
Makes any time special ®

AMERICAN *Romance*

Upbeat, All-American Romances

HARLEQUIN®
Duets™

Romantic Comedy

Harlequin®
Historical

Historical, Romantic Adventure

HARLEQUIN®
INTRIGUE

Romantic Suspense

Harlequin Romance ®

Capturing the World You Dream Of

HARLEQUIN® *Presents*

Seduction and passion guaranteed

HARLEQUIN® *Super*ROMANCE®

Emotional, Exciting, Unexpected

HARLEQUIN® *Temptation*

Sassy, Sexy, Seductive!

eHARLEQUIN.com

Looking for today's most popular books at great prices?
At www.eHarlequin.com, we offer:

- An **extensive selection** of romance books by top authors!

- **New** releases, Themed Collections and hard-to-find **backlist.**

- A sneak peek at Upcoming books.

- Enticing book **excerpts** and **back cover copy!**

- Read recommendations from other readers (and post your own)!

- Find out what everybody's reading in **Bestsellers.**

- **Save BIG** with everyday discounts and exclusive online offers!

- Easy, convenient **24-hour shopping.**

- Our **Romance Legend** will help select reading that's *exactly* right for you!

Your purchases are 100% guaranteed—so shop online at www.eHarlequin.com today!

INTBB1